LAURENTIAN DIVIDE

LAURENTIAN DIVIDE

A Novel

Sarah Stonich

UNIVERSITY OF MINNESOTA PRESS
MINNEAPOLIS
LONDON

Published by the University of Minnesota Press
111 Third Avenue South, Suite 290
Minneapolis, MN 55401–2520
http://www.upress.umn.edu

ISBN 978-1-5179-0562-0 (hc)   ISBN 978-1-5179-0249-0 (pb)

A Cataloging-in-Publication record for this book is available from the
Library of Congress.

Printed in the United States of America on acid-free paper

The University of Minnesota is an equal-opportunity educator and employer.

24 23 22 21 20 19 18   10 9 8 7 6 5 4 3 2 1

For Aaron, swimming.

W hat could Hatchet Inlet here at the edge of the wilderness have in common with third-century Rome? You might not know that the St. Lawrence River Divide that T-bones our own Laurentian Divide is named for a Roman. St. Lawrence was the Archdeacon of Rome, where he held the purse strings as treasurer. A good man when Rome had its share of bad ones, like the Emperor Valerian—think Darth Vader, only not too bright. Kicking Christians out of Rome wasn't enough for Valerian, so he decided to kill them. He sentenced Lawrence to death, but only after he ordered him to turn over the church's treasures. Lawrence stalled, claiming he'd need three days to pull the coffers together since they were scattered all over Rome. But on the sly he was doling out the treasure to the needy. All of it. Then he gathered his entourage—widows and peasants, lunatics and orphans— and presented them to Valerian as the "true treasures of Rome." You can imagine the emperor wasn't amused, and he ordered Lawrence to be roasted on a spit. The story is that when he was half-seared, he said, "Stick a fork in me, I'm done," or something like that. For his trouble, Lawrence was declared patron saint of cooks and comedians.

I chose Lawrence for today's sermon because he was an immigrant: he'd gone to Rome to do good work and find a better life. An immigrant just like most all of our grandparents, like the Mexican boys working over at the pulp mill, or our own Kam down at the noodle place. And we all know Veshko here. We see the faces on the news every day, refugees drowned by the boatload, countries shutting their doors to those in need, fools making noise about building walls. This is what we've come to. I want to think here in Hatchet Inlet we are better than that. Because we have to be better than that.

This congregation has suffered mighty blows and we have plenty of healing ahead of us. Farmers' Almanac *says this winter is going to be a doozy, people. Let's take these coming months to reflect, mourn, and pray. Spring* will *come—even on days like this, when it doesn't seem possible, spring will come. In the meantime, if you see a stranger, welcome them. If you see someone is lonely, sit down and share a coffee. If you know someone in these families grieving or in pain, listen. Pull out the earbuds and just listen. Don't turn away. Make it a point to give of yourself, and it will come back to you in spades.*

Okay? One housekeeping item before we begin: I'd like to remind everyone that plows are out and that odd-side parking begins this evening.

And now, without further ado, I invite the accordionists to approach the lectern from the left. If the brass will line up on the right, we can get this show on the road. Go with God.

Now, let's polka.

—Pastor Dan Huttala, St. Urho's Church of the Pines, transcript of polka service sermon on November 10

THE TOPIC OVER BREAKFAST IN PAVOLA'S IS DEATH.
Not the sort occurring weekly up at Senior Cedars, where
grannies in mobility scooters and walkers thump along
in their derby to the finish, and not the tragic sort that floored
Hatchet Inlet last fall after Kelly Rantala and Jessica Wiirtinen
were killed in a drunken swerve. The death patrons of the diner
mull over this bracing May morning is theoretical, regarding the
current status of Rauri Paar, who may be dead, or—not to split
hairs—is maybe not alive.

Pete Lahti holds the little metal pitcher just so, watching half
& half meet his black coffee in a tiny Hiroshima bloom. Indeed,
if Rauri is dead—and this might be a rugged image for so early
in the day—somebody'll have to go out there and peel him off
his cabin floor or search his island for gnawed remains. Maybe
drag the bay. Pete listens as the caffeine-fueled debate revs and
idles across booths, down the straightaway of the counter. Sitting
next to him, Pete's father, Alpo, only nods. Every morning since
ice-out on the big lake there's been talk. Usually, ice-out this far
north in Minnesota is in April—in a bad year like this, as late as
May. As soon as ice on the big lake breaks up, Rauri's smaller
lake follows suit. Once it's navigable, he straps on a harness like
some husky and humps his Alumacraft up the corduroy portage.
Beyond Rauri Lake (no one remembers its actual name) it's an
easy enough slide down the south side of the Divide, which lands
Rauri on the banks of the Majimanidoo, where snowmelt can
roil it into a carnival ride. Dodging ice chunks the size of coolers
is no easy feat in a twelve-foot fishing boat with only a 10-horse

Evinrude. Rauri could be bobbing like a cork around the Laurentian Basin.

Pete's made the journey to Rauri's place a few times, once years back and again on his own last fall when he went out to put down Rauri's old spaniel, Scotty. It's no stroll.

The one thing everyone in the diner agrees on is that Rauri should have shown up by now. You can say "Spring is here," or you can say "Rauri's back." His arrival marks the start of the season, and when weather is slow to warm and cabin fever's not yet broke, you might hear someone mutter, "Where in hell is Rauri Paar?" Some won't set seedlings in their windowsills until they've see the whites of Rauri's eyes.

When he does show, it's first things first: he drops a toxic load of laundry at the Wash & Gogh, then it's straight to the barber for a haircut and hot lather shave. Once his bushman's eyebrows are trimmed and he's wearing a fumigated shirt, he'll beeline to the produce aisle at Putzl's and stand gawking as if at a centerfold, stuffing himself with fresh anything—gnawing parsley while juggling limes and tangelos into his cart. Mumbling "abundance" while snuffling a peach or "cornufuckingcopia" as he gropes tomatoes.

Lastly, Rauri makes his way to Pavola's, where he takes center stool to enjoy his first fresh eggs since November. Regulars ignore the yolk on his chin and coax an account of his winter out of Rauri. No great storyteller but a wiz at figures and facts, he regales them with a litany of temperatures and wind speeds, snowfall totals, ice depths, pounds of propane used, boxes of Bisquick consumed, cords of birch burnt.

They prod for more. The core of their curiosity regards loneliness, but no one asks outright how he hacks it—every winter out there by himself. Instead, he offers a picture of his season like a paint-by-number of facts: biggest fish, wildlife visitations, vermin infestations, magazines read. Monochrome at best, the sections are slowly filled in with what DVDs got watched and how many times, what supplies were run out of—the previous year it had been cooking oil and Preparation H. Rauri might describe notable meals cooked: his personal best had been a haunch of wolf-killed doe with chanterelles glazed in a reduction of maple syrup and vodka, a side of fiddlehead ferns sauced with condensed milk and nutmeg. Worst was a stew of jerky shards and limp carrots in a base made from the last bouillon cube, garnished with moldy Parmesan and consumed sober.

If anyone had taken note of the Northern Lights over the winter, Rauri could remind them of the exact dates and times, and how many minutes or hours they had waltzed. No nuances from Rauri, barely an adjective, but if it's facts you're after, he's your man.

Pavola's patrons assume that Rauri is thrilled to be among them, and they unconsciously note who his gaze returns to, whose hand gets shaken most vigorously, whose back is slapped most mightily. Who had Rauri missed?

As always, he saves revealing the exact date and time of ice-out for last.

Nearly everyone in Pavola's has a sum wagered, and while Joe Pavola collects the money and manages the kitty, Rauri reserves the honor of doling it out to those with the closest guesses. This year there's more than two grand in the kitty, ice has been out on the big lake for four days, and since Rauri is MIA, there are implications. The names and times are listed in a spiral notebook under the counter. If more than one person bets on the same day, they must pick morning, midday, or evening. Rauri arrives with the date and time written on a scrap in his wallet so there can be no fudging like the time he split the pot between the Jenson boys the same day they got their pink slips from OreTac. They weren't even close. The rightful winner that year was Kip Karjala, his guess confirmed by Erv at the DNR. Kip hasn't spoken to Rauri since.

Pete no longer has a stake in the kitty—his own date has passed by two weeks, placing him well out of the running, which is fine with him since it's the guys working seasonal that need the cash—their guesses cluster across the three consecutive most likely dates. It's them that might be thinking hardest about Rauri's predicament.

He could have just sprained an ankle or busted a rib and is out there tethered to his recliner, living on ramen and peanut butter. Whatever the case, no one in Pavola's seems particularly motivated to haul ass out to his island to confirm. Not even Rauri's closest friends—*close* being a relative term, *friend* being another.

Sissy leans across Pete to top off his father's cup despite its being nearly full, saying, chirpy as always, "For all we know, he could be dancing the Macarena out there. He could barge in this minute and say—Whatsit? 'Rumors of my demise are very exaggerated'—who said that, Spock?"

"Twain," Laurie sighs from two booths down without looking at her sister like sisters do. "It was Mark Twain, and it goes, "'Reports of my death have been greatly exaggerated.'"

"Well, he can't be dead," Sissy bangs the carafe back onto the Bunn burner and folds her arms. "He just can't."

For several reasons.

Besides being the presenter of the kitty and harbinger of spring, Rauri is the closest thing Hatchet Inlet has to a living legend. His death would mark the end of an era. He is The Last Holdout, the only private property owner left in the Reserve. Everyone else was bought out years back, but Rauri refused the offer and stepped up to defend his grandfathered-in right to bear a gas can. On Pavola's wall map of the Reserve, all mint-green land, sage-colored bogs, and baby-blue lakes, Rauri's narrow islands remain fawn-colored—*private property,* according to the key. He alone holds a permit to use combustion engines and live within the Reserve borders.

When the ruling came down in Rauri's favor, the press swarmed, locals were captured in man-on-the-street sound bites, and camera crews thrashed their way out to his islands. Two-page articles were printed in Twin Cities papers. Eventually the hubbub settled, but Rauri would occasionally be trotted out when there were new pushes for motorized access into the Reserve, or when some Vibram soul would come up from the Sierra Club to debate the Sportsmen's Coalition, when a new picture would appear—Rauri with a firm grasp on the throttle of his outboard motor or two-stroke ice auger—always under the same tired headline FROM MY COLD, DEAD HANDS. No one can accuse *The Siren* of being original. If anybody really dug, they'd discover Rauri has never been a member of the NRA and in fact doesn't even own a gun.

Rauri's deal with the Feds is that he's allowed to occupy his islands and rev his engines and machinery for as long as he ticks. But should he die or leave his islands for more than sixty days, his lease reverts to the government to become the final piece of the jigsaw that is the Laurentian Reserve—a million acres of motorless wilderness, nearly pristine. Nearly.

For now, his outpost with its corrugated roofs and piles of salvage remains a fawn-colored stain on the map. "Until I croak," he jokes, "I'm the skid mark on those tree huggers' boxers."

Since Rauri does not trap or hunt, some wonder what he does out there. But Pete's seen his workshop, stockpiled with scavenged antlers and bones. He'll trail a dying old bear into veils of mosquitoes to score a set of claws. When there is a wolf kill, Rauri will hang just far enough in the periphery so the alpha can see he poses no threat. More patient than carrion, Rauri moves in with his plastic sled only after the pack waddles from the carnage. Elbowing aside ravens, he wrangles the antlers and jawbones and pelvises from the puzzles of the dead. He dries and polishes such prizes before fashioning them into chandeliers or wall sconce skulls with LED stares. He hollows hooves for cufflink boxes. He tans belly hide for lampshades stitched with sinew. It all sells for stupid amounts down in Minnetonka and Deephaven in shops with names like Up Chic Creek and Lichen It.

Pete's dad keeps clippings from back at the height of the debate. He remembers one from a Sunday supplement of the Duluth paper, Rauri looking like a runty Viking, holding his Husqvarna aloft, the article harshly portraying him as an antienvironment bumpkin. Folks pitching left of the argument are too PC to admit they are wild for him to expire, though they will be dancing the tread off their Keens when he does. It is true that when the wind is right, his generator can be heard a mile or two into the Reserve, to the chagrin of canoeists. What doesn't get mentioned is all he's done for the same people wishing him gone: Rauri's pulled many an inexperienced camper out of jams of their own making. His icehouse walls are lined with salvaged aluminum from canoes wrecked by paddlers too stupid to avoid big timber in straight-line winds. If you need help in the Reserve, Rauri, being the only guy, is the go-to guy. The pickets of his garden fence are lost canoe paddles and broken cross-country skis. Mobiles hanging from his porch are fashioned from snapped rods strung with snagged lures. Rauri probably couldn't count the number of gashes he's stitched up, broken bones set, or dislocated shoulders he's relocated over the decades. He's pumped the stomachs of mushroom-hunting idiots and has sat up all night more than once nudging awake some concussed fool.

Pete, curious about Rauri's medical knowledge and impressive first aid kit, had asked about his training, but Rauri's mumbled answer was somehow out of sync with the movement of his Adam's apple. "Field medic."

"When?"

"'69, '70."

"In 'Nam?"

"Dau Tieng." About the war itself, all Rauri would offer was a shrug.

Hadn't his dad mentioned something about meeting Rauri when he'd first hitchhiked into town? Pete's about to nudge Alpo when Junior Gahbow pipes up.

"You know those islands aren't really his."

"What do you mean?" Alpo asks.

"They were ours," Junior says.

After a gulp of coffee, Pete says, "Junior, you could say that about the whole reserve."

"No, I'm only saying about his islands—they're sacred ground."

"How?"

"They just are. After Rauri parked himself there, my pa and

Eddie Drift and Noble Wakemup went out to pay him a visit. Story
being he had paper proof he'd inherited the islands from an uncle
who'd got them in some land grab by the pulp company."

No surprise there, Pete thinks but only asks, "What'd they do?
Your dad and the elders?"

"Told him what's what, I s'pose," offers Junior.

Alpo leans in. "Then?"

"Rauri said he'd leave if they asked him to. Offered up the
deed on the spot. Said he'd sign a quit-claim deed and hand over
the islands."

"They didn't take him up on it?" Pete asks.

"Nah, told him they'd think on it."

"And?"

"And what?" Junior shrugs.

"But that was forty years ago."

"Far as I know they're still thinking on it." Junior nods to the
ceiling, *"Boozhoo, Nimishoome."*

If Rauri is laid up with some manageable injury, at least he's
got the splints, antibiotics, and meds to see him through. Pete
has seen examples of Rauri's sutures, every bit as neat as his own.
With enough morphine, an able medic could set his own bones.

Between concern over Rauri and concern for the kitty, conversation has escalated. Everyone in Pavola's has an opinion or a
should. Should County Rescue be called? Should somebody go
check things out and report back? Alert his next of kin?

Earl Rantala raises a hand. "That time he left? I heard he
got a trader's license in Chicago and made a killing on the stock
exchange. He could have a fortune hidden out there for all we
know."

"You know fuck-all. He worked as a pipe fitter in Ohio."

"Nu-uh, he was a Merchant Marine," Juri Perla interrupts,
"working the Great Lakes."

"Wasn't he an intern down at the VA hospital?"

"I think you mean *orderly.*"

"Jesus." Pete sits back. What is becoming clear is how few
facts of Rauri Paar there are. He puts his coffee cup down none

too gently and says, "Conjecture." A few old-timers at the counter give him that look: *college boy.* Pete swivels so his words are evenly distributed: "You're guessing, is all. Anybody remember when he came back that time?"

"Yup. Just after Reagan got elected." When Alpo speaks, heads turn, but when he adds no details, Laurie tosses out the idea of drawing straws to determine who might make the trip out to Rauri's island.

"It's an all-day ballbuster out there and back. Who's got that kind of time?"

A dozen eyes land on Dusty Heikala, built like a Navy Seal, and having nothing *but* time since his court-ordered leave for sending three bikers to the ER after a brawl in the Legion parking lot.

"Hell, I would but . . ." Dusty tugs up the leg of his jeans to show the tiny green light on his ankle cuff. "I got a two-mile radius."

"And if he's dead?" Laurie asks.

Junior gestures to his own foot with the amputated toes. "Somebody take me out there, I'll go. I'll bring the tobacco and keep his fire lit."

Dusty nods. "Or, maybe just light up his cabin like in *What's Eating Gilbert Grape,* which is only what the Feds are gonna do anyway once they get their mitts on the place."

Joe comes out from behind the grill. "Or pile one of those cairns of rocks over him to keep the animals off. We seen that on our trip to Ireland last summer. Irish got nothing on us in the way of rocks."

"Assuming he's dead, Joe."

"Well, say he is—what do we do?"

After a silence, Sissy says, almost to herself, "Somebody's tried calling him," she cracks a roll of dimes into the till, "haven't they?"

Everyone looks at everyone else. A frenzied mining of pockets nets a dozen cell phones, but no one has Rauri's number. Pete calls Lynn at the clinic and asks her to pull up Rauri's account, then scribbles on his napkin. Punching numbers, he feels all eyes on him like deer, blinking along with each ring. He looks up, shaking his head, "It's rolling over to voicemail." After the beep he hasn't the faintest idea what to say and so punts, sounding the opposite of casual: "Hiya, Raur, it's me, Pete. I just was wondering what you've been up to, sooo . . . hey, give us, *me,* a holler. It's Pete Lahti?"

As he hangs up, Joe whistles. "Not quite Oscar material there, Lahti."

Pete makes as if to hand over the phone. "Feel free, since you're such the Russell Crowe."

Nunce Olson, retired county coroner's assistant, sniffs. "Whoever goes out there should make notes of how and where his body is, get some idea of his last days by poking around. And if it looks like foul play, for God's sake don't touch anything that looks like evidence." Nunce makes no secret of the fact she is an aspiring crime writer.

Laurie swivels. "You'd *like* him to be dead."

Nunce ignores the comment. "You gotta be realistic. There are wolves. He doesn't carry a gun. Depending on where he died, he could be half-eaten, parts of him dragged off." Forks hoisted midway halt; images hang in the air alongside the hiss of breakfast sausage on the grill.

Sissy nearly stomps a foot. "Stop talking like he's dead."

Laurie plants an order of pie in front of Nunce and asks, "What if he died inside?"

"Inside?" Nunce pries the lid of crust with her fork and peers. "Inside there are voles, not to mention what beetles or maggots will do."

Gimp Wuuri touches both eyelids.

"And don't underestimate mice . . . ," Juri adds. "I mean, if ants can move a rubber tree . . ."

Laurie sputters.

"Mice," Sissy says to the cash register. "I don't know why that makes me think of those velvet paintings of dogs playing poker, only with Rauri and a bunch of big mice. What is it about him that reminds me of a mouse?"

"His eyes are close together," Alpo says.

"Slopey forehead," Laurie adds. "And his ears are sort of far back?"

"Hard to say with the hair."

After the door to the walk-in freezer clunk shuts, Junior shrugs. "They say freezing to death is actually a pretty peaceful way to go. Wouldn't-a taken much in January."

The mention of January elicits moans—not yet far enough in the past to laugh about, not yet warm enough to wear their *I Survived the Polar Vortex* T-shirts. You will find few climate-change deniers in Hatchet Inlet, where extremes are felt and seen daily—moose withering, tree diseases and gray squirrels migrating north, lake temps running hot and cold. After the third subzero week in a row, a camera crew from the Weather Channel came up to film folks trying to do mundane chores dressed as if for bomb disposal. Days when Pete was out on calls, he'd zip into a snowmobile suit upon rising and peel it off only when tripping toward bed. Over at the junior high, ninth graders set oranges outside at lunchtime and an hour later dashed out from shop class to shatter them with hammers. The winter *had* been a doozy, dangerous even indoors, where it was so dry just walking roused carpet sparks to singe holes in socks. One house was burned to cinders after its woodstove overheated; another half-dozen had damage from chimney fires. All across town, propane was sluggish and water pipes burst. A record number of frostbite cases were admitted to the ER, and there was a suicide over in Greenstone. Attendance at the Sokol Hall AA meetings went rock-bottom—sometimes only Pete, Jon Redleaf, and Granger showed up, and Jon hardly counts, not being a real drunk himself, but there's no Al-Anon in town.

"Okay, who's been out to Rauri's most recently?" Alpo asks.

"I ain't been since Labor Day," Juri says.

"Not me," Pete says. "Not since last fall."

"You put his old spaniel down?"

"Yeah, it was just after . . . *after.*"

After the merest slice of silence, Alpo continues. "So, mid-October, say?"

"Sure."

Scotty had been in renal failure, and while Rauri had the drugs, he couldn't bring himself to load a syringe, let alone a rifle he did not own. The dog was crippled with arthritis, blind, and at sixteen well beyond the average lifespan for the breed. Pete packed a few doses of ketamine and a quart of Jameson, disguised in an empty Sprite bottle. It was the last gasp of tick season, he remembers that. The final mile had been a bit hairy after the steep portage past the narrows, and with the autumn sun setting early he had to book to make time.

Once Pete arrived, Rauri kept apologizing. "I'd do it myself, but you know the way spaniels look at you . . ."

Beyond that, Pete actually remembers very little.

"How was he?"

"How? He was just Rauri." Pete shrugs. "Okay, considering." He reconstructs his visit in a most-likely scenario. His trip to Rauri's had been only days into the start of his relapse. What had surprised him most, after having been sober for months, was that just into a bender he was already having blackouts, and that it took as much booze as it ever did to numb up. The first part of the visit he remembers in yellowed flashes like a filmstrip—Rauri petting the little dog's head as if memorizing its contours. He kept topping off his glass when Rauri wasn't looking . . . hoping that when the Sprite bottle was drained there'd be something else in Rauri's cupboards.

"And?"

"And we fed Scotty popcorn and some hamburger." He thinks. It may have been Doritos and chicken.

"Then?"

"You want a blow-by-blow? I put Scotty down, then put Rauri to bed. Rauri buried him in the morning and I left."

In reality Rauri had put Pete to bed, and he knows this only because Rauri had told him the next morning, not making a big deal out of it, not judgy, just passing on the information with his head cocked, a little like Scotty. In fact, he can't picture Rauri with any expression on his face other than the slightly distracted half-smile chiseled there.

"I meant to get out there again," Pete says. "I knew a breeder over in Black Falls had a liver-colored runt."

"But?"

Pete regrets the disclosure. He had every intention of getting the pup out to Rauri, but one thing led to another and the weekend got misplaced and Monday was spent making up for lost time and by Tuesday it was too late. "I didn't get there in time and he'd already snuffed it."

"Oh, Pete." Sissy comes out from behind the counter. "You're not saying Rauri's been out there alone all this time without a *dog*?"

Alpo sighs. "I doubt Rauri's alone or dogless because of Pete."

"Still," Junior nods, "that makes you the last person to see Rauri alive."

"Oh, c'mon."

Out of patience, Pete stands. "Talk is cheap. I'm going over to the credit union, see what I can find out from Mackie." His cousin is a loan officer. "Mackie might tell us if Rauri's checks are getting deposited, at least." He nods at Alpo. "Dad. You coming with?"

"Sure. I'll drive."

Pete fishes in his pocket before dropping an oddly folded bill on top of his receipt.

Alpo winks in Sissy's direction. She blows a kiss back before pulling an order of waffles from under the heat lamps.

At Borderlands Credit Union, Mackie pretends to be outraged that they would even ask about somebody's private banking transactions. But as they are pulling out of the parking lot Alpo's phone rings.

"Uncle Alp?" Mackie whispers. "Actually? There hasn't been any activity on his account yet this month."

"So we know but don't know. The circumstances. Thanks, Mackie."

"Hey, while I've got you, can you ask Pete if he could stop out and take a look at Molly? Her nipples are oozing something."

"Sure." Alpo looks at him. Pete sighs and nods.

Mackie whispers, "But only if, you know, he's—"

"Sober?" Pete leans. "You're on speaker phone, Mackie, I'm right here."

"Oh, geez, Pete, I'm sorry."

"No biggie. I'll stop by after supper."

"I've got pie?"

"Pie would be good."

Alpo hung up. "Square one."

Pete reclines his seat so that he's staring out the sunroof. A few minutes of shut-eye on the drive to the clinic would be nice. He'd been roused at three a.m. to swivel a breach. Thank God, it's the end of lambing season—this is no climate for sheep, but a fad comes down the pike and people get some Instagram vision in their heads of curly lambs, of selling sheep cheese or boiled-wool mittens at the farmers' market. Or they decide they want antibiotic-free eggs and so order a chicken coop from Restoration Hardware and a brace of chicks, but winter comes and the novelty wears off and feathers fly. Down in the Cities the chicken rescues can't keep up.

As his father drives, Pete blinks at the puffy clouds, the sun behind them slicing upward in a razored benevolence. As a child Pete was convinced there was a heaven and that there were angels, having been told his cousin Andy had become one upon drowning when they were both eight. By the time Grandpa Corrigan died, Pete had grown less sure about angels. Santa Claus and the Tooth Fairy had been debunked by then and the pearly gates were looking less pearly. The Easter Bunny's cover had been summarily blown by his sister, coincidentally named Candy.

It used to annoy him at the clinic when parents, rather than explain the concept of death, would pull the angel card. *JoJo is going to a farm in the sky, Sweetie.* Or *Pinky's in a better place,* suggesting their mower-mangled bunny is happily crapping on some great cloud of wood shavings. Pull the angel card because *Mommy has a busy day.*

At the girls' funerals, Pete listened to the minister declare such destinations as *hereafter* and *thereafter* as if they were as real as Bloomington or Coleraine. He observed mourners' desperate need to embrace images of Kelly and Jessica somewhere sunny, wearing robes, sporting wings—easier than picturing them as they were pried from the wreck, neither completely intact.

Whatever works.

Both had been in their twenties. Kelly was in grad school studying water quality and working on her thesis; Jessica was cramming for the bar, keen to practice tribal law. Though they were grown women, Pete still frames them as the adolescents they'd been during an Easter break ten or so years back. He and Beth had been in town with their daughters, little then—to visit Gappa Appo (neither could pronounce *Grandpa* or *Alpo*).

Pete had gone for one of his "walks" in the unseasonable warmth, the flask a solid comfort in his shirt pocket. Passing the Wiirtinen house he saw Kelly and Jessica on a blanket on the flat part of the garage roof, trying to sop up heat from the dark asphalt. They were thirteen, maybe fourteen. One was painting the other's toes—he can't recall who was painter and who was paintee. Pages of a magazine flapped, an Easter basket rolled. At that stage, Pete was managing his job and keeping things under control; it was well before Beth had begun to suspect.

As he passed below the girls unseen, the laughter spilling over from the roof cut him with a pang of something he could not identify. Once out of range it hit him. They seemed such intimate conspirators. He could have used such a friend himself at that point, one who might demand he get his shit together and stop being an idiot: he envied their friendship.

But by the time he'd reached his father's mailbox he was considering the upside—that *not* having a friend meant there was no one to keep him from spending the holiday afternoon popping in and out of Alpo's fish house to visit the fifth he'd hidden there.

* * *

Letting his head roll, he takes in his father's silhouette, wondering if he thinks much about his mother anymore. Pete has long ago stopped trying to understand his mismatched parents. Because they seemed so often to confound one another, Pete believes what kept each bound was some quest to solve the other.

He hopes Sissy with all that life in her can make his father happy. An old Robyn Hitchcock tune weaves into his head—he wonders if his father has ever heard it. *My wife, and my dead wife.* He grunts the lyrics away before they can lodge.

Pete chooses to remember his mother as he remembers those girls—long before her end, before becoming ill, at her most vivid. About the age he is now—younger, actually. *Am I the only one who sees her?*

"I'm older than my mother."

After a beat, Alpo says, "You're thinking out loud, son."

He opens his eyes. She'd always been quick with advice—annoying, really. But now he'd give anything. What, for instance, might his mother suggest they do about Rauri?

He knows exactly what she would suggest—that they hightail it out there and check on him. "I should paddle out there," Pete says. "To Rauri's."

Alpo considers, then shakes his head. "I could go. You have work."

"You've got this weekend to think about, remember?"

"I do . . . ," Alpo brightens. "I s'pose I do."

"That's right, Dad, just keep practicing the *I do.*"

2

SISSY HAS HAPPIER THINGS TO THINK ABOUT THAN A nice old guy dying alone without even a dog. Honestly, hasn't everyone had their fill? And now with Rauri missing here's the grim reaper shaking his bony finger at Hatchet Inlet again. Maybe. Sissy looks around at the regulars. She'd prefer their usual complaints about lakeshore taxes, the tailings pond at OreTac, and union dues, because the tedious for-and-against, for-and-against at least has a rhythm to it. Now it's one-upping each other on how many grisly ways one person can die, from how long it might take to bleed out, to arguing whether spontaneous combustion is really even a thing.

Sissy's got half a mind to tune the radio to *Morning Edition* and give them all something to take their minds off Rauri.

In sixty-some hours her wedding day will commence. This time Saturday she'll be having her hair teased into an updo and her nails French-manicured. Thirty-six hours after saying "I do," she and Alpo will be in Cozumel on their all-inclusive honeymoon, where for ten days *she's* going to be waited on, and when not being waited on, she's going to bake on a Mexican beach. Sissy's coming home with a tan or she's not coming home at all.

The dress hangs in a zippered garment bag on the back of the Ladies' door. Either it's come unzipped on its own or someone's snuck a peak. She unzips it the rest of the way and runs a hand along the champagne-colored silk. Inching closer to sniff, she recoils and yells to her brother, "Joe, turn that fan to high! My dress smells like the special."

He yells back, "What the hell's it doing *here?*"

Does he expect an answer? After picking it up from the alter-ations lady, she hadn't wanted to leave it in the car. The rash of break-ins has been blamed on the meth heads, but as far as Sissy's concerned, meth is a problem in Hatchet Inlet only because Janko Junior isn't half the sheriff his father was. No surprise when some-body slapped an *I'd rather be fishing* bumper sticker on his squad. No surprise when Junior didn't peel it off.

She looks to the wall where Pine Pig hangs, as if he might have something to say. Back when her great-grandfather Turk Pavola opened his butcher shop, a logger gave him a huge wafer of pine with two hundred wobbly rings of coniferous history. Turk carved it into a sign for the shop, seven feet across and eight inches thick, chiseled on both sides with a relief of a hog wearing a crown, his quarters sectioned and labeled with the different cuts: Hock, Shoulder, Trotters, etc. Arching over in san serif is *Pavola's*. Sissy likes to imagine old Turk working on the sign by lamplight, wood chaff in the mighty beard of his photographs. If Pine Pig could talk he might sound like her great-grandfather in some yowly-vowelly Finnish cadence. But because Pine Pig never says any-thing, he seems all the wiser. Sissy has been caught more than once talking to him (so what?) and has suggested Laurie try it herself sometime, "Because the thing is, you talk out loud for long enough, you eventually start hearing yourself." And if Lau-rie could hear herself, she might dial it down.

Carved at the bottom of the sign is the sentiment that more or less still applies ninety years on at Pavola's: *Where Bacon Reigns*.

Joe gets his pork from a farm in Wisconsin and cures it in his pole barn before hand-cutting it. Laurie and Sissy have worked the bacon craze—making bacon-caramel syrup for sundaes; bacon brownies; bacon jam; bacon-glazed donuts. After the novelty of those wore off, Laurie washed her hands of bacon, but Sissy hit the bulls-eye with her cashew-bacon brittle, and now summer people are hooked on SissyBrittle as if on opioids. The counter does a brisk business with no one blinking an eye at eight-fifty a pound. And since it's Sissy's deal, she gleans a hundred percent of the profits, shrugging off Laurie's suggestion that cashews are an extravagance, that peanuts at a fraction of the price would increase her profit margin. With her first season's take, Sissy had a logo designed, got a Website, and had boxes made. Her pre-Christmas orders went ballistic. The FedEx driver good-naturedly blames his extra pounds on Sissy when she tops off her orders with a box of seconds for him. She needs to decide whether to make SissyBrittle a real business or keep it small.

Bacon may reign at Pavola's, but damned if her wedding dress is going to smell like it. From the short-order line, Sissy hears the *thunk* of Joe's cleaver and a mumble. She's about to holler again when the fan ramps up and green order slips flutter on the spinner as if in a gale.

She pries open the back door and hangs the garment bag outside on one of the old meat hooks where Joe hangs deer carcasses during season. November is the month she most dislikes, each day a narrowing corridor of light, deer hung upside down with their impossibly huge eyes filming over. One year Joe hung a whole family: doe, buck, and two yearlings, skin stripped away, all sinew and bare muscle bound by cauls the color of dusk. Some deer are given to Joe by the DNR when culling the herds; some come from hunters that don't even like venison but kill for sport. Sissy covers her ears when Joe names them: sometimes living in a small town requires willful ignorance. That's what Alpo says.

But this morning she's just happy it's May—it's spring and in every way opposite of November. In spite of its being only forty degrees, Sissy lingers, thinking of something their mother used to say when shooing them out of doors: *Go blow the stink off.*

Two bearded millennials driving one of those new Cube things slows near the alley lot. The passenger squints at the back entrance. Most tourists turn their noses up at the diner, put off by the pressed-asphalt exterior and the faulty neon *Pa ola's* sign. But Laurie insists that Rural Gothic is in now—plaid is all the rage down in the Cities, where hipsters are happy to drop three hundred dollars for steel-toed boots identical to those miners pay fifty-five for with their union discounts over at Shaw's. These urban boys with waxed mustaches are "lumbersexuals," according to

Laurie. Most of them work in tech and graphic design but wear the reverse mullet of early loggers—party up top and sides buzzed. Alpo says he would pay money to watch one try to cut down a tree.

Both roll their windows down to get a better look at the parking lot. The one with geek glasses wears an Elmer Fudd hat. The Cube slowly moves on as if reluctant to park its puny self next to an F150 or Ramcharger.

Some tourists turn away at Laurie's *No Free Wi-Fi* sign, or upon discovering drip coffee where they'd hoped for cappuccino. Laurie has hinted that Sissy's incessant questions drive others off, as if being friendly would. There's no half-full glass for Laurie—she's a quarter-cup or nothing, while Sissy's billows over the rim in that way (she can never remember the word for it) but what's the harm when she only wants to know who these people are and what's compelled them to travel across the country or even an ocean? There are the resorts, the lakes, and the Reserve. That's all. She understands the draw of escaping the rat race of big cities, but her own version of vacation would not include portaging thirty-pound packs or eating freeze-dried food, and she would rather not use a pit toilet in the woods while being watched by creatures with teeth bigger than her own. Now one of those houseboats with a full kitchen and bath—that she can see. This place can look beautiful in the brochures, all glittery water and sunsets, but at the end of the day, here is just that—*here.*

Some even have rooftop decks with water slides.

Pavola's best patrons are the longtime summer people, cabin owners, and retired snowbirds who believe the diner is their discovery and let everyone know they are forgoing the Perkins down the street to support a mom-and-pop diner. They come in mid-morning after the regulars file out, around the time Laurie fires up MPR. They joke about cholesterol specials and leave huge tips that Sissy and Laurie are happy enough to rake in.

Sissy unzips the garment bag all the way to let the breeze rustle the silk. It is hands down the nicest dress she has ever owned, and she wishes the clerk at Nordstrom's hadn't referred to it as a bandage dress. It's not white, and not an actual wedding gown—who could face that? Even hearing the word conjures torn lace. She's chosen a very elegant calf-length dress-up dress in champagne silk, with the palest robin's egg blue piping that matches the lining on the little three-quarter-sleeve bolero jacket. When she'd called Laurie in to the dressing room, her sister had nodded, half-approving, "Not bad. It makes your waist look smaller than it is."

"But?"

"I didn't say *but*."

"You're thinking it."

"I'm not. I just think it's an interesting choice for the over-forty bride."

"Because it's strapless?"

"No. Just cross fingers for the weather, or you might need more than that little bed jacket."

"It's a *bolero*."

"Well, this isn't Spain and you're not going to a bullfight. You'll need more."

"I'll freeze before I wear some jacket."

"Well, not a *parka,* something classy—a *wrap*? How about a mink from Annie's?"

"And smell like mothballs? No, thank you. Does my back flab hang over?"

"You don't have back flab." You never knew when Laurie would be kind.

Sissy, suddenly feeling too large for the dress, lifted her arm for Laurie to undo the side hook and zip her free. She let out the breath she'd been holding and watched the dress pool to the carpet. "I wish Kelly was here."

After a breath Laurie says, "We all do, Sissy."

The last time she'd shopped for clothes was for the funerals, and the excursion to Duluth had been awful—navigating the mall, poking useless hands and useless elbows into dark sleeves. God knows her mind hadn't been on back flab then, just finding something fast so she could get back to the pod of her car where she'd taken to holing up like some den animal—her Mazda being the one place besides bed where she could let loose the eerie moans she didn't know were in her, let go the tears that leaked as if from some cracked hose. For ages her passenger seat was so thick with balled tissues it looked like a craft project.

At first, Sissy had been in shock like everyone else. The thought can still stall her in midstep. Her beautiful niece, killed along with Jessica Wiirtinen. *Along with* is how the grief counselor has urged Sissy to think of it, not killed *by* Jessica, which is how Sissy cannot help thinking of it sometimes, though she has managed to never say it aloud once.

At the bachelorette party they'd all been drinking. Just Chardonnay for Sissy and Laurie, but the bridesmaids were drinking Red Bull and vodkas. Plus a few obscenely named cocktails like a Blowjob, which Sissy learned was a shot of Bailey's knocked back with lips stretched around the rim of the shot glass. A Stiff Dick was basically a Long Island Tea with half & half. There'd been a lot of laughs when it nearly gagged Tammy.

"Gross." Sissy had grimaced.

"Which is the *point*." Kelly had snorted, "Hel*lo*?"

It bothers Sissy that these were the last words between her and Kelly. Why couldn't it have been something less sarcastic than hel*lo*?

Good-bye?

Who could have known they weren't just going to the Ladies'? Later, the security footage showed how they pinballed across the Duckblind parking lot, giggling and armed with a glue gun and a Rubbermaid bin of crepe streamers and paper roses. They were off to decorate the honeymoon cabin up at the Narrows for the bride and groom. At the inquest, evidence against the bar included grainy images of them climbing into the van, still wearing their thrift-store wedding dresses spattered from their afternoon at the paintball field, wrangling their filthy trains along.

Approximately fifteen minutes after leaving the lot, the van's brakes engaged at the tight curve after the gravel pit, and the vehicle launched through a copse of young birch, snapping them like bones before crashing into the girders of the DM&IR trestle bridge.

They had been best friends since kindergarten. Just before the dual closed-casket visitation had begun, the florist delivered a horrible wreath of pink and blue carnations, spelling out *Friends4Eternity*. Laurie tossed it into a coat closet before either of the mothers could see it.

Someone planted a cross out near the bridge. People wedged bouquets, Beanie Babies, candles, the usual things. Mourners could peer past the busted trees to see bits of pastel-colored crepe paper fluttering from bushes and trees. Not knowing what else to do with herself that first month, Sissy had driven out nearly every day after lunch rush. She watched the crepe twist amid the last flutter of birch leaves. The stuffed animals became a soggy mess and the colors of the crepe ran together. By the time the pin oaks were naked, the streamers had bleached to white and lay limp on the ground. Then snow fell to cover it all.

She had retrieved one of the paper roses from near the base of the bridge where deep scrapes were scarred with Dodge red paint. The rose is still taped to her dresser mirror. Sissy knows it should be taken down soon. Kelly would want her to. Wouldn't she?

There are only so many reminders one can take. Maybe the rose does belong back at the bridge. Sissy's yoga teacher is always suggesting ways to "shed the negative" and leave thoughts and emotions behind with little visualization tricks—to shuck whatever is weighing you down, toss grief like a rose into a ditch.

She's better off than others on the obituary's survived-by list. Sissy's brother Dan—Kelly's stepfather since she was barely two, so basically her father—has only begun to shake the underwater quality of his speech. Kelly's sister Bailey has developed a sort of leaning shrug to the empty space where her big sister should be. Janine is still drinking like a fish in the privacy of her upholstery shop. The Pavolas are standing—hollowed some, but still standing.

Tammy's wedding had been postponed, of course, and when it did happen six weeks later, it was simply the saddest wedding in the world. Which is one reason Sissy's been so insistent on a cheerful event for herself and Alpo. Defending her extravagance, she says, "Hon, this town *needs* a party."

"Fine," he agreed, "but I am not going to Minneapolis to any cake tastings. And I want food that's food, nothing *artisanal*."

"Okay."

"No pan flutes, and no tux. *Nada* on the tux." They'd both been listening to Rosetta Stone Spanish in preparation for their honeymoon.

"Ok*ay*," she'd said, assuming there would be some wiggle room. "But maybe you'll get a new suit at least? I mean, your good one is nice but are you going to—"

"Wear the same suit I wore to the funerals? 'Course not. That suit's so old I wore it to Rose's."

When Sissy frowned, Alpo pulled her to standing from her kitchen chair. "I may be cheap, but I'm no chump." He spun her in a half-turn. "Men's Warehouse, here I come."

Two things Sissy loves about her fiancé: one, he knows his own mind. And two, he's thoughtful. Not something she could say for Gerry, ever. She wonders if Gerry is on Facebook, and if he'd seen her status change to "engaged," and if so, what he thought. As if she cared.

Out on the loading dock Sissy stretches up on her toes and breathes in a huge breath of dirt-scented air. On the south side of the dumpster a cluster of red dogwood has muscled open its buds. An alley stream trickles from under the last of the blackened scabs of snowbanks on the north sides of garages.

Rauri Paar or no Rauri Paar, spring has arrived.

As Sissy steps back in, she notices Pete and Alpo have left their tips on the table. She has asked them not to, but her request seems only to have prompted a challenge for each to outdo the other. They fold their bills into origami—at first just simple things like paper airplanes. Then Alpo Googled *origami frog,* which was one-upped by Pete's windmill, trumped by Alpo's rabbit, and so on. The contest has nothing to do with her, really. What she knows but they don't is that her little collection of folded dollars represents the beginning of something better between the two of them. A tiny way for Alpo to dole out forgiveness without having to say anything, and Pete's way of showing he's making the effort.

Today one of Sissy's prizes is a horse's head fashioned from a five, and the other is either the Empire State Building or a rocket constructed from two ones.

By nine a.m. the first breakfast crowd has thinned, by ten-thirty the second wave is beginning to clear out, and she has a half-hour before the early lunch crowd descends. When Marna comes in to spell her, Sissy slides into a booth with her notebook and iPad. She checks again on the florist's delivery time and her remaining to-dos. Her Friday pedicure is scheduled for five p.m. Another weather update assures her that while Thursday and Friday look dodgy, there will be no rain on Saturday. Early May can be unpredictable, from blizzard to broil, but the forecast for her wedding day promises midfifties and sun. Fingers crossed nothing blows down from Saskatchewan.

Her hair appointment at Tresses is doublechecked. The wedding is at five-thirty, reception from six-thirty until whenever. Sober-Cabs and Uber drivers will trawl the Sokol Hall parking lot—no one is driving home drunk from her wedding, she's making damn sure of that.

Sissy understands that the usual traditions aren't what make a wedding memorable, so she has cherry-picked a few elements she hopes will. No bridesmaids or maid of honor for one thing means not having to favor one friend or relative over another. So hurt feelings are avoided, mostly. Laurie had only frowned and nodded, and while her friend Nancy might be stinging right now, she'll come around, if only for being spared the expense of a bridesmaid's dress. Sissy herself has a cardboard wardrobe in the attic stuffed to the gills with a hideous pastel lineup from the eighties and nineties—ruffles and puffed sleeves and shoulder pads that made big girls look like linebackers and petite Sissy look like a fifth grader playing dress-up.

No gifts. It's not like she and Alpo *need* anything. The opposite—they have two households of accumulated stuff to winnow through. Only the best of their furniture will go into their new lakeside townhome at the Landings. Not to say guests are getting off scot-free—donations to Malamute Rescue Minnesota will be encouraged (not *extorted,* as Joe implies) and collection boxes will be scattered over the tables. Thanks to SissyBrittle, she now has Square on her phone and iPad, so not carrying cash won't be any excuse. She's ordered a hundred refrigerator magnets shaped like paws and printed with the Website URL for those preferring to donate online.

The wedding will be fun. People need fun. The Erbach Brothers of Superior get booked a year in advance for a reason: they can sing and play anything from Taylor Swift to Tony Bennett. Joe says be thankful they are as homely as they are or they would be lost to *American Idol* by now. She'll be given away by Jeff. Joe let it be known his feelings were hurt by saying, "No biggie," and as much as she'd like to, she couldn't risk asking her brother Dan, who would probably bawl the length of the aisle.

Alpo jokes, "Even I'll be outshined by Jeff," which is only the truth, because there is not a man alive except maybe Clive Owen who approaches the brand of handsome Jeff has in spades. He is currently being groomed and probably not liking it, which is why Sissy asked Alpo to drop him off at Doggie Style. It takes nearly three hours to bathe, blow-dry, trim, and express the anal glands of a 140-pound malamute. Plus, it being May, there's his undercoat to rake out. Sissy's requested Jeff's nails be clipped and buffed. The pale aquamarine studs on his new collar match the piping on Sissy's dress, and, as it happens, his eyes.

List ticked, Sissy relaxes and pries off her shoes to sit cross-legged in the booth with her two folders, one marked TRIP, the other marked WEDDING. Cathy O'Hara jibs into the diner wearing one of her flowy Indian things. Once the door closes, she deflates some and heads for the booth, all smiles. She will be playing piano during the ceremony. Sissy likes Cathy well enough, but sometimes she's that person who, when you mispronounce some word like *expresso* won't correct you on the spot but will manage to find a reason to say *espresso* a sentence or two later. Alpo says that is the definition of passive-aggressive. Cathy is muscley and tan, recently back from her winter working at a goat ranch in New Mexico, where in return for beanful meals and a stall-sized bedroom with views but no central heat, she made chèvre cheese from goat's milk and taught Iyengar yoga. Cathy calls herself a *sojourner* instead of *snowbird*.

She returns each spring to live out at Naledi Lodge with her niece, Meg. Cathy is a very social person, and Naledi has turned out to be more remote than she'd bargained for. Sissy sees this happen—people move here for the quiet, not counting on quite so much of it. Cathy is in town often, wanting to be part of things, determined to fit in, volunteering for this and that. Every third word out of her mouth is *community,* but you cannot blame her for being enthusiastic. She's taken a job two days a week at Pebbles & Bam Bam, the hot stone massage place Veshko the refugee operates. Sissy has wondered if Cathy might not have a thing for Veshko and reminds herself to pay more attention to him during her massage, because for a man she lays herself out nearly naked for twice a month (thank you, SissyBrittle), she couldn't even say how tall Veshko is or what color his eyes are. After the massages she is limp and blurry without her contacts and he is all manners. There is a thing he does down each side of her spine with his oiled elbow that makes her imagine being pressed right through to the underside of the massage table, reborn. Veshko is from Sarajevo, where he lived through The Siege. Everyone has their trouble and loss, but she imagines Veshko has had more than most—though it's hard to know since he's not what you'd call chatty and could hardly be accused of overdoing the eye contact.

Cathy settles in across the booth and glances at the papers and brochures Sissy has fanned before her. "All squared away?"

Sissy begins ordering her stacks back into the folders. "I hope so. Flight info, Sandals reservation, et cetera." She holds up an official-looking envelope. "Marriage license!"

"Nice. Can I see?"

"Sure. You want some coffee?"

"Mm, just hot water." She fishes a jar of something that looks like soil from her bag. To Sissy's questioning look, she shakes it. "Chia."

When Sissy returns with a cup and a pot, Cathy is frowning over the certificate.

"You're changing your name?"

"Yeah . . . ?"

Cathy looks as if she's been slapped. "Why?"

"Why?" Sissy sits.

"Did Alpo tell you to?"

"*Tell* me? No, we haven't even . . . we haven't actually—"

"You haven't *talked* about it? Well, then, there's still time." Cathy leans. "It's an archaic tradition, Sissy. Your name is your identity. It's who you *are*. Taking on a man's name labels you as *his*—you're subsumed."

"Subsumed . . ." Sissy knows what it means, it just seems a little dramatic. "Cath, my name isn't who I am. It isn't my *identity*."

"How isn't it? How?

"Well, I—"

"It's insidious misogyny women still buckle under, and *why?* I could list twenty reasons it's a bad idea—thirty." Cathy raps at her breastbone like it's a door. "We deserve equality, Sissy, but if we don't respect ourselves enough to keep our own identities, how can we expect anyone else to?"

Sissy tries to reply but Cathy is on a tear.

"Seriously, if the educated women of the First World don't set an example . . . I mean, girls in Nigeria are being kidnapped and sold."

Sissy nods and pours more hot water into Cathy's cup, hoping she will pause to drink because she looks a little flushed. Besides being a cheese-making *yogini* (according to her card), Cathy is also a Life Coach and holds weekend retreats out at Naledi for women from the Cities. It seems to Sissy that all Cathy does is what smart girlfriends do for each other: give advice. *Leave him! You're good with hair, open a salon. Whatever you do, don't adopt his kids. Try Vagisil.* Commonsense stuff. Sissy supposes it's always easier to tackle someone else's problems.

"Listen," Cathy's tone shifts, calmer now, as if speaking with a client. "You've been Sissy Pavola for how many years?"

"Forty-five. But I don't think changing my name to Lahti will get anyone kidnapped."

"Maybe not, Sissy, but it won't do any *good.*" Cathy dabs the corner of her mouth. "Just think about it? There's a war on women, Sissy, and you have a voice. And if you use your voice, you're a *warrior.*"

Sissy pounces on the diversion of Joe wheeling out a rack of Cornish pasties to cool. "I don't know about you, Cath, but I'm starving." She has two pasties served up as Cathy is beginning to slow down.

"An entire gender shooting itself in . . . *that* smells amazing."

"On the house." Sissy pushes the plate under Cathy's nose as aromatic steam wafts from the little vents in the pastry. "Protein for the battle? The beef is grass-fed and the lard's free-range."

Cathy grabs a fork, giving her a look. "You're a terrible liar." The way Cathy goes after the pasty, you'd never guess she drives all the way to Fargo to picket stockyards.

It's the Pavola recipe, the crust downright airy—the secret being the cold half-dropper of cider vinegar added to the water mixing it with flour cut with beef lard. Besides seasoning, there are only three ingredients in Pavola's pasties: meat, potatoes, and onions, period. Sometimes butter. Some cooks will add rutabaga, but Sissy suspects that's to distract from fatty meat or tough crust. A pasty containing carrots is just wrong. On a trip to Wisconsin Dells, Sissy had been served a pasty with *peas* in it, leaving her to wonder if the Badger State hasn't lost the plot in more ways than one.

People do often take Cathy's advice—maybe because for as preachy as she can be, there's something about her that makes you think she knows something you don't.

Sissy's thoughts skip back to the morning.

"Cathy, you know Rauri Paar?"

Cathy takes her time to chew. "Sure. I see him around."

"He talk to you much?"

"Some, here and there." Cathy closes her eyes a moment, considering the mouth-feel of a perfectly diced potato.

Sissy waits it out, not wanting to distract. "Do you get any sense he's, you know, down?"

Cathy swallows. "Down? He's never really, ah, up is he?"

"True, but . . ."

"I haven't seen him since last fall, anyway. Why?" Cathy asks.

"He's what . . . missing, I guess." Sissy's gaze wanders to the window. "Darn Rauri."

Maybe it was nothing, but there had been something, some little thing about the last time she'd seen him . . .

"If Rauri is dead," Laurie is suddenly at the next booth, stacking dirty plates along the plank of her arm and hooking a syrup pitcher with her pinkie, "I'll kill him." She meets Sissy's eye and narrows her own. "We don't need any drama this weekend. You're getting married Saturday and that's that." Laurie hips the swinging door into the kitchen and disappears, the hinges squealing in her wake.

Cathy captures crumbs on the back of her fork before licking it like a Popsicle. "I miss having a sister."

"You do?" Watching the door thump to stillness, Sissy blinks back to Cathy. "Sorry, of course you do." Cathy's sister was Meg Machutova's mother, killed ages ago in a plane crash. Sissy is about to offer a word, but some bulb appears to be going off for Cathy.

"Hey. You know that public radio couple? This place could be featured on their show. They tour the country looking for greasy spoons?"

Sissy stiffens. "Greasy?"

Cathy waves the comment aside. "We all know how clean this place is—I'd eat off the urinal."

"I'd like to see that! You've *been* in our Men's?"

"Well, no."

Thank goodness, thinks Sissy. Cathy would have a bird if

she saw the wooden stalls in the Men's, where crude and complimentary comments about girls and women have been carved into the walls since Roosevelt—from soldiers' initials entwined with their sweethearts' to a list of girls doling out free love next to *Class of 1970*—the zero made into a peace sign. More recently are invitations to troll something called Grindr. The more offensive stuff gets sanded away, but some of the funnier lines and old limericks have been spared. Laurie even chose to leave the etched cartoon of herself saying, "There are plenty worse things to be called than Puss & Boots. The scabbard's a bit butch, but I wouldn't mind that hat."

"You're out of the water closet at least," Sissy observed. Neither has been in the Men's since going on strike and tasking Joe with the responsibility. Lord knows what's in there these days.

Laurie is out in Hatchet Inlet, but with a force that seems unnecessary to Sissy. The wide berth given Laurie has nothing to do with her liking women—no one has ever said boo about Miss Rappaport, that writer Polly, or the ex-nun who owns Bucksaw Sisters. Why would they bother with Laurie?

"Oh," Sissy remembers the radio couple. "I know what show you mean. He's skinny, she's not. Jack and Mrs. Sprat?"

"That's them." Cathy is now using her index finger to clean the plate. "They'd go crazy over these pasties. Your brittle, too. You could be bigger."

Cathy has hit on exactly what Sissy's been gnashing over. Does she want to be bigger? As it is, she can visualize every single counter where her brittle is sold—little tourist shops on the route to Hatchet Inlet, cafés down the North Shore, the Roadhouse out on 98—places like that. But if ratcheting up orders a notch or two meant working fewer hours in the diner . . .

"We could get in touch with that cook-show host who always sounds like she's salivating."

"Sure, but can we talk about the music now?"

After Cathy has left, Sissy considers her warning. Does a marriage subsume? That could apply to a lot of things people get sucked into: the Shopping Channel, restoring an El Camino

(Gerry), Facebook (Laurie), and even lifestyles—like Cathy's holistic, Prius-driving, non-GMO, organic-cotton *simple* life that looks anything but. Would the opposite of being *subsumed* be to turn your back on it all, like Rauri Paar? Choose to live life in the woods, alone? Nobody else's thoughts budging in, no needs, opinions, no pressure? No neighbors but wolverines and whisky jacks. That's just a different sort of being sucked into something— *yourself.* Sissy wouldn't last a week on those islands without going over some edge. Could that be where Rauri's gone, over? Not far from where he lives is the literal edge—the Majimanidoo Falls— where little whirlpools twirl around a larger whirlpool, a giant drain that never ices over, called Satan's Basin. What goes into the Basin rarely comes out, including tourists or idiots who read the warnings and see the chain-link fence as a challenge. The Basin is a convenient choice for suicides. Neater than a gunshot, quicker than pills. Those tossing themselves in usually leave notes—like that poor bullied Greenstone boy who drowned himself just to have the last word.

Sissy blinks at her distorted reflection on the chrome of the sugar dispenser. If anyone would have time to think about and plan their own death, Rauri would. Sissy sighs. Maybe there's something to be said for being too busy to think about such things. The thought just reminds Sissy of all she'd miss, like every single thing that will happen next. One week you might be handed someone's brand-new nephew to hold, or watch the next Susan Boyle win *Britain's Got Talent,* or taste the best peach ever on a trip to Florida. She hopes Rauri hasn't done something stupid (unless he's been diagnosed with something horrible, which is a different thing altogether). It seems backward to Sissy that her mother's neighbor over at Senior Cedars sits waiting to die from lung cancer with each breath sounding like something dragged, while Pete can put down a sick cat in less than a minute with a syringe.

Then there's her mother, but Louise is just too much for Sissy to be thinking about right now.

3

A LPO ROLLS TO A STOP AT THE FIRE HALL AND CUTS the ignition. "I do," he says aloud—not practicing, as Pete suggested, more like a repeat of the "I do" he'd mumbled much earlier that morning.

At five a.m., he'd opened his eyes to Sissy's naked silhouette, framed in fluorescent from the bathroom fixture. His first thought was *how slight she is,* then, how unfair that she must haul herself out of bed six days a week in the pitch dark to get in a cold car to work in a hot kitchen and listen to bullshit that gets lobbed across the booths at Pavola's like pearls of wisdom.

She'd been shivering and hopping into a pair of panties when Alpo patted the covers.

"Back to bed, Red. Ten minutes."

"Now?"

"Yup."

"I gotta be at the café in thirty minutes and you want me to come back to bed?"

"*I do.*"

The spooning that ensued became more than spooning. Alpo became engrossed by the fine joinery of Sissy's shoulder blades, then with meshing the salt-and-pepper stubble of his chin with the blond stubble of her armpits. Ten minutes turned into thirty—he'd made her late, and when late there's the wrath of Laurie.

He's thinking of Sissy as she'd been, sleepy and languid, her shoulders dewy from the shower. The back of his hand aimlessly travels the steering wheel, its leather-wrapped knuckles feeling

as skin-warm as her spine. Alpo is in fact still planted in his blue
Bronco because he doesn't want to walk the ten feet from his parking spot to the fire hall with a woody. You worry you're too old
and then . . .

For most of Alpo's life, sex has been more a physical act than
one of emotion—of *passion*. His marriage to Rose, while loving,
hadn't exactly been an erotic garden. She had been willing with
limitations, and while they'd had their moments, Alpo could
count on one hand occasions he'd heard her cry out in pleasure
or saw her naked with the lights on. The irony being that she'd
been built for sin, with the perfect-ten proportions of a Rockette:
skin like polished quartz, breasts like a Valkyrie. Aside from one
ancient relationship with a girl who flipped burgers at the Anchor
Bar in Superior back in the '60s, little in Alpo's experience suggested sex might twine so deeply into a union—into *him*.

It seems so normal these days to toss around terms like *fuck*
or *masturbate* in the same tone used to ask for the pepper. And
how casual nudity seems to be for Sissy's generation. She pads
around the house in a thong and nothing else, has hauled him to
Hoodoo Point to skinny-dip, and even dragged him out at midnight to stand peeled in the rain. Being needled by a downpour
had felt cathartic.

She's made such fun of his pajamas they are now crammed
deep in a drawer: it does make him feel younger, waking up in
just his skin.

Then there's the selfie, which if it ever got out would mean
the end of his dignity, to say nothing of Sissy's. She'd been peep-
ing from under the green fleece blanket, a jaunty fold of it fallen
across her forehead just like an elf cap. Her eyes were comically
wide and the blush on her cheeks matched the hue of his penis,
which she had comically smashed up against her nose. Bulbous
is a terrible word but the only one. He didn't even know she'd
had her iPhone down there until the flash went off. Later, sitting
on his lap and flipping through the pics, she'd laughed so hard
she'd peed a little on his thigh. Alpo laughed until his C3 and

C4 throbbed, because in the photo no one else can ever, ever see, Sissy looks exactly like a Disney character and his penis looks exactly like a dwarf's nose. Naturally, he begged her to delete it.

"Ho," she'd held the phone away, "not likely."

"Then I'll have to . . ." His attempt at sounding menacing was laughable.

"What? You'll have to *what,* big man?"

"Marry you."

By the time their mutual shock evaporated Alpo realized that he *would* like to marry Sissy, if she'd have him. And so, he asked her properly, down on one knee, dangling left.

Alpo has fallen in love before but has never had fun doing it.

Sissy sometimes laughs when having an orgasm, which could be a real blow to a man's ego if he didn't know the woman better. She's often cried too, and while those first tears had been a bit of a shock, she swears it's not sad crying, just her body letting go of what-all gets pent up during the course of a day: kitten videos, asshole drivers, the news. Probably thoughts of Kelly, but Alpo doesn't press it. Besides, lately her outbursts hold more delight than sorrow.

Alpo unzips—just to relieve the pressure—and gazes through the windshield awhile at nothing, then shakes his head at his own lap and gives in with a robust hand, as if meeting some old buddy shown up out of the blue. It's not ten a.m. on a Wednesday, and here he is wondering if there isn't a Wendy's napkin on the floor of his Bronco.

There is.

Only when he's finished and breathing like a bear does he remember what he'd been trying to remember at the diner. About Rauri Paar.

There are, he supposes, worse ways to clear your head.

The day Rauri Paar first arrived in Hatchet Inlet it was Alpo who had ushered him in. He hadn't mentioned this earlier because he's not one to share half-assed details, and his memory of it is forty years hazy.

* * *

He'd picked up the hitchhiker just north of Mountain Iron. Alpo had been testing the suspension of his not-quite-new red-and-white Dodge short-bed. He'd been savoring the quiet ribbon of road between the din of the machine shop and the din of home, where at two months Petey was full-throttle colic, and little Candace toddled and clanged around in the pot cupboard, accompanying herself with yodels in a pitch that triggered sinus pain.

The bestraggled stranger on the side of the road looked several years younger than Alpo, or maybe just seemed young because he was small and looked lost. Closer, it was harder to tell. When he went to hoist the kid's Duluth pack to the truck bed, Alpo nearly sprained his shoulder. The thing weighed sixty pounds at least.

"Jesus." Alpo had given him a look.

"Canned goods," he explained. "A few books."

"You visiting? For how long?"

The kid shrugged. "A while. I guess."

Alpo looked him over. Sheepskin coat, battered boots. Skinny. When he pulled off his cap, his ginger hair tumbled out just like in the song, shoulder length or longer. He was no hippie, though, considering his calloused and brown hands, maybe a farm kid with no money for a barber. His forehead was sunburned and peeling. In March? Given his eyes, he was either utterly exhausted or utterly stoned. He didn't look like he was from the area, but he didn't look like he wasn't. When he revealed his ignorance during the ride, Alpo wondered if the kid even knew where he was. *What do folks hunt here? When's fishing season? Is lake water safe to drink?*

"What growing zone's this?"

At that, Alpo suppressed a snort. "Two," he said. "Same as Unalakleet, Alaska."

"Shit." His passenger sighed.

They stopped at Amoco for the toilet. Alpo went last, and when tossing his paper towel saw the damp wad of fresh pocket trash: candy wrappers, a spent matchbook, knotted twine, an empty Lucky Strike pack, and a hospital bracelet twisted in with the cellophane—its blue letters blurred—the patient name illegible, but he could clearly make out *WR Med Ctr.*

Whatever the kid's story, whatever brought him to Hatchet Inlet was none of Alpo's business, yet something made him pluck the bracelet out of the bin before shoving the rest of the trash deeper. Back on the road, the kid fiddled with the radio knobs until he found the rock station in Duluth, and when the reception failed, as it always did near the Divide, he found a Canadian program in French and went silent for the remainder of the ride, giving no indication he understood what was being said.

Dropping him off, Alpo offered his hand along with his name and girded for the inevitable, *Like the dog food?*

But the kid only said, "Raur-ri," stuttering over the name as if making it up on the spot, "Paar." Alpo remembers thinking he'd never met a ginger-headed Finn. The veins on Rauri's exposed wrists were so blue and vulnerable looking they made Alpo think of his children.

At the corner of Main and Third, Rauri shouldered his pack easily and nodded. "Hang loose" was his good-bye. He didn't say thanks for the ride.

From flashes in the periphery Alpo knew he'd stayed around town in one of the cheaper rooms that outfitters rent to paddlers, biding his time at the library during the day. No clue what he did at night. Alpo gleaned that Rauri had kitted himself out for god-knows-what with maps, dry goods, a compass, tools, kerosene, tarps, fishing gear, a bush radio, and a battered Old Town canoe.

As soon as the ice went out, Rauri drifted away to a back-of-beyond border lake to settle on a trio of islands shagged with jack pine. He shored up the old trapper's cabin and built a greenhouse from salvaged storm windows, splurged on a Jøtul, and there he stayed. In the four decades since, Alpo has hardly given Rauri's history much more thought. He's giving it some now. What had he ever done with that hospital bracelet? Back then, besides working fifty-hour weeks, he'd been building a new foundation and a proper basement for the house, Rose had just gone back to teaching, and they were raising two little kids. Digging into Rauri's business wouldn't have been high on his list.

How word got around about Rauri's ferry service to Canada is anyone's guess, but during the remaining draft years a dozen or so kids with high numbers had gone fishing on Rauri Lake, drifting over the border to Ontario shores but not drifting back. The code for the whereabouts of such young men was that they were *drinking Molson*. After President Carter declared amnesty, most returned but some stayed for the vibe and for the socialized medicine. One that did return was Alpo's younger cousin Jay. He'd taken young Pete to Jay's welcome-home bash, basically a kegger with fireworks that could be seen from the Canadian side.

Pete had lost his first tooth that night, quite literally, so that Alpo and six other grown men found themselves on their knees poking around in pine needles and duff with flashlights and Zippos. After Pete had bawled himself to asleep, Bo Baltich shucked off a boot and sock and trimmed off a thick section of his own toenail with his pocketknife. They all sat in a semicircle drinking warm beer and watching Bo whittle it to the approximate shape of a child's incisor. They woke Pete under the light of a ritual moon and somberly if not soberly presented him the tooth and a jangle of coins. Rauri happened to have a Canadian centennial silver dollar in his pocket. Alpo wonders if Pete still has it.

The few older vets down at the Legion frowned on Rauri's shenanigans—it's okay to be a pacifist, just not an active one—but the 'Nam vets cut him more slack, having been there, half-wishing they'd done the same, still trailed as they are by serrated dreams, phantom wafts of wet bamboo and cordite. Or worse.

After amnesty, Rauri took off without a word and was gone a year—so it's not like he's never disappeared before. There was a rumor of a woman, possibly a kid. Recently, a new rumor of that old rumor had resurfaced, that Rauri's rumored kid was now either a rich dot-com executive or gay or both.

But no clue where rumored son might live.

Rauri returned just in time to become the bull's-eye at the hot center of the Reserve debate, so any curiosity about what he'd been up to was shunted to the rear. The issue was motors: open the park to snowmobiles and outboards, fly-in floatplanes and four-wheelers, or limit it to canoeists, cross-country skiers, and backpackers. By the long drawn-out end it came down to the existence and rights of one person. Rauri Paar became the sole pin in play. Because he held outright ownership, Rauri was granted a provision: he could relinquish his property for a sum above fair-market value, or be grandfathered in to dwell on the islands until his death.

Which only postponed the final designation and postpones it still. In the meantime, each side has had decades to keep appealing, time to ratchet their senses of entitlement off the charts. Alpo understands that nothing pisses off the righteous like having their convictions put on hold. Outsiders believe control of the Reserve is theirs, and locals believe they own the place and are wolfish about territory. All along there have been threats, commotion. Just last year a young couple was caught trespassing on one of Rauri's islands, puncturing holes in his boat—perhaps hoping Rauri would go down in a sinking runabout? Rauri had shrugged it off, refusing to lay charges. There's been vandalism, and most probably more threats by mail than Rauri lets on. Mischief goes part and parcel with disputes, property line challenges, and zoning infractions—practically rites of passage north of the Divide, where obtaining the simplest easement is anything but easy.

Alpo has known the crew at Pavola's since they were in grade school. Some are jealous of Rauri's special privileges—of being able to run a motorboat where they can't, live where they cannot camp without a permit. But would any of them act on it? He hopes not. Still, Alpo's not sure why Rauri would make light of threats. Other times he wonders if Rauri is really as hapless or uncomplicated as people think.

Back at the house Alpo has a drawer full of clippings from the Reserve battle, many mentioning Rauri. There could be something he's missed or forgotten; maybe that hospital bracelet got stuffed in there. He makes a note to check.

It's a warm enough morning he can open the fire hall garage doors and air out the fug of cigar smoke from Walt who volunteers nights. He likes having the doors open so that folks driving by can be assured that the two gleaming fire trucks and the boxy ambulance are at the ready and well kept. Not that a few pampered vehicles will stop anyone from being an idiot with a chainsaw or driving drunk, but when the worst happens, these vehicles are in prime condition, even if only to rush EMTs and volunteer firemen like himself out to deal with the aftermath.

Alpo had been one of the first on the scene after the accident—something Sissy need never know. Upon arrival, everything was smoke and murk and a chaos of shouts delivered on clouded breath. The plate number of the totaled van was repeated into a shoulder mike and copied.

It was the first hard frost, with a ground fog so he could see the beams of high-powered flashlights crossing each other. Men crashed through brush, and with each discovery things slowed and muted a notch; ambulance lights throbbed in the bare treetops as if the place itself had a pulse. Alpo's boots crushed frost-furled leaves, snapped twigs. Someone muttered a steady *Jesus, Jesus* at intervals. Radio transmissions hissed. The sky lightened to a flat gray somehow eerier than the darkness. Maglites snapped off. Positions of the bodies and wreckage were marked. It was determined there was no second vehicle involved.

"Two confirmed DOS" was the message passed on man to man, radio to radio.

The road was chalked, the skid trajectory notated as a clear case of lost control. The driver might have swerved to avoid a deer, hit a patch of frost. Considering the state of the wreck, excessive speed was implied.

There was the sound of plastic rustling, then the long rasp of a zipper the length of a body. The first zip Alpo heard, the second he felt. He did not know at that point who the victims were and to this day does not remember actually picking up the arm, only that he'd sat down hard on the bumper of the ambulance and held it in his lap. He examined the charm bracelet dangling from the wrist, slowly recognizing it, and puzzled as to how it could have wound up at such a surreal scene. It was a college graduation present from Sissy to her niece Kelly. At this point Alpo wondered if he wasn't dreaming, then hoped he *was* dreaming, then felt his breath seize upon realizing he wasn't.

The bracelet had a golden ice skate, a jade Buddha, and Kelly's sorority emblem. There was an enamel Eeyore, and a run of little gold letters sassily misspelling FUKC. Sissy had had the sterling Minnesota charm custom-made with a tiny sapphire like a lake set approximately where Hatchet Inlet sits.

"So," Alpo remembered Sissy telling Kelly, "you'll know your way home once you've conquered the world." It took his recalling Sissy's voice to burst back into the moment.

As long as he held his palm over the carnage where the elbow had been wrenched free, it just looked like any arm lain across his lap. It made him think back to watching television with his daughter, Candy, her sitting on the floor with her back against the couch, elbow thrown casually across his knee to reach for the popcorn bowl.

He remembers taking the medical ziplock bag handed to him, but not who gave it to him. The plastic had a slightly waffled texture through which he could still make out each charm on the bracelet. The plastic was just blue enough to tint the blood an inky purple, as if a Bic had leaked inside. With his cuff he carefully wiped away the smears of blood. He dug for a hankie, found a puddle, and made sure the exterior of the bag was immaculate, wiping, then wiping again. He sat back down on the ambulance bumper and kept the arm safe. There'd been so little weight to it. When the EMT came to ease it away, Alpo was unaware that he was even speaking, let alone reciting *Everything nice.* He stood as they filed past with the stretchers and filed back with the body bags. The young women in those bags were not going to be fixed. Alpo did not possess the tools, had no sugar and spice.

* * *

Alpo unrolls the folded canvas hoses on the fire truck, turns them on for a quick fill, and checks for leaks and wear. Done, he uses the water to hose winter grime from the planters made of truck tires that edge the station lawn. The ground is flax-dry on the surface but spongy and cold beneath. He rewinds the hoses, making sure the bearings are oiled. Machinery is absolute. Nothing so fallible as a girl's arm.

Admittedly, like Pete, Alpo thinks too much lately. Not because he has too much time on his hands—his hands are actually quite occupied as the only volunteer who maintains equipment. His duty at the station is a litany of brief tasks that take all of an hour each shift—a romp compared to tending the mining machinery he was once responsible for. Here it's mostly just checking and rechecking. Also, Alpo tinkers. Since people know he's here and can fix things, they bring him their broken toasters, electric can openers, sewing machines, and dust busters. He's happy to oblige, drawn to the sort of mechanical minutia that require dainty tools and a little patience. It's meditative, fixing snagged bobbin cases or wonky Hoover cords, and he sleeps like a baby knowing his work won't result in any OSHA disasters.

Now that he's retired, his thoughts are supposed to be his own, but what they do is tug him around as if on a leash. The theme over the past week has tended toward choices—those he has made and those he didn't. What if he had taken another path, considered other options? *Regret* is too strong a word, he actually has very few: one pops up like a cowlick—that he'd settled for the mines when he could have become a mechanical engineer, maybe seen more of the world.

He'd had a chum back in junior high, Tommy Machutova. Alpo didn't see much of him outside school because Tommy lived out at Naledi and worked the resort all summer for his old man. They'd been on the same team in applied science class and wrote a paper together about the invention of the television based on the Aha! moment Philo Farnsworth had while watching a field being plowed—the inspiration from which sprung his patent for an image dissector photo tube and, subsequently, television tubes.

Their instructor, Mr. Urho, knew exactly what he was doing when he took each boy aside and told him he was first in the class but would need to hustle to keep his lead. It worked: both Alpo and Tommy dug in to compete, fierce but friendly. They shared similar aptitudes and both had drive—the big difference being that when it mattered most, crusty old Vac tutored Tommy in algebra and helped him apply for a scholarship to a prep school in Lake Forest, Illinois, and Alpo's own father got off his bar stool just long enough to march him down to the Shell station where there was an opening for a mechanic's assistant. The prevailing tide in Hatchet Inlet in the sixties was that the mines were good enough, that logging and outfitting were good enough, and that aspiring to more suggested attitude.

Once Tomas went away, Alpo at least got Ruthie Amundson, the girl they'd both been crazy for. He envied Tomas for his ivied school where learning was revered, where shirt cuffs stayed clean. He imagined his own hands working a slide rule instead of dismantling carburetors. Inevitably, Tomas's next step was a good university while Alpo's was a two-year stint at VoTech.

After starting at the Gulliver Mine, Alpo only saw Tomas once or twice a year when he was home on break from CalTech. They'd have a drink, talk fishing or girls, but avoided topics of work or study—the gap in their futures already too wide to bridge.

Vietnam was the static background on radio and television. Since wars need steel, work at the mine went into high gear pulling ore to make choppers and jeeps—and weaponry, Alpo assumed. When the topic of their mutual deferments came up, Tomas vaguely mentioned working "on something" for the government and had been recruited by an engineering firm in the Pacific Rim.

Alpo met Rose, got promoted. There was less leisure for a beer with Tomas at the Duckblind, not that he was home often, and by then he'd married Anne. After the war, Tomas took an offer from a firm in Chicago that built bridges and bought a house in a leafy suburb. Alpo buried his father and moved Rose into the Lahti homestead in time for Candy to be born. Life happened.

He couldn't say why he'd felt more guilt than grief when Tomas's plane went down. His little daughter Meg already looked like an orphan with her curls and Annie freckles. It was hard to fathom a motherless girl with only old Vac for company.

Alpo sighs. Yes, there are things he'd like to do differently. He dribs tiny orbs of 3-In-One oil onto the flywheel of a Kenmore, pushes his chair back to stand and stretch.

Though the fire hall is a volunteer gig he sets a schedule. Lunch is from 12:30 to 1:15. He never peeks into the lunch box because Sissy asks him not to. Today it's cabbage rolls *and* coleslaw, in case he wasn't getting enough cabbage. But that's Sissy—if cabbage is on sale, cabbage is what's cooking.

As Alpo lines up the Tupperware he thinks of Rauri and the night Bo Baltich carved the tooth, when they all sat on the forest floor passing Pete from lap to lap like a little sack of sleep, keeping him off the damp ground. Rauri had made a joke nobody got about a writer Alpo hadn't yet heard of, suggesting the evening was very "Robert Bly."

Years later, Candy gave him *Iron John* for Father's Day, which Alpo dutifully read half of until realizing there was not going to be a punch line. Recently, he'd begun sorting through the bookshelves and it's popped up again, sitting in a box destined for Goodwill. He wonders if he should give it another go . . . it seems that these days men only make statements and voice opinions, react rather than reflect. Rauri would have read the book, since he seemed to read everything—the walls of his cabin are lined with shelves, books stacked two deep. He claimed the R-value was terrific. Maybe he's out there bent over some novel, hopefully with something to eat, chewing it with a jaw in working order.

Alpo's own sparse shelves hold mysteries and crime novels written by former lawyers and cops—the sorts of books that if lost or forgotten can easily be replaced by another in the series.

Rose had been a picky reader, reverent about the books as objects, and handled them as she did the family china, keeping the best behind glass. Her people recited poetry at the drop of a hat—at two whiskeys the genetics would kick in and the one-upmanship reciting Keats and Kavanagh would commence between Rose and her sister and the priest brother who always struck some chord out of tune with Alpo.

"Guilt for your Godlessness," Rose would chide, to which Alpo would grunt.

"Jealousy over the name, then?"

Not jealousy. Something else—to suggest he resented little Pete being named after her brother? Alpo wouldn't have wished his own name on an enemy, let alone his own son.

Clannish, the Corrigans pulled little Pete into their games early on, enlisting him to compete in word games, the crossword puzzles, urging him to lisp the entirety of "Jabberwocky" through the gaps in his teeth.

Alpo thinks of Rose's many books and sighs. He'll have to ask Pete to sort them and take what he wants and donate or sell the rest. He won't bother Candy, who won't stand for the clutter of books in her modern box of a house where she and Dentist Dennis (she begs Alpo not to call him that) are raising his youngest grandchildren, pretty Maisie and peevish Paul.

Rose would say the key to a person's character is there on their bookshelves, but Alpo has his doubts. How many actually get read and how many are for show? Rauri is a bookworm, but what kind? Has he been one of those quietly philosophical types all these years? Does he read to escape reality? His past? Has he been out there all this time wrestling with a poet's heart? As Alpo rinses the Tupperware and sets it on the drainboard, he realizes how little he knows.

4

"WIPE THAT OFF THE WINDOW, PLEASE," HIS father said. "And next time use a tissue."

Pete tucked the offending finger into his sweatshirt sleeve and frowned. "I don't got any tissue."

"Don't *have* any tissue," his father corrected, shifting to pull a handkerchief from his hip pocket, but Pete was already grinding the snot across the passenger window with a cuff pulled over the heel of his grubby hand.

"Great." Alpo exhaled.

"This drive is boring. Will we get to swim?" Pete's finger was auguring again and his heels whacked the bench seat. "How. Much. Longer?"

Alpo reached over and tugged Pete's hand from his nose. "*Leave* it. Ten minutes, tops. And do not tell me you have to pee. And no, you can't swim. It's too cold yet."

"It is *not*."

"Besides, you didn't bring trunks."

Pete sulked as the road narrowed. Ahead was a series of signs for the resort, planted one after another Burma-Shave style.

Alpo pointed. "Can you read those?"

Pete glanced out the pickup window. "Yup."

"Can you read them *aloud*?"

With as world-weary a tone a seven-year-old could muster, Pete read.

Vacationland is getting nearer,
Put your feet up and relax here.

He sniffed.

Land of Sun and Sky Blue Water,
Watch the Deer and Moose and Otter.

Pete nodded his head to the rhythm in spite of himself.

Northern lights and peace a-plenty,

As they reached the arch he frowned and finished robotically,

Wel-come, cam-pers, to Na-le-di.

"That's good, son. Do you know what an exclamation point is?"

"Yeah," Pete muttered, looking ahead at the string of cabins, his forehead furled in dismay. "It's not a camp!"

"No, it's a resort."

Past the cabins stood the lodge, anchored on one corner by the tiny store. BAIT SNACKS BEER POP nailed above the porch windows in twig letters. Pete pointed to the fiberglass Arrowhead Dairy Cone. "Can we get ice cream?"

"We can get ice cream."

"Same-*same,*" Pete sang.

"Same what?"

"Two sen-ten-ces, same words."

"Is that so?"

"Rearranged." Pete watched his father think that over and tapped the window. "*Re. A. Ranged.*" He pressed into the bench seat. "I don't want to play with some *girl.*"

"Some *girl* might not want to play with you. Ever consider that?"

In the lodge, Pete's father turned him by the shoulders to a freckle-faced girl with eyes that didn't focus so much as take aim. "This is Meg."

He folded his arms but did not look away.

"Meg, this is Pete." Her own greeting was a mere shrug but enough to set her curls bouncing, putting Pete in mind of Slinkys, a headful of miniature Slinkys the color of the copper wire in his dad's workshop. All over this girl's head.

Vac sidled out from behind the bar, looked Pete over, nodded, opened the screen door, and said to both children, "Get some fresh air." As if they lacked it.

His father followed, herding them to the play area. Vac stepped out to watch a moment, then disappeared inside. Alpo was just getting Meg positioned on a seesaw when Vac was approaching, holding up two beers, indicating the bar with his thumb. Alpo reluctantly let go of Meg and nodded to Pete.

"Play nice now."

Before his father reached the door, they'd abandoned the see-saw and ambled off.

Near a cabin that was being cleaned, Pete was drawn to the Radio Flyer the maids pulled from cabin to cabin. Big girls, college girls with kerchiefs on their heads like Aunt Jemima on the syrup. Meg told him Vac fixed up the wagon by welding on racks to hold the mops, rags, and cleaning supplies—a long dowel at the rear pointed up like a lance to spear a dozen rolls of toilet paper. A transistor radio attached to the rack was rigged with an antenna made from a coat hanger. When Meg's back was turned, Pete stole a little bar of Camay for his mother.

At the horseshoe run, three resort kids listlessly tossed bean-bags, dressed almost identically. They were so bored they invited Meg and Pete to a game of hide-and-seek. Neither made any attempt to hide, and as the countdown began, Meg offered a polite, "No, thank you," and in a show of ownership took Pete's hand to pull him along. "I have a *guest*."

There were better things to do than play.

Pete followed Meg to the farthest cabins. Just as they rounded the corner, they heard a soft thud. A hummingbird had flown into the glass sky reflected in the windows. It lay on the path, its body inert on the orange needles. It didn't even twitch when Pete held it. Its neck was hinged.

"It's broke." He held it out to Meg.

She picked pine needles from it and they examined the tiny corpse together, turning it every which way, watching its colors change in the light, gingerly tugging the wingtips to their full span. Its beak was surprisingly long and sharp. Even as he held it, Pete could feel the warmth draining from its body. Meg declared the number of tail feathers was uncountable, and while Pete was able to count beyond five hundred, he pretended he couldn't. They decided the rest of the body was covered in fur because they could not fathom feathers so small. They went off to look in the garbage bins for a box that might do as a coffin but could only find an egg carton. After laying the little bird in it they thought it looked too alone surrounded by eleven empty places, couldn't bring themselves to lower the lid. They set off to hunt for other dead things to keep it company. Meg found two minnows belly up in the bucket. She knew where there was a squashed tree frog on the road. Eleven corpses was a tall order, so rather than keep searching they decided it would be easier to find more living things and *make* them dead. They killed a worm, a leech, and a beetle. Neither relished the acts, but they were necessary. Then having lost their appetite for blood, they decided a chicken bone counted, as did a handful of dead bluebottles from the fish house windowsill. The husk of a big spider harvested from a smaller spider's web gave them pause. When there were only two empty egg sections to go, they decided personal belongings would be fitting tributes: Pete dug in his pocket and produced a sticky watermelon Jolly Rancher, then helped Meg untangle one of the platoon of pearly plastic barrettes restraining her curls.

The ceremony was brief, because Meg knew no prayers other than the good-night one. She haltingly recited, *Now I lay me down to sleep, I pray the Lord my soul to keep. If I should die before I wake. . . .* Pete knew a phalanx of prayers in both English and Latin, learned from the High Mass his mother took him and his sister to on Sundays. Saturday mornings his mother went to confession while his father would stand in the driveway wrapped in a towel and tersely wave her off—Saturday was Alpo's sauna day. Pete and Candy didn't go to confession. Their father forbade it, so on Saturdays they were allowed cartoons and Captain Crunch. By the time Sylvester the Cat and Road Runner had worn themselves out, Pete and Candy would be sugar-fraught and cranky. Their mother would return bright-eyed and forgiven, and their father would emerge from the sauna the color of an eraser.

Pete knew the kiddie prayer too; he rushed in to join Meg, *I pray the Lord my soul to take.* They topped the little mound of earth with a Popsicle stick cross. Meg led him through the boathouse, a blind box of chill after the bright sun. The walls amplified the sounds of water lapping at the interior walls. Pete didn't like it. Even his whisper was loud and echoing.

"I wanna go back outside."

"Don't you want to see the boats?" Meg was clearly disappointed, intent on showing off her territory. "We sleep here sometimes when it's real hot."

"Sleep *here?*"

"Me and Vac, on air mattresses. In the canoes. It's nice."

As Pete's eyes adjusted to the darkness the boathouse corners seemed a little less sinister. He could make out two wooden canoes bumping together and a few fishing boats. In one corner was an oddly bulged figure, like an alien or one of the starving children in Africa from the commercials his mother wrote checks for. It was only an outboard motor clamped to a sawhorse.

Just as he was saying, "Wait," Meg grabbed a snorkel mask from a hook and clomped to the far door to open it onto a sudden rectangle of daylight. He followed as she led him around the *H* of the docks. Forgetting she was annoyed, she took his hand and tugged him to the end of the dock. They lay belly down on the boards with their heads and shoulders over the end and Meg stuck her face in the snorkel mask, her voice funny as she said, "I'm gonna see what's down there."

"*I* want to see what's down there!" Pete knew what an exclamation point was.

"We have to take turns." She wriggled on her belly and commanded, "Sit on my butt so I don't fall in."

Pete sat on her backside and waited, chin planted on fists. When he grew tired of waiting, he bounced a little and each time he did, a hoot came out of the snorkel tube and a garbled "*Stop it!*" erupted with a spurt of water. After being patient for nearly two minutes Pete nudged her. "My turn."

She'd wanted to see what was waving around on the bottom; he wanted to see what kind of fish he might catch to cut open to see what was inside. While Meg sat on him, she hummed a tuneless hum. The end of the dock cut into the flesh under Pete's ribs. He tried to see a fish. There were none, only some old beer cans half-buried in the mucky bottom, reeds, and a clump of some kind of jelly eggs growing on weeds.

Meg pulled his head out of the water by yanking on the snorkel. "You really want fish?"

She led him back to the fish house, where two dads were filleting a stringer of pike. They asked for the carcasses the men were only too happy to give over, watching with some amusement as the two laid them out on a flat rock and examined the skin and bones with sticks.

The skeletons were slimy, with rough fins and teeth so razor-sharp Meg insisted they could saw a Popsicle stick in half with the jaws. "I bet you could."

"Maybe," Pete was dubious. The mention of Popsicles reminded him of his father's promise of ice cream.

They had passed maybe a few dozen words between them in three hours. When they got back to the lodge, Alpo asked them what they'd been doing.

Both blinked in tandem: "Nothing."

His father brought him out to Naledi many times that summer. Pete didn't remember those other visits nearly as distinctly, though he could imagine they had spent their time similarly, walking around looking for things to take apart or put together. There was sand to be dug, dolls to be dismembered, sticks to be sharpened, things to do.

A lifetime ago. A yellowed catalog from the time they were fast friends, long before he and Meg were more.

Their most recent encounters he'd just as soon forget. But his sponsor Granger has urged him to go over every humiliating moment. See yourself through the eyes of those on the receiving end, spare yourself nothing. He'd last seen her just as he'd relapsed, only weeks after the accident—the night of the freak October blizzard that froze everything in place, the debut of the worst winter in decades, in such surreal circumstances that if Pete were to write it as fiction no one would believe it. What do they call it in detective novels? The hook—usually in the first paragraph.

I was minding my own business, drinking myself blind, when I got the call to go pick up a severed hand.

From where Pete had been splayed on his sofa, it looked like a record breaker. When snow blasted the glass, he turned toward the snow-scalloped pane, a Hallmark card view. Outside, drifts had covered over the open crates of recycling at the curb and the sodden couch on the lawn of the house opposite. The two cars up on blocks were buried to the bumpers. As curb appeal goes, the snow was a win-win in Pete's neighborhood.

Pinned by inertia, Pete was occasionally distracted by a loose corner of wallpaper flapping in the draft. He could get up and do something about it right then, if he'd felt like it. Instead, he flipped from one end of the couch to the other so he wouldn't have to. His porch steps were engulfed in a graceful drift, suggesting the house was afloat on a sea of snow. The corner stop sign shuddered. He felt around on the floor for his World's Best Dad mug and managed to drink the last of the Dewar's without raising his head. He was just about to get up for a refill when a weather announcement interrupted the *Polka Peggy Show*—nothing Pete would deliberately tune in to, but he rarely shut the radio off, because it's a voice in the kitchen, companion audio to the television and the *Breaking Bad* marathon he'd embarked on earlier when he'd still known the location of the remote.

"Plows have been called back to the county garages. Travel recommended only in emergencies, folks."

Pete collapsed back to the cushions. When the plows get

pulled, there's no going anywhere. He queued up another episode and five minutes in realized he'd already watched it. He closed his eyes for what he thought was a minute. An hour later the phone vibrating across the glass coffee table woke him. He recognized the number from the county offices and was about to ignore it, but then it was four a.m. Nobody calls for nothing at that hour.

"North Country Vet. Lahti here."

"Pete? Janko here. Sorry about the time."

The last time the sheriff had called was the morning of the accident. He worked himself into a sitting position, feigning nonchalance. "No problem, Janko. Don't tell me Bubba ate more socks?"

"Nah. He's good. Pissed about wearing the cone, though. Listen, you won't believe this."

"Try me," Pete said.

"You know Hal Bergen?"

"Sure, sort of."

"He's been 'coptered down to St. Sebastian's in Duluth. At least most of him has."

That roused Pete. "What?"

"Bandsaw accident. Lost his hand out at the mill."

"Jesus . . ." Pete stood too quickly so that shapes in the room kaleidoscoped. "Christ."

"Yeah, well, what was lost has now been found. 'Cept we don't got any vehicle that can get out that way to pick it up."

"*Have* any vehicle." Pete rubbed his stubble.

"Say what?"

"Nothing. What do you mean *pick it up*?" Pete wasn't convinced the conversation was actually happening. He pinched the skin of his Adam's apple. Apparently, it was.

"We can't pull an ambulance for this, and I doubt one could even make those back roads with these drifts. I know you got your snow machine out and was thinking maybe you know something about limbs. And since you already know your way around there?"

"To do *what* . . . ?"

"Get it. To get the hand."

"Yeah, Janko, but where?" *Jesus. Hand?* Poor fucker, Hal. Pete was moving in the direction of the kitchen and misjudged the step, nearly pitching. The phone launched from his hand to spin across the linoleum. He caught up with it just as Janko had finished answering.

"Sorry, Junior. This phone. Where, again?" He remembered too late that Janko hated being called *Junior*. His father had also been sheriff, as had his grandfather. Big boots to fill, then bigger.

"The Machutova place. Across the bay from the mill. Didn't you work out there summers for old Vac?"

"Naledi?" After a pause Pete inhaled. "Hang on. How in hell does a hand from the mill wind up at a boarded-up resort?"

"A dog is how. And it's not boarded up. Vac's granddaughter what's-her-name is back up there. With that husband."

"Meg." Pete shaded his eyes against the fluorescent glare of the kitchen. "You mean Meg?"

"Right."

"You want me to go out to Naledi. To pick up Hal's hand?"

"If you're, you know, up for it."

He looked out the window. The thermometer was juddering, snow slanting sideways. Where frost had formed on the inside of the glass, Pete scratched a letter.

"Pete?"

"Okay, Janko." He scratched another letter. "I'll get out there."

"Bring a cooler."

"A cooler?"

"For the hand."

"Ah. Will do." After hanging up Pete looked from the blank iPhone screen to the window where he'd written MEG in the frost. He scraped away the letters. This storm was the real thing—sober he wouldn't chance it. Had he thought to bring his snowmobile suit in from the garage last spring? Of course not. It would be ice-cold, same for his Sorels.

Pete took pride in his *high-functioning status*—a term picked up at rehab. He was able to sober up on a dime, or at least appear to go from drunk to less drunk in fifteen minutes, an accomplishment when the bar was set so low. Dousing his head with the kitchen sprayer, slamming a Red Bull, and eating slices of bread, and he's nearly Steady Eddie. The irony isn't completely lost on Pete that it's easier to pull himself together when it's to tend to some sick or torn animal or to change someone else's tire.

Or rescue a hand. Pete stepped into the bathroom for a leak and swayed over the bowl, blinking as the stream splattered up from the rim, thinking it might be best that the snowmobile suit is cold after all.

He'd seen Meg around town a few times during the previous summer but never approached. It was never the right circumstance. Either she was with her husband—tall, smug, hoity English accent—or she'd be chatting with somebody or in her car or on her phone or pumping gas. Something. She'd looked right at him more than once and smiled the way you smile at a stranger. He zipped.

Pete blinked at the mirror, striving to recognize the version of himself voted Most Mysterious in the senior Wolverines' yearbook, lean with dark good looks. These days he looked how he felt: bloated, fifty instead of forty. The muttonchops only made him look greasy. His eyes were bloodshot, the skin underneath like hammocks.

"Fuck."

He briefly considered shaving. As if there were time, when Hal Bergen was down in the hospital waiting for his hand. *Whatever the hell that must be like.* Just the thought merited draining the breakfast mug just there on the toilet tank, a measure of whiskey laced with cold tea.

Meg used to hire Rob Perla and his wife Katie as summer caretakers when she was living overseas, but even when the place was closed up, Meg had the driveway plowed in case of fire. Pete occasionally went out there during off-season to check propane lines and snow loads on the roofs. He knew where all the keys were hidden and would fire up Vac's old John Deere just to keep it running. Stale oil's no good for a motor.

Sometimes he let himself into the lodge and went to her old room, nothing in it but boxes and a stripped mattress. He stood in the room she shared with the husband to check out the sort of books someone like him would read. He never felt he was trespassing.

In summers the old Canadian lived there. Polly—bit of a stiff until you got her talking, and then she was pretty entertaining. Once Pete realized her vision was going, he picked up her groceries and gin when Jon Redleaf wasn't around. Vac had deeded Polly one of the few remaining cabins and had more or less deeded her Meg, too, in some sort of guardianship deal, though it was all pretty murky to Pete.

Now Meg's out there with a *hand* and her professor who does not even own a driver's license, let alone a fishing license or carry permit—one of those pillars of academia who might as well be covered in ivy himself for how useful he is. He plays tennis.

If anyone could handle a hand, it would be Meg, the most unflappable girl Pete had ever known. The best and worst thing about her, he supposed. And no one really changes all that much. Do they?

The Polaris started on a dime. Main Street was like a church aisle, each lamppost casting a snowy veil like a first communion lineup. The weight and rate of snow would guarantee a real mess once arctic air bore down to freeze it all. A mother to shovel—the ER would have its share of cardiac admissions.

With the ice barely formed, there was no traveling across Little Hatchet. The general rule of thumb was that a local wouldn't drive an ice road until weekenders from the Twin Cities planted their shanties and had gone back and forth in their four-wheelers or trucks a few times. Canaries in the coal mine—usually a few got fished out before things set up.

No matter. Pete could travel faster on the road, take a few shortcuts on trails. Speeding through a tunnel of blinding flakes, Pete battled the angle of snow, trying to keep his goggles clear. A half-hour out he was exhausted with eyestrain. By the time he rounded the curve of the lake to move opposite the wind, his arms shook with fatigue, reminding him of the days he'd split and stacked wood for Vac out at Naledi.

All the kids had summer jobs. In May the tourists swarmed to the resorts, to town, to the lakes, looking for anything to do, catch, buy, or eat. Local kids like Pete and Meg got counter work, or stocked shelves, washed dishes, did grunt labor for the outfitters and resorts. Pete's first job was at Chummy's stocking bait, netting floaters from the concrete minnow tanks, keeping the algae down and the water aerated. He packed Styrofoam to-go cartons with night crawlers and moss, taking care to poke holes into the lids after his first hard lesson: several returned containers of suffocated bait came out of his paycheck, which at $3.10 an hour hadn't amounted to much. He measured leeches into clear bags of lake water and topped them off with squirts of oxygen until the bags were drum-tight. He herded crickets into grassy beds of Chinese take-out boxes. He was adept with his net and could scoop exactly a dozen minnows in one try—at fifteen, you took points of pride where you could. He battled his own reek each night by washing his hair twice with a Lava bar or the Lemon Up his sister suggested, which turned his sable-dark hair a rusty brown. His dreams had the coppery taste of minnows.

By his second summer at Chummy's he'd worked his way up to the counter. Because he fished on his half-mile paddle to work, he knew what was biting in the mornings and on what—pike on leeches, sunnies on slugs. He gave customers tips on how to keep bait alive with club soda, how to float an onion bag of chubs to an anchor rope.

During one early commute, he encountered Meg at the shore on Goose Point, her little runabout anchored and nodding. She was onshore, utterly absorbed in the watercolor pad balanced on her knees, a brush clamped in her teeth. He hadn't seen her much since their days as children at Naledi. She sat on a fish-cleaning board nailed to two level stumps. In the pink sunrise, she was a little like a painting herself, one side of her hair looking ready to ignite. She moved her charcoal stick along with her whole arm, elbow, and knobby wrist. He assumed she was making some waterscape, but as he got closer he could see her looking at a pile near her feet, something rank and haloed with flies: offal and fish skeletons, the sort of mess fishermen leave for turtles. He noticed that her hand did not stop when she cocked her head to the gore, just kept working like an oiled tool.

He didn't want to scare her, so he stirred the surf a little with his paddle before placing it on his knees. "Hiya."

Without looking up, she lisped around the paintbrush. "No need to whithper; they're already dead."

"I remember you."

She looked up. "I remember *you*."

Meg was old enough to run errands for the old man by then, maneuvering the resort's jeep through town like a union driver, though Pete knew she was younger by a year and not old enough for a provisional license. If Janko Senior took any note, he let it slide.

"What the heck are you painting?"

She dipped her brush in water and dried it on her T-shirt before parking it in her hair. "Mostly drawing—just adding some color to show what's guts and what isn't."

"Sounds pretty."

"Actually, it is." She met his eye. "Wanna see?"

He didn't think it was pretty but lied.

As it happened, Naledi needed a dock boy that summer and suddenly Pete had two jobs. Vac worked Pete hard, but he and Meg managed to find time for the sort of mischief you'd get up to with a buddy: raiding the leftovers to bring to the landfill for bear-baiting, drinking sweating bottles of pilfered Schlitz. They trapped red squirrels to a dual purpose—keep them out of cabin rafters and to supply Vac's taxidermy hobby. The old man's ongoing project was to create a squirrel symphony with enough "musicians" to conceivably play Mahler and possibly make the *Guinness Book of World Records*. Meg pitched in by carving dozens of tiny cellos, violas, and violins out of balsa wood. She made timpanis out of acorns and bassoons out of chopsticks. After skinning the squirrels, Vac would give the naked carcasses back to

Pete to dissect and take anatomy notes. He dried the bones and reconstructed the skeletons the way other boys glued together model cars.

Meg did her best to annoy Pete on a daily basis, doing things he wouldn't do on a dare, like climb the old fire tower though it was fenced off with bold warnings. The steps weren't just rickety; some were rusted through. Once, she had gone up and climbed out the roof hatch to hang on to the flag post. It had been raining and the corrugated slope was wet and dangerous as hell. Shouting himself hoarse for her to get down, Pete realized he'd never been so angry with anyone, ever. On the way back to the resort he would barely look at her.

"Why did you do that?"

He didn't realize Meg was shaking until she spoke, wobbly, grinning like an idiot. "Because heights scare the crap out of me."

Most girls made little sense to Pete: this one made none.

Looking back, he'd missed a few hints dropped like lead. They'd paddled across the border to Lulu Island once where she showed him the spot where she was "pretty sure" she'd been conceived. Meg dragged Pete up a rock and pointed down to a sickle of sand. "That's where I got started. I think. Dad had this joke only my mom laughed at: 'I went all the way to Lulu Island and all I got was this goddamned kid.'"

Pete had been standing close enough to smell Meg's hair, piled in a way that made her look like she was balancing a sewing basket. A trickle of sweat on her neck traced down to her collarbone like an invitation. It physically hurt Pete to not lean over and press his tongue to that shallow dip. He began to inch forward, then stopped—because how weird would it be to kiss a girl at the same location where her parents had done it?

After an awkward minute Meg shrugged. "So I guess that makes me Canadian."

Was there something wired differently in an orphan? He wondered.

His own mother had been sick with cancer that year. Her bright cheeriness got brighter but was punctuated by scrimmages of whispers between his parents that stopped abruptly when he walked into a room. Their bedroom door was closed at odd times, and he knew for a fact they weren't in there doing it.

She was the real thing, orphan-wise, having lost both parents in one go when their plane hit Lake Michigan—dad, mom, and the unborn brother or sister she never got to meet. So she never knew her parents the way you would by fifteen. Pete sometimes regretted being rude to his mom, but he hardly seemed able to help it. How many times he hadn't done what she'd asked—kept his room neat, been more polite, come in at a decent hour—even knowing she was sick?

Females. The problem with mothers was that there were no clear perimeters like there were with fathers, where things were more cut and dried with tasks, rules. You knew exactly how you'd messed up because there were facts. Pete was discovering that there were simply not that many facts regarding the overall makeup of females.

Another time, after Lulu Island, Meg took him to a boarded-up mine shaft, a place he wouldn't have gone unless coerced since it was rumored to house undetonated dynamite. Meg scoffed, claiming that was just a scare tactic to keep kids out—she'd been down it a *thousand* times. When he hesitated, she met his look with her steady green stare. "Ohhh," she said knowingly. "You're afraid."

He had to go then. In the tunnel his headlamp kept flickering so he could barely make her out, though she could see him, her beam like an interrogation. They popped up into a shaft entry the size of a small room where slices of light cut through wallboards. Meg pointed to a pallet and told him how one of the resort guests—a married man—had taken an underage girl there to have sex with him. The girl, Lilith, had had a reputation. "Jailbait," Meg said. That's what Lilith's cousins called her behind her back—also called her "nympho"—and Vac, who never said much about anybody, had called the girl "wanton," leaving Meg to puzzle over what being a slut had to do with Chinese food.

She'd shown Pete where the nympho and the man had done it, matter-of-factly recounting how the man had asked Lilith to pinch his nipples. Meg looked up as if truly perplexed. "What would that even do for a guy? Would that even work?"

Pete had hung his head, unsure he could take any more tours of landmarks where people had screwed.

By the following summer Meg had made her own fake ID to get into the rural taverns like Without a Paddle and Bucksaw Sisters. She had taken to hanging with an older crowd, college boys up from the Cities, a few locals. All were shitheads, as far as Pete was concerned. Meg was sixteen and acting like she was twenty-one. One of the guys who hung around her was nearly thirty. Pete told her she'd better be careful. He warned she was going to get into trouble. "I wouldn't trust those guys as far as I could throw them."

"You're the expert on the sort of guys I should date?"

"Date? You play pool with them. They buy you drinks and then make out with you in the parking lot."

"You've *spied* on me?"

"One of these days one of them is going to get you into his car. That's all I'm saying."

Meg bit her fingertips in mock terror. "Not into his car!"

"You know what I mean."

"Unreal. You sound exactly like my grandfather."

"Well, Vac isn't stupid," Pete said.

"I suppose you think I should date somebody like *you*." She fingered little quotation marks in the air.

"Yes, actually." It just came out.

She did this thing then that the old man did—went still and silent so that what you'd said just hung in the air as if spelled out. She reached out and laid a hand on his chest just over his thudding heart and said, "Well, *that* took you long enough."

Meg was seasonal, packed off each Labor Day. Pete usually tagged along to see her off at the airport in Duluth, helping Vac hoist the green school trunk. Meg lugged Dayton's bags containing new loafers and uniforms. She'd told him the uniforms allowed her to blend in among the rich girls, and she hid her orphan status by speaking of her parents in the present tense. When classmates and dorm mates talked about vacationing in places like Gstaad or St. Barts for Christmas holidays, she'd mention her family's winter "lodge," which is only what Naledi was during winter. When they headed to places like Provence or Rome for summers to be dragged through museums Meg would kill to see, she'd admit being stuck at one of the family's summer places, which was hardly a stretch since Vac did own thirty cabins.

In spring Pete would anticipate her arrival with feigned nonchalance. Once the ice broke up and buds popped on the birches, Meg would be delivered north along with the mayflies as if borne on the wings of a hatch.

Years later Pete would read some interview in which Meg joked about her years at St. Agnes as her "plaid period," that even at forty the sight of McGahern tartan could conjure an emotional grab bag of boarding school ennui: homesickness, impatience, and confused sexuality. Once she was off to art school in London, Meg "fell to fashion," as Vac put it—just as a Catholic schoolgirl cut loose would. Fetching her from the airport, Pete never knew which Meg might breeze through the arrivals gate. She'd shown up wrapped in a serape with hair dyed Frida black; in a maxicoat and fur hat like some Russian bride; looking cheap in vinyl thigh-highs and a rabbit ski jacket; and once, slouching in a man's raincoat, topped by vintage bowler, finally having finished the Milan Kundera novel he'd sent. Meg read very little, which was forgivable because when she did read it was with investment. During the bowler hat period, Meg's paintings resembled Magritte's.

During her last years abroad, it was left to Pete to fetch her in Duluth when she came home. They would take an entire day to make the two-hour trip along the North Shore of Lake Superior, stopping at a few out-of-the-way picnic shelters where they would proceed to exhaust themselves in various positions, refueling with warm Coke and foods Meg had pined for—smoked trout, pasties, maple toffees. Sticky with food and each other, they would drive on to the next park. Pete would later write a paper on the formation of the Civilian Conservation Corps within the New Deal: a glowing tribute to FDR and the young workers who erected so many isolated shelters and the trails leading to them.

Through openings in the cloud cover Pete could see the half-moon setting: the storm was moving on. What in hell was Meg doing at Naledi so late in the year?

Nearing the resort, he saw the clouds had thinned and there was a swath of clear sky. As he navigated his sled through the coldest gash of time just before sunrise, ice crystalized his mustache. The wind suddenly abated; even the engine seemed quiet.

Approaching Naledi, wired and hungover, the weirdness of his mission had begun to register. *A hand?* His stomach was sour enough. He left his machine to idle and climbed the stone steps, snow-sloped and hard to get purchase on in his boots. He banged the glass door to give Meg a heads-up, then let himself into the porch. He could see her in the kitchen, lifting her head groggily from her arm, a pile of sketches in front of her. She rose and rushed to do something at the stove. When the smell of scorched coffee met the diesel stink rising from his own gloves, he nearly puked.

No sign of the professor anywhere—probably still in bed. Pete opened the kitchen door and stuck his head in.

"Hiya, Meg."

Meg spun and nearly lost her balance. "Pete?" She looked as punchy as he felt.

"I'm here for the hand." *Like dialogue from some bad film.* Pete pushed up his goggles and shoved back his parka hood. The kitchen was day-bright under the lights. He tried to shape his frozen mouth into a smile. Feeling the dribble of melt from his mustache, he plowed it away with his sleeve.

She frowned at his bloodshot eyes, pausing at the mutton-chops, opening her mouth as if she might challenge if it really

were him. He could imagine the sight of himself—not that he'd
want to.

He looked away quickly to the blue plastic cooler on the
counter. "That it?" he asked.

"Yes, but . . ."

Meg hadn't changed all that much. Her face had lost the plush
of adolescence and her eyebrows were plucked to surprise. She
looked tired, but who wouldn't be, up all night in the company of
a stranger's hand? The top sketch on the stack featured a charcoal
rendering of the hand, the severed bone end in full color. A soft
whistle escaped Pete. Classic Meg. Hand her lemons and she'll
draw them. *Hand her a hand . . .*

His gaze swept from the drawings to her smudged knuckles. She pulled her hands into the sleeves of the cardigan she was
wrapped in. He nearly let slip, *You weirdo.* Something he used to
say to her on a regular basis. Had she understood that he'd always
meant it as an endearment?

While middle-aged and self-possessed, she still hid her hands
as she'd always done. He felt it in his throat, his chest—the old
twist of longing. He averted his eyes and planted his feet to quell
the sudden urge to flee.

"Sorry, Meg, no time to chat here."

Meg seemed surprised. "Oh, right. Of course . . ." Picking up
the cooler she held it out like an offering. "How weird is this?"

"Right?" He took the cooler, his grimy glove meeting her
hand, ochre paint under her nails, the heel of her palm gray from
pencil lead.

"Yeah. Hey, we oughta . . . at least, ah, grab a beer sometime?"

"Sure." She wrapped herself tighter in the sweater. "A beer.
Why not?"

"Right on." Buoyed by the little curl of her lip, Pete grinned
back. She looked at him exactly the way she used to. As if she
knew something.

"Hey, Meg?"

"Yup?"

He'd had years to think what he might say—how many times

had he imagined this encounter? And yet he had . . . nothing. He opened his mouth and heard the words tumble from his dry tongue. "You sure held up." As that verbal turd dropped, her smile froze. Pete fought the urge to punch himself in the throat.

Idiot.

She gave one of her long, slow nods. Before she could speak, he held up the cooler as a shield and backed out the door.

And while their train wreck of a reintroduction was only last autumn, it seems a lifetime ago. Pete had gone back to treatment days later, his second twenty-nine-day stint at Birchwood in six months. He'd returned to Hatchet Inlet sober and set upon staying that way, ninety meetings in ninety days, working the twelve steps, gluing himself to his sponsor. He worked all hours at the clinic and coached Peewee hockey on Saturdays. He'd hit a meeting before or after supper. Three nights a week he drove to the YWCA pool in Petit Falls and drove home in the dark, alert and smelling of chlorine.

He'd heard the husband was gone, that they'd separated shortly after that storm. Pete knows she'd spent the winter at Naledi because Jon Redleaf had been designing the studio she was going to build on the bluff and was living in one of the cabins. She drives an old Land Cruiser now, wears a serious parka, and walks a younger version of her old dog.

Spring has been slow to make up its mind, receding like a difficult breach. But to Pete, finally, it feels like the other side.

He's back. Or at least on his way.

5

SISSY AND LAURIE HAVE BROUGHT BLUEBERRY COBBLER. No sooner does Laurie set it on the coffee table than their mother whacks the container away. It lands upside-down on the carpet. They have read the literature and recommendations and accordingly do not acknowledge certain behaviors. "Think toddler," the family counselor had suggested. So Sissy counts to five and pretends nothing has happened. They are still in their coats.

She knew her mother wouldn't eat it, but the staff might have enjoyed it. Righting the Tupperware, she peeks under the lid to see that the perfectly crunchy oatmeal topping is ruined. Shame, for it might have motivated someone on the Memory Care ward to pay Louise more attention—to act when noticing her editing the carrots out of her soup and into her pockets, or unraveling her hems, or digging her hands deep in the soil of the lobby plant- ers. *We'll just get you spruced up now, Lou. Those daughters of yours can sure bake!*

Cobbler was once a favorite, but Louise's latest quirk is eating only white foods: mashed potatoes, bread, Cream of Wheat, rice, fish with the breading peeled off, buttered spaghetti. She drinks gallons of milk in spite of the gas. As if proving the old saying, she is becoming milk-colored herself.

"You are what you gum." Laurie cocks her head.

"Maybe she's pale because she rarely goes outside anymore?" Sissy says.

They are in the third-floor lounge.

"Hello, Mom," Laurie says, overly bright.

Sissy says only, "Hi," bending to adjust her mother's glasses, one stem careened up from the effort of knocking away the Tupperware.

Laurie eases the glasses Sissy has just straightened from their mother's face and begins cleaning them.

Sissy takes the cobbler to the wastebasket. Inside the liner is a brand-new pair of men's socks and a pearl necklace. She fishes the items out and lays them on the nearby mantel, higher than wheelchair height, then dumps the cobbler in the wastebasket, container and all.

As Laurie does every visit, she closely examines their mother's blank stare before stating the fact of herself, like an accountant: "It's me, Laurie, your daughter."

Visits have pull-tab odds. Ninety-five percent of the time their mother returns their looks as if through wax paper. Sometimes the scales fall from her eyes—or whatever the saying is—and they are treated with a glint and a few sentences, some memory either on the mark or off. Today, Louise scrabbles for Laurie's hand, saying, "Oh," and then quite clearly, "Kelly."

Sissy and Laurie look at each other. There have been numerous family discussions about what or even whether Louise should be told about her granddaughter. They'd nearly hoped she'd forgotten about Kelly; it had been months since her name had come up.

"No, Mom." Laurie takes extra care to poke the glasses' stems back into the white perm, avoiding her eye as she lies. "Kelly is in Minn-e-a-polis. I'm *Lau-rie*."

Sissy sighs. Lately she's been thinking about visiting alone.

Kelly didn't even look like Laurie—in fact, Kelly wasn't even a Pavola. Her father, Mike Rantala, had been working as a military contractor in the Middle East when Sissy's brother Dan took up with Kelly's mother, Janine. Kelly was a toddler at the time. Janine called Mike to tell him she wanted a divorce and admit the rumor was true: that she was pregnant and it wasn't his. Soon after Mike found out his buddy Dan was the father, he drove his kitchen supplies truck through a checkpoint without stopping—possibly intentionally—was fired on, and killed. Janine and Dan, wracked with guilt, wanted Kelly to have something of her dead father besides the insurance and so did not change her name after Dan adopted her. When she was old enough to be curious why her name was different from her parents' and was told the basic facts, Kelly crayoned an official certificate adopting Dan as her father "for ever and ever."

Sissy hopes it's a solace to Dan, knowing he'd been loved like that. She wishes he would stop feeling he doesn't deserve to mourn the daughter he "stole" from another man—at least that's how Sissy sees it.

Steering back to the script they'd agreed on while walking over, Sissy turns from the mantel and bends to Louise's chair.

"You know I'm getting married this weekend, Mom." She has long since stopped posing questions to her mother. Statements are best. "And *you* are coming to the wedding."

At least for the ceremony, or for however long Laurie can deal. Sissy has hired a familiar face to help out, Kitty Orjala, to see that Louise doesn't roam too far or get into trouble. They've chosen a dress for their mother to wear on Saturday and have brought it along for a run-through. Louise is eating miniature marshmallows from her housecoat pocket. After popping one in her mouth, she points a finger at Sissy. "You're not getting *married.*"

"Yes, I am, Mom. To Alpo Lahti. You remember Alpo?"

"That fucker?" Their mother's voice is high and feminine, the same tone she'd used with the kindergartners she'd taught. The foul language is fairly new; until a year ago, Sissy had never heard her mother use anything stronger than *damn,* but now she holds forth like a stevedore, making every f-bomb or *goddamn* sound as if it's being read from a picture book. While Louise's diet might be drained of color, her vocabulary is bright and primary.

Sissy and Laurie must look away from each other before either busts up. Sissy won't bother to ask why her mother has called her fiancé a fucker, because the answer could be anything from *Radio Flyer* to *two tablespoons* to *hairy armpit*. You never knew where in the coop of her brain Louise might be pecking.

While Laurie shows their mother what she'll be wearing for the wedding, Sissy's gaze drifts to the window. Below, a group of resident "guests," unmistakable in their neon-green vests, are shuffling one by one around the hedge like a caterpillar headed toward the van. The vests slip over their heads like bibs and snap with reflective straps in the back so they can't be taken off without help. The fronts are embroidered with the Senior Cedars logo of the gnarled tree clutching a rock, smack-dab over the heart. Many of the ladies don't like having their hairdos mussed by putting on or taking off the vests, so the field trips are composed of mostly men. Naturally they all need to be kept track of, but wouldn't it make sense to just plant the same sort of chip in them, like dogs get?

Sissy keeps such thoughts to herself.

She has watched the Day Trippers' van-cam on the Senior Cedars activity site (Laurie claims that "Night Stumblers" will be next). Usually, the field trips are to places like the Hockey Hall of Fame or the Pioneer Farm, or a Saints game down in Duluth or the Miller Hill Mall. Online screen-captures of the van's interior show a dozen old guys spaced like eggs, all tinted Herman Munster green. Alpo watched the van-cam for one minute before saying, "Even if I didn't know my ass from home plate, I'd know something wasn't right."

Laurie is holding up the dress for Louise's approval. Sissy would love to see her mother in a new outfit for the wedding, but the navy dress and sequined mohair cardigan will have to do because Louise will only wear clothes she is familiar with. Put something new on Louise and she will peel it off along with every other stitch. Faced with so much as an unfamiliar stocking, and the gloves come off along with everything else and Louise will be found somewhere at the end of a trail of clothing, cellulite quivering. She's not had new underwear in more than a year, and the state of her old panties is becoming an "issue" with Monica, the ward manager. Since underwear is the last thing Sissy wants to see on the floor of the church, she's been hoarding a pair of melon-colored tricot panties in reasonable condition.

The bras with ruined elastic are constantly mended, but when Sissy suggested they let Louise go braless, Laurie and Monica looked at her as if she *had* suggested they chip her mother like a dog. Sissy's since ordered three JCPenney bras, which she has laundered a dozen times and has dried in the dryer with tennis balls so they are nearly broken in.

As Laurie wrangles Louise's arms into the cardigan sleeves, Sissy is reminded of trying to stuff Kelly into her pajamas. Such a squirmer she'd been, going all noodly in Sissy's grip, then giggling like it was the funniest thing in the world.

Once the sweater is on Louise, she pets her sleeve; the mohair passing muster. "That's a very pretty outfit, Mom." When she doesn't respond, Sissy kneels. "Did you go to chair aerobics today?"

"No. The music's too orange. Do I know you?"

Sissy cocks her head. "Sometimes. Sometimes you do."

Louise's eyes brighten, as if a corner of the curtain has lifted. "Of course I do. I was just talking about you two, telling him my two grown daughters still work in that shithole of a diner."

"Who were you talking to, Mom?"

Laurie budges in. "Tommy? Or the other one?"

Tommy and Alan are Louise's current "boyfriends." They were perhaps once real boyfriends recalled and reconstituted from the past, but there are no residents at the Cedars by those names.

"Not *them,*" Louise sniffs, as if Tommy and Alan are total losers. "Rauri."

"Rauri *Paar*?" Laurie pulls a face.

"Oh, yeah?" Sissy leans in. "How is Rauri these days, Lou?"

"Fine, just back from the beach."

"That's nice. He came *here*?"

"Ya. We had tea. And intercourse."

"*Did* you?" A snort escapes Sissy. "And . . . how was that?"

Laurie is mouthing *no* and giving the look.

"Good!" Louise blinks at them. "That man has . . . stamina."

"Really, Mom." Laurie gets up briskly. "Let's get you to your room, see if this dress still fits."

"For a short guy," Louise takes Laurie's arm and grunts to her feet, "he's got a thing on him like a core drill."

Sissy has to turn away as Laurie and Louise continue down the hall. Hanging back, she stops at the desk to complete the paperwork to check their mother out of the facility on Saturday, from four till ten p.m. She ticks the boxes: *yes,* she'll be fed; *no,* she will not require medication or spare clothing; *yes,* she will be supervised and regularly "toileted."

As Sissy is signing, Ruth from Activities comes by with a cart of craft and scrapbooking supplies. "Hi, Sissy."

"Hiya, Ruth." Sissy turns. "Say, Ruthie?"

"Yeah?"

"My mother didn't have any visitors this week, did she?"

"Besides your brothers? I don't recall any."

"Right. I didn't think so."

"But feel free to look in the book." Ruth nods at the guest register at the end of the counter.

"Thanks, Ruth."

"Oh, wait. Janine was here."

At the mention of her sister-in-law, Rauri is instantly forgotten. Sissy meets Ruthie's eye. "How was she?"

Ruthie shrugs. "'Bout the same. I could smell it on her a little. I guess it's a long road back from something like that, isn't it?"

"It sure is."

"You take it easy now." Ruthie winks. "You'll need your energy for Saturday."

Once outside and heading down the steps with Laurie, Sissy starts laughing and has to sit down. "What the heck is a core drill?"

"Some tool from the mines." Laurie keeps going and turns once without stopping. "Laugh *now.*" She juts her chin toward the third-floor windows. "You know that's *us* up there in twenty years? Maybe ten?"

"Jeez." *Killjoy,* Sissy thinks. Getting to her feet she brushes off her bottom. "They'll have a cure by then."

"And you think I'm unrealistic?"

As they say good-bye, Sissy hugs Laurie extra tightly and adheres the two plastic googly eyes snatched from the scrapbooking cart to the back of Laurie's jacket, just between her shoulder blades.

"What's that for?" Laurie frown-grins at the intimacy.

"You're my sister," she says. "I love you."

After watching Laurie goggle off toward her duplex, Sissy heads home to feed Jeff. Then she's going to Alpo's to perform the chore she's been dreading—choosing pieces of his furniture for their new place. The Landings are side-by-side condos near the marina, built to look like a string of lodges. Sissy has never lived anywhere brand new, nor has she ever owned a place of her own— her mother's house doesn't really count since she's only taken over the mortgage. She and Alpo scored a choice end unit on account of her being a cousin to the Perla brothers who are partners in the development. And since her Uncle Juri is the cabinet contractor, Sissy's getting some special kitchen options at cost: a marble pastry slab, a deluxe pantry with a second sink, and a bump-out breakfast nook overlooking the lake. Who cares that the logs aren't actual logs or that the cedar-look roof shakes are a composite? Just that morning she and Alpo had been discussing them.

"Much safer. We won't have to worry about chimney fires."

"Doesn't the new fireplace have gas logs?"

"Point." Alpo winked. "Couldn't burn the place down if you tried."

Sissy drops her keys on the table in the kitchen her mother has set fire to—*twice*. After cranking open a can of chunky beef, she mixes it with kibble and an egg for Jeff. The avocado Kenmore range is scorched where Louise stuffed kindling down one of the burner wells as if it were a cookstove like her grandmother had. That time, the fire department had come. The beadboard in the alcove shows char cracks under coats of paint. The second fire, when Louise put recycling in a roaster and set the dial to broil,

Sissy put the flames out herself. Rather than file an insurance claim, she began making applications to nursing homes.

She feels a thud from above and braces for Jeff, who will be bounding down the stairs from the bed he's not supposed to be on. He barrels into the kitchen thwacking his tail in greeting.

Of course, Sissy has had the discussion with Alpo—about the Alzheimer's and how early it claims Pavola women. He insists it doesn't matter, but it matters to Sissy that he might end up taking care of two wives in his lifetime. "You wouldn't make a very good martyr, Lahti."

"Who says anything about being a martyr? I'll just set you off on an ice floe."

"You say that now."

"You're not even fifty, girly."

Sissy slides down the wall to talk to Jeff while he eats. "Ready for new digs, bad boy? I am." She is. Mostly looking forward to living where there are no one else's memories to navigate. "*You* have a special nook on the landing with your own little window so you can bark at the ducks." The only history their new place will have is what she and Alpo construct there. She will have a six-burner Viking gas range. She mutters at her mother's seared electric stove.

"Good riddance, Old Paint."

After Jeff has eaten, she takes him out and follows him with a bag until he goes.

She drives north on 88. At the crossroad just before Alpo's driveway, the road sign reads LAHTI'S HOBBY. She can remember coming by with friends when they were in their twenties, seeing Alpo up on a ladder working his topiary. They'd thought of him as an old kook then, though he'd have been younger than Sissy is now. She'd half-heartedly joined the others in making fun of the Hobby, some dumb remark like *If I ever go that nuts over macramé or decoupage, just put me away.* Silently, she'd thought it romantic—a man pouring his grief into making something weirdly beautiful in memory of his wife. Now that she actually knows him, the Hobby makes utter sense. These days it's overgrown and barely registers, save a few unexpected shades of nonnative evergreen.

On his back porch she hesitates, fingering the key. Stepping across the threshold, she heels off her shoes and pads down the hall to the den, where the blinds are shut tight against the glint off the lake. Upon opening them, thick sunlight stripes every surface. Sissy toys with finding a duster, if only to delay her task. She is here to do one thing and should do it quickly. Boxes are stacked in the corner. The file drawers of Alpo's desk are open, sparse and neat, recently reordered, as evidenced by the recycle bin overflowing with a mountain of old bills and documents. Mostly medical and insurance papers, the familiar logos and printouts much like the piles Laurie deals with monthly for their mother's Medicare, Senior Cedars, Caremark, clinic bills. She lifts a corner of a St. Sebastian's invoice. Rose's name is on everything.

"Poor Alp," she mutters, imagining him sitting here, going through it all piece by piece. To herself she says, "Go." He's asked Sissy to leave the Post-its on what furniture she likes.

The little dinette is adorable, but they'll have a built-in at the Landings. There is a massive antique bureau in Alpo and Rose's bedroom, in which Sissy spends exactly two seconds. Meaning to take measurements, she'd brought a tape measure and notebook but has left both in the car, along with her cell phone to take pictures. Suddenly thirsty, she goes to the kitchen and drinks half a tumbler of water before the iron taste comes scraping. Remembering that the fridge has a filtered pitcher, she dumps the water and pours fresh. One of the cupboard doors is open, Rose's handwriting inked and penciled right onto the wood, a list of phone numbers, and there's Sissy's old home phone number from when she used to babysit Pete.

During the two summers Pete refused to go to camp with Candy when he was twelve and thirteen, Sissy was the Lahtis' mother's helper, hired to keep an eye on things, meaning Pete.

This was before Rose's diagnosis, when she still traveled to Ireland each July to visit cousins. In Rose's absence, Sissy did light cleaning and made lunch for Pete. He wasn't much bother, his nose usually in a book, leaving her to her dusting or weeding until it was time to make grilled cheese or hot dogs, which they would eat in silence at the picnic table, Pete always annoyed when the pages of Sissy's magazines flapped.

"Why do we have to eat outside?"

"Because there's a picnic table, dope." She's always wondered how anyone could live on a lake and just go about their business as if it weren't right there glittering. Pete and Sissy were only a few years apart, but at the time she felt infinitely older. After doing the lunch dishes she was free to go hang her feet off the dock or wade in the shallows while Pete dissected something or went to watch television. When Alpo came home from the machine shop she would pedal back to town, unless it rained, when he'd insist on tossing her bike into the back of his truck and driving her. He was just someone's dad then, a nice man. Memories of him then are nearly nonexistent, save one time he had to work till nearly dark, when she came out of the house to find him attaching reflective decals to the fenders of her Raleigh. When she'd thanked him, he'd only mumbled something, then checked the batteries on her headlight.

That's Alpo, she thinks. Kind but not crazy about being caught at it.

There is a mantel clock in the living room, brought from Finland by Alpo's grandfather. Sissy likes the idea of a clock that once marked time for a different generation in a country so foreign from this place. It has a lovely, old-world sound, and Sissy doesn't care that it's not accurate, in fact likes the notion of it keeping its own time. She slaps a Post-it on its face.

Going room by room, picking through the history of Alpo's marriage and family doesn't feel right. This isn't her place. He had given her an out, saying, "'Course you might not want— we might not want any of it."

She's about to leave when she notices the painting of the Hobby set halfway between the moving boxes and the pile destined for the Salvation Army. He can't be thinking of giving it away? When the Hobby had started failing from some disease, Alpo had commissioned Meg Machutova to paint it before all the trees could die. Aside from the big canvases hanging in the downstairs bar at The Rectory, it is the only real painting of Meg's that Sissy has seen outside art magazines or in newspaper articles. Sissy didn't live in Hatchet Inlet at the time Meg painted it; she'd been off doing her catering certificate, living in an efficiency in Minneapolis, uncertain if she would ever return. Gerry had just proposed to her, and she'd come home for a week to pack up her things while he looked for a house. Joe enlisted her to make some tree-shaped cookies for the unveiling of the painting—the "opening," as he'd called it. Sissy had happily overdone it, having just aced her pastry and cake décor courses. She spent hours mixing royal icing in coniferous colors and finding just the right cookie molds. At the opening she walked around with a tray of shortbread spruce trees and juniper boughs and pinecones that everyone said were too pretty to eat.

She'd watched Alpo's reaction when Meg unveiled the canvas, saw his eye first flicker with approval and then go blank, his smile looking pasted. Drinking white wine and chewing on little cookie trees, Sissy watched him go out to the sidewalk and stand as still as the telephone pole while the party churned along inside.

Maybe she has romanticized that encounter in hindsight, but it seemed some dawning or realization overtook Alpo there on the pavement. It *did* seem something was slightly different about him when he came back in. He stood next to Sissy and examined the painting again and that time his smile was sincere.

She stole looks at him. It was twenty years since Rose had died. Not that Sissy could read minds, but she got the sense that the painting sparked something, maybe acceptance. She made some comment about it being calm, dreamlike, then offered, "I think Rose would've liked this, don't you?"

Until that moment, Alpo may well have had Sissy lodged in his mind as the teenager he once knew, but when he turned to answer she felt she was being looked at in a completely new light. As a woman.

"I think so too." He laid a hand on her arm and leaned. "She was very fond of *you*. Did you know that?" He seemed pleased to be able to relay that.

Rather than cry, which is what she felt like doing, Sissy only nodded. She poured herself a full Dixie cup of Blue Nun and walked down the hall to the storeroom to sit on a crate across from Pine Pig.

"If I marry Gerry," she said to Pine Pig, "and if I die first, do you s'pose *he* would mourn for twenty years?"

She'd already begun thinking more critically of Gerry, noting his slights—the impatience, his reluctance to visit Hatchet Inlet. What really gnawed was the way he was with Jeff, who was still a little puppyish, but settling down. Gerry was nice enough to the dog when she was around, tolerant, but she worried he might not be when she wasn't. He complained daily about dog hair.

Sissy drained her Dixie cup, then said to Pine Pig, "I'm not going to vacuum twice a day for the rest of my life—for anyone." She went back into the dining room, where the crowd had thinned. Alpo sat in a booth with Chim, Juri, and her brother Joe. Ignoring them, she turned to Alpo and asked, matter-of-factly, "Would you like to go out sometime?"

They nearly always sleep at Sissy's place—she can count the number of times she's been to this house. At some point Alpo must have entertained the thought of her living here, but she's glad he never asked. The house has been in the family for generations, and while no mansion it's probably worth a lot on its pine-covered peninsula. Alpo had worked hard to keep it in the family after his father nearly drank it into foreclosure. Alpo was born in the driveway in a snowstorm while the car radio played "Goodnight Irene" by the Weavers. He raised his kids here. Sissy has to wonder if walking away from it will be as easy as he thinks.

The painting of the Hobby will have sentimental value to Alpo, even if he doesn't realize it now. That Meg's painting has meaning to Sissy is something that might surprise him altogether. She shifts the heavy frame to a prominent position in the hall, finds a Post-it, and writes: *This, please. I also love the clock. You choose whatever else. XOXO, S.*

Leaving the key on the hall table she shuts the door behind her.

Back home she thaws chicken and makes another blueberry cobbler. This will be their last night together until the wedding. Tomorrow is Alpo's bachelor party and the night after is the eve of the wedding so they won't be "bunking," as he jokes. Not seeing each other seems yet another ritual Sissy hasn't thought to question until now—doing something a certain way because it's always been done that way. You'd think that would be the one night you'd *want* to double- check—kick the tires, as her brothers put it.

They will sleep in the same bed every night after the wedding, eat most meals together, do dishes, pay bills, go about their days, but the paper is no guarantee a marriage will work. If anything, Sissy suspects, marriage can seem an excuse to not pay attention. She's seen that enough times. Just as she's thinking it, his key clicks in the lock and Jeff's ears prick and he's up from his spot and skidding into the entry. In the hall mirror she can see Alpo laughing as Jeff overcorrects and plows into the crock of rock salt. He's down on one knee to unlace his boots while Jeff nudges, hoping for a tussle.

"I'm hooome," he calls out, as if she might not guess.

"Hey, handsome," Sissy calls. He doesn't realize she can see him as he mimics Jeff's play stance of downward dog. When Jeff barrels forward, Alpo pretends to snarl, then lets Jeff snuffle his neck.

* * *

She says little over dinner. Alpo is quiet too, as if both have done their share of talking for the day. Midway through the cobbler Alpo sets down his fork and reaches for her hand. "Cold feet?"

"Nope." Sissy puts a hand on his chest and nods toward the stairs.

Alpo smiles. "What about the dishes?"

Thinking of her mother, Sissy says, "Fuck the dishes."

She wakes alone in the gray box of time just before dawn. For a split-second she panics, then remembers it's the hour when Alpo often gives up on sleep to sidle away downstairs. He could be on the couch reading, or out for one of his treks to check on the sunrise—that's how he puts it, *check on,* as if a sunrise might need oiling or tightening. After a moment of lying still, she hears a cupboard door bump closed, the kitchen radio come on, and muffled voices lull her back to sleep until the alarm goes off.

In the shower with suds rolling down her back, Sissy recalls the feeling of Alpo's lips along her ribs, her hip bones. She gargles warm water and laughs. At the point he'd crawled out from under the covers she'd panted, "You were a long time down there, mister."

He grinned. "Not like I have to punch in and out."

"Something to be said for having a retired lover."

He'd winked. "Once you go AARP, babe . . ."

"Ha."

He doesn't seem to feel his age or even acknowledge the difference in theirs except to joke about it. Watching the Oscars, she'd looked over to see he'd been paying zero attention to the screen, had been watching her as she mindlessly pulled up the shoulder of her nightie each time it fell. Just as Best Actress was about to be announced, he pointed to his fly and deadpanned, "Hop on Pop?" Sissy had laughed hard enough to fall off the couch and promptly forgot to care who might win.

As she steps from the humid bathroom air, the scent from her shampoo gives way to the smell of coffee curling up the stairwell.

She stands at the bureau buttoning into a shirt, and her gaze drifts to the folders marked WEDDING and she thinks of her mother again.

Louise had been a sharp cookie. Brilliant—before her mind began to dull like beach glass. She'd sit in the kitchen arguing with the suits on *Firing Line* on the little black-and-white TV, rattling off facts in her teacher's manner, never dropping a stitch from complex patterns that clinked from her knitting needles in slow woolen falls. Louise could dispatch the crossword puzzle in under two cups of coffee using a pen while helping Sissy with her algebra. She'd raised four kids on a lousy insurance settlement and a kindergarten teacher's salary, and that wasn't nothing. When Louise Turnquist married Rudy Pavola, she'd been only twenty. Sissy doesn't remember her father, being just a toddler when he'd died. He'd whacked his head slipping on ice outside the café after closing for the afternoon, came home with a headache, sat down in his recliner, and never got up. Checking out can be as simple as that, which makes Sissy wonder why people don't pay death more mind since it's just *there*—as the worm of some disease, a van crumpled into a metal fist, or a simple bonk to the head.

She'd said to Laurie, "We're all just in the same boat, right? All headed for the same rocks."

Laurie shrugged. "What you don't get, Sissy, is that people don't want to live in reality. Where've you been this past year?"

Sissy knows enough to avoid certain topics of conversation with Laurie, especially politics, because even if you agree, she gets worked up. "Even so. I just don't understand why more people can't seem to enjoy the trip, rocks or not."

"I dunno either," Laurie tisked. "I don't think Dad enjoyed it so much."

From what Sissy's gleaned, her father had been quiet and a little moody, quick-tempered but funny. Laurie, who remembers him, says he was kind to her and Sissy, but hard on the boys. Her brothers shrug at the mention of his name.

"He doted on you," Laurie mumbles.

"I was the baby, Laur."

Laurie maintains that the last thing Rudy Pavola would have wanted was having one of his kids work in the diner—that he'd spin in his grave to know *three* do.

Sissy's only certainty is that he'd loved their mother. He must have, because she does—still, even though she's only a fraction of herself. Sometimes she studies Louise's face, looking for her. Recently, she'd dreamt that Louise's head was glass like a gumball machine and her brain was made of balled-up bits of pink paper printed with words and codes in her neat handwriting. Sissy was thrilled to discover this because it would be so helpful to the researchers and scientists after her body was donated for Alzheimer's research. In the dream her mother was intact, and all anyone needed to do was insert a coin in her ear and a coherent thought or some fact would fall from her mouth like a gumball.

No one in Hatchet Inlet would have remembered her as Louise Turnquist. Originally from Cohasset, Louise "married in," produced four children, and would be fondly remembered by hundreds she taught kindergarten to. Still, to most everyone here her own age, she is Rudy Pavola's widow.

Sissy takes the WEDDING file and heads down to the kitchen, through the living room with its bare picture hooks and half-packed boxes everywhere. She has accepted the Johnstons' offer on the house. After the honeymoon, her siblings will come fight over their mother's better belongings and Sissy will deal with the dregs.

Her fiancé has a towel tucked into his khakis as a make-do apron and is setting the breakfast table. He turns. "Hey, Sleepy."

"Mornin', Dopey." He's folding cloth napkins. "Aren't we fancy?"

"Can't find the paper towels." He grazes her with a kiss.

She sits, tucking the folder on her lap—there are only so many places to set things these days. The white boxes are for the kitchen things she'll keep, and stacks of brown boxes along the wall for rejects to be hauled to Animal Ark. The little café table that had been so darling in IKEA but wobbles on its three legs like a rescue dog is definitely going.

"French toast." Alpo sets a plate in front of her, saying, "This is one husband you're not going to wait on."

"My only husband, I hope." His kindness makes her twinge a little for what she's about to say, but before she can pull out the papers, he sits and begins reading the egg carton aloud like a public radio announcer: "'*These Cage-Free Brown Eggs come fresh from Hens that are never confined to cages. Our Hens are raised outdoors where they are allowed to roam freely and engage in their natural social behaviors.*' That's *Hen* with a capital *H*, Sisu."

Sisu is his nickname for her. He says she's that kind of Finn.

"I know," she says, "but summer customers keep asking for organic eggs, so I thought I'd try them at home. The yokes are yellower, but they're four cents more per unit wholesale—we'd have to raise prices on egg dishes by a dime."

"A whole dime. Well, there *are* social behaviors to consider." Alpo taps the wording.

"Yeah, you'd think for that price the hens would be allowed in*side* the coop. Maybe with the rooster?"

He laughs. When she doesn't, he says, "What's up, Sissy?"

"It's . . ." She pulls the folder from her lap and eases the marriage license out. "I've been thinking . . ."

Alpo frowns. "Not too hard, I hope."

"No, no, nothing like *that*."

"What, then?"

"I'm going to keep my name."

He exhales. "Yeah?" He picks up the license, reads the amended line, and hands it back. "And?"

"You don't mind?"

"Mind." He seems to chew on the word. "Should I?"

"No."

Alpo shrugs. "Kind of an old-time thing, isn't it?"

"But don't husbands want to, I dunno . . ."

"Put their brand on things?" Alpo laughs. "Like livestock?" He looks her up and down, tapping his lip as if thinking. "Don't change a thing."

"You don't need me to be Sissy Lahti?"

"Well, aside from that being a stupid-sounding name, it's not who you are, is it?" He doesn't wait for her to answer. "Besides, your credit cards and e-mail and what-all—checking account." He stands to flip the French toast. "Jesus, the driver's license alone . . . imagine not having to wait in line at the DMV."

"Final answer? You don't mind?"

"Nope. But can we have buffalo wings at the buffet?"

Sissy snorts. "No."

He hands her the butter knife but doesn't let go. "You *can* talk to me, you know. About things. About anything."

Sissy nods. "Knife, please? I'm starving."

6

A T FIRST HE CAN'T TELL IF SISSY'S BEEN THERE, THEN sees the Post-its on the painting and clock. Of course she'd choose just the right things. Alpo feels a little sheepish for having asked her at all, given all there is to deal with at her own place. She shouldn't have to navigate his stuff as well.

He showers and pulls a six-pack from the fridge, having promised to stop next door for happy hour. He couldn't say why he doesn't visit Perry and Sheila more often, and now that he's moving he feels a bit of a pang. Early on, Alpo took them under his wing—such as it was. He's coached them in requesting a zoning variance to renovate their boathouse; suggested who to ask for at the lumberyard; advised on which electrician to hire. *Tell them Alpo sent you* is his most frequent advice, hoping to spare them the gouging sometimes imposed on cabin owners and retirees thought to be rolling in it.

Much of his North Country wisdom doesn't register as such until standing next to Perry, who only has less by dint of not being born to it. Last week Alpo found him scratching his head over large landscape stones pulled from a retaining wall and into his driveway. Perry assumed vandalism, but Alpo pointed out the disturbed ant colony where the stone was pried from—dislodged by bears grubbing for brood.

"They root it out with their tongues—the larvae. See there? That's caviar to black bears."

They talk about the price of propane, the road fund, taxes, or staying sane through March—easier this year with the arrival of high-speed cable and Netflix. Alpo reminds himself to thank Sheila for the suggestion of *Fortitude,* a show about another northern outpost with its own troubles, even more remote and colder than Hatchet Inlet.

Considering the bumper stickers on their hybrid car, it's obvious Sheila and Perry are liberals, though they rarely touch on politics, which is the prudent thing to do north of Hinckley. These days it's hard to know what if anything is safe to talk about. Alpo's no knee-jerker, but he will say in no uncertain terms that he does not support the maniac poised to tweet the country into the toilet.

They are good neighbors, closer over the years as they grow grayer. He's opened up to them about his concern for Pete. Perry sought out Alpo at the onset of his prostate cancer before even telling Sheila. And Sheila was the first person Alpo told after proposing to Sissy. Good news doesn't always play well with some of the boys at Pavola's who don't like to have their grousing interrupted by someone's happiness.

He's been meaning to invite Sheila to come by the house and outbuildings to scavenge. Scattered around her neat red-and-white buildings is a museum of scythes, ice-block tongs, milk cans. She's trained vines to grow on pitchforks, and the wall above her kitchen range is loaded with vintage cookery tools resembling implements of torture. Her bat houses and birdhouses are made from exactly the sort of clutter and crap that Alpo's been meaning to get rid of.

Rose, who never darkened a door without some offering for the host, would frown at his paltry beers in a pack. He hesitates in the hall near the bookshelves. Perry—a retired English professor—collects obscure volumes of poetry. Most poets on Rose's shelves are Irish, but a scan reveals an old one with a Minnesota theme. For Sheila he chooses an illustrated guide to wildflowers in a fancy cloth sleeve.

Halfway up the path he wonders if poetry isn't a bit personal. He stops at the bench that looks out over the Divide. He'd recently dragged it across the property line so Perry and Sheila can claim it, in the event whoever buys his place would begrudge somebody

sitting to enjoy a moonrise or sunset. Balancing the poetry book
on his knee, he fishes a beer from the sack, cracking it at arm's
length to spare the book any spray. *Odes of the Arrowhead,* by J. H.
Fleming is embossed with the profile of an Indian with a fierce jaw
and hatchet nose, like a Comanche or Cheyenne—nothing like the
softer-featured Ojibwe and Lakota that actually settled the region.

He considers the introduction:

The Pioneers of Thirty Years
Appeared on the scene,
among them being the Author of this volume,
"Odes of the Arrowhead."
I respectfully submit this BOOK OF VERSE.

The publication date, 1929, seems late out of the gate for pio-
neering—by then much of the state was settled, the forests shorn,
watersheds flooded, Native kids shunted into residential schools
in hopes of knocking the Indian out of them. Not quite his fore-
fathers' shining moments.

Flipping pages, he drinks his beer. The book reads like rhym-
ing Chamber of Commerce drivel to Alpo. Why do exclamation
points annoy him so? Texts and e-mails from his daughter resem-
ble cavalry charges.

He considers leaving the book on the bench, then decides to
give it as a novelty.

Indeed, Perry gets a kick out of it, hooting over passages while
Sheila plies Alpo with chips with hummus and a crumbly cheese
Sissy would know the name of. Two beers in, Perry stands to read
in a dramatic voice:

THE MINNESOTA ARROWHEAD
Broadcast the news, let it be read—
The story of the Arrowhead.
Where lakes abound and pine trees spread

Broad sheltering branches overhead.
The Arrowhead! The Arrowhead! The Minnesota
    Arrowhead!
Resort of bear, moose, caribou,
That from the haunts of whitemen fled
Where Redmen oft' the eagle slew
With arrows of the Arrowhead.
The Arrowhead! The Arrowhead! The wild romantic
    Arrowhead!

Perry bellows the last lines, holds the book to his chest, and claims, "Truly terrible. I'll treasure it."

Sheila settles on the couch while Perry flips to another page with a very short poem titled "A Genius" and holds it out to Alpo for his turn to read. He doesn't bother standing.

A poet may be a genius
It depends on what he wrote.
But a man can be a Genius
And still not be a Poet.

Keeping cadence, he adds his own line:

"But a Gasbag nonetheless."

Alpo plays a game of cribbage with Sheila in the kitchen while Perry stuffs morel mushrooms he'd found that morning. After they've been sautéed, he sets them on the table with a flourish.

Alpo is hungrier than he knew. "Maybe I'll marry you instead, Perry."

"Sorry. He's taken." Sheila lays down her hand. "Fifteen six and a run for twelve. I win."

Sheila turns to Perry. "Let's go to Duluth Friday? I can't fit into my linen suit, and I'm not wearing flannel to a wedding."

LAURENTIAN DIVIDE ⤜ 87

Alpo laughs. "You wouldn't be the first. Used to drive Rose mental, people showing up at formal dos like they portaged there."

"I'm with her," Sheila says. Sheila had known Rose only slightly, and only at the end. Yet she'd stepped up repeatedly to do a last-minute errand here or there: pick up groceries or prescriptions; fetch the kids from the Greyhound station; deadhead the flower garden. Perry helped move the hospital bed in and weeks later helped move it out, along with the oxygen trolley and commode. Sheila performed a hundred kindnesses, from a smile to a cup of coffee to silently handing over a jacket when Alpo would come over to stand on their deck just to be somewhere different. The kindness didn't end when Rose died. The day Pogo was run over, Alpo was at a loss as to what to do—stash the dog in the chest freezer until Easter when the kids would be back? Perry talked him out of billeting Pogo in with the fish sticks and took a pickaxe to the permafrost so Alpo could bury him in the Hobby. Sheila marked the grave with a lovely flat piece of banded jasper.

Sheila looms a bit over Perry, a tall woman with a kind face that furrows in concern. "Anything new on the hermit?"

"Rauri? Nothing."

"It's just—that woman at the bakery said he's missing and likely drowned since he can't swim a stroke."

"Maggie, the town horn?"

"That's her."

Alpo settles back. "Rauri's not exactly *missing*. More like misplaced."

"She said he's not quite right in the head, living out there all alone."

"He's fine in the head. He might have his reasons for holing up out there."

"Like?"

Alpo shrugs. "Everyone has their history. Maybe Rauri just saw too much back in Vietnam."

"PTSD?" Perry asks.

"Hard to say."

"There must be somebody who knows him well, knows *something*?"

"Honestly . . . ?" Alpo trails.

"Who goes out to his place to check on him?"

"No one, that I know of."

"No one?" Sheila seems surprised.

But Rauri lives out there and apart for his own reasons. As she suggests, his well-being might be another matter. Alpo tilts his glass and peers through, as if Rauri's whereabouts might be divined from the foam.

Sheila says, "I mean, even living way out there, he's still one of you."

One of you. Sheila and Perry know they aren't accepted here. They are called 612ers behind their backs, and even though they've inhabited the local area code and their house for twenty-five years, the place is still called Pujanens'. Folks don't think to include them other than as second thoughts at the end of a guest list.

He turns to Perry. "The boys are throwing a little get-together tomorrow. Not exactly a bachelor party, but you know."

"Yeah?" Perry looks pleased. "I'm in."

"Pete's found some place in town." He turns to Sheila. "Don't worry, it won't be a strip joint."

"*Is* there a strip joint?"

He could tell her about the White Tail at the crossroads between the two mines but thinks better of it. At the door Sheila presses a headlamp on him despite the rising moon. "This time of night deer are rowdy—always crashing across that path like the bars have just closed."

On his way down the hill Alpo can make out a few does and yearlings traveling from their watering hole up to grassy encampments on higher ground, taking their time. On a steep run of the path, Alpo is astonished when a buck leaps so near him he feels the whoosh of air and a draft of warmth off the animal's flank. As it crashes back into the brush Alpo staggers and scrambles to connect with a slender birch. How had he not heard *that* coming? As he sways, the tree bends with him.

Another step and he might have broken his neck. Heart pounding, he reaches the bench to catch his breath. The moon crests just above the trees. He stuffs the headlamp in his pocket and sits watching the moon until it is high and bright and his pulse has stilled. There's a dozen ways to be hurt or killed on his own property. There would be even more out at Rauri's.

Once in the house he grabs the phone.

"Janko, Lahti here."

"Hey, Alpo. Timing. I was gonna get ahold of you earlier today. My sister Linda's been asking after your place. She's got her license now and is wondering what realtor you're going with."

"Hertzog's. Tell her sorry, I had to go with them. They got Pete out of the lease with the owner of that house he was renting."

"Too bad. Woulda been a nice commission. You know Linda's Ron has Parkinson's?"

"I do know that, Janko. I hear you, though."

"Because, I was just thinking . . ."

"I signed a contract, Jank."

"Oh."

"So, you hear anything about Rauri?"

"You're about the tenth person to call. Funny thing, though— none of them wanted to be the one to file a report. Had to do it myself, so that's done."

"You don't have to wait forty-eight hours or something?"

"Nah, that's cop-show bullshit. I already requested an expedited search. State highway's been notified. So's county sheriff and border patrol. It's on everybody's radar. There's a crew going out tomorrow if the weather holds. We got it."

After putting the phone down, Alpo goes to Rose's old sewing room. The desk sits under a tower of boxes. He pulls out the entire bottom drawer and takes it to the dining room table and upends it. Stacks of newspaper clippings have yellowed and curled to the shape of the drawer. He starts sorting, using salt and pepper shakers to hold the pages flat. Running out of weighted things he goes to the bedroom and sweeps Rose's paperweight collection from the shelf into a shoebox, certain he has never seen one of these tchotchkes employed for its intended purpose. The grandkids will love them, he hopes.

He pins articles with the Eiffel Tower, jade Buddha, London Bridge, in order of date. He hefts the apricot marble rose he'd found for their tenth anniversary, sets it aside. He pins down a grainy shot of a small crowd picketing and moves on. Most articles from the early '70s chronicle the fight to get the Reserve designated as roadless wilderness. There are minutes from town hall meetings; articles on the pushback by pulp and mining interests; a mishmash of op-ed pieces ranging from opinionated to vicious; graphs and photos of environmental disasters in other states that resulted from mining and clear-cut logging. There are full-page ads taken out by various factions deriding or minimizing opposing concerns. The '80s and '90s were relatively quiet, but in the early '00s, mining interests reared their heads again. Leases were contested, lawmakers got involved, politicians sparred. More recent articles are heavy on facts, statistics, studies. State agencies and watchdog organizations have been chiming in. Since scientific proof is irrefutable, mining interests go after the agencies that compile facts to discredit or mitigate them. When laid out on paper in front of him, the evidence of forty-plus years is conclusive. The only guarantee that Hatchet Inlet won't be a ghost town in forty more is in preserving the Reserve. Its value only increases exponentially as the rest of the planet's wilderness gets chipped away.

These days both sides are barely responding to each other. Even among neighbors the fight has grown ugly, people posting things on Facebook they would never have the balls to lob over a backyard fence. It's not just the online shenanigans. Alpo has known of grown men engaging in vandalism from petty to felony larceny, from stealing election signs from yards to arson—a timber-frame Conservation Corps shelter was torched by a former mayor, who waltzed out of court with a misdemeanor slap from the judge he fishes with.

On the left of left, zealots chain themselves to bulldozers or shimmy up old-growth pines to park themselves for weeks, sleeping in hammocks like bats. Alpo wouldn't like to imagine what they do when they have to take a crap. But right or wrong, those protesters make plenty of misery for local law enforcement.

Alpo sees no gain in voicing his own opinion. There was a hit on the radio around the height of the debate that often looped through his head: *Clowns to the left of me, jokers to the right.* Stuck in the middle indeed.

Rauri was for opening the Reserve to motors, of course. Alpo scans each article for any mention of him and sets those aside. Earliest pieces characterize Rauri as a sort of gnarly hermit or backwoods nut. Alpo hops online to Google his name for more recent hits. Surprisingly, there is a profile in a *Mother Jones*–style quarterly from six months before. It's the only account that includes Rauri's own words. There are two photos, one of him holding a bouquet of stunted carrots and turnips in his greenhouse, another in his workshop looking through the tangled antlers of one of his fancy chandeliers.

> *Rauri Paar has lived on his remote trio of stony islands in the Laurentian Reserve since the early seventies. Born in Ames, Iowa, in 1948, he's lived on Lower Shield Lake a mile from the Canadian border for nearly four decades.*

Alpo scrolls down a page of Rauri describing his craft, how he procures his materials. There's a sidebar interview with a gallerist curating an exhibit of Rauri's work for a high-end boutique in Santa Fe, which sheds no light other than to suggest that Rauri's making more money than he lets on. In the article, Rauri's earthy tone makes him sound like someone from the co-op:

"I grow root crops, harvesting and drying berries and other edibles, like mushrooms." Paar extends his growing season in an eight-by-ten-foot greenhouse sunk four feet into a berm. "I tried to keep goats but in the end they were too hard on the ecosystem of the island, not worth the milk and cheese they produced."

Ecosystem? Alpo laughs, clearly remembering when Rauri sold his goats. After tethering them in his kitchen one subzero night, he woke to find they'd chewed through their ropes and had devoured several books, including a mystery he'd been in the middle of.

Paar will buy a brace of laying hens each spring for the eggs, but by late fall has usually lost most to predators. "I don't like to cage them. Besides, I've yet to see a pen that can keep out a pine marten, so, they roam free. If they make it, they make it."

The islands are also visited by mink, badgers, wolves, and bobcats. "You can't begrudge them," says Paar. "That's just the way it goes here. Everyone needs to eat."

Paar does not trap or hunt, but he does fish and occasionally accepts meat that "shows up" by whatever means, including wolf-kill and gifts from deer hunters and trappers. There are many trade-offs living the wilderness life, but Paar claims they are worth it. When this reporter asked how he passes the time, Paar smiled, "I don't pass it, I live it."

About the ongoing controversy of his home in the Reserve, he says, "I'm all for nature, but you cannot pull a man's home and livelihood out from under him."

More words in two pages than Alpo might hear out of Rauri in a year. The article concludes:

After touring his greenhouse and outbuildings, we were treated to Labrador tea with mint, sweetened with syrup collected from his sugar maple camp, and warm blueberry spoonbread (recipe on page 6). As a parting gift, he handed over a quart bottle of

the birch beer he brews and sells to canoeists. "You come on back
in another ten years," he told us. "With luck I may still be here."

Alpo goes back to the paper clippings, trying to separate two
that seem stuck together with something. The something is the
hospital bracelet. W. R. Med. Ctr. That would be Walter Reed, he
assumes. The little rivet is rusted and powdery to the touch, the
plastic covering so brittle it cracks apart when Alpo extricates the
paper tab from within. The typing is little more than a series of
blue hatches reduced to watercolor. But when he smooths it open
he can read the back where the words clearly show through. There
is a have yellow the name PAAR, RAURI ELDON; a long patient
number; military ID number; unit and ward number 2207. The
patient designation reads PSYCH.

Alpo can't say he's surprised. He pulls his laptop closer and
searches for a database of U.S. Army units. After finding Rauri's name and rank, it's surprisingly easy to find out where he'd
been posted, near Da Nang. Adding search words *Dau Tieng, medics, M.A.S.H.,* he's led to a site compiling the writings of troops
deployed there. Apparently, Dau Tieng was a besieged post fre-
quently shelled and ambushed by snipers. Actions and skirmishes
usually resulted in high North Vietnamese casualties—in fact, the
American troops usually wiped the floor with the enemy that kept
coming back for more.

Alpo scrolls to an account written by an anonymous medic
after a February attack:

> *2.23.69 Soon as we (medic crew) landed on the pad, the pilot had
> to lift. The Dust Off went up and south, we assumed it would cir-
> cle back, but just then sniper fire started. We took cover when we
> heard the tracer shells. It lasted hours. We had no sense of casu-
> alties. Early after the first round of shelling—around 18:30—I
> was covered and sent to a perimeter bunker after a mortar strike.
> The bunker was partly stove in. A few of the boys had shrapnel
> lacerations. A kid named Monty was on the floor, in and out. I*

*administered morphine, but they couldn't let me turn on a flash-
light so I covered myself in a tarp like an old-time photographer
and attended his foot using my own light. Privates Johnson and
Westerburg held him down while I removed his boot. The ante-
rior tibial artery was sliced by shrapnel and the top of the boot
sliced also. I eased the boot off to discover it half-filled with blood,
three toes floating in it.*

The writer could have been Rauri, for all Alpo knows. Before
reading on, he goes to the china cabinet for his bottle of Christmas whiskey from Dentist Dennis.

The accounts are unnerving for how matter-of-factly they present carnage. Alpo stops reading to examine photographs. Some
correlate to specific accounts, others seem randomly posted: pictures of units; billets; mess halls; and groups of soldiers around
tables, around fires and radios, around games of cards. At first,
he scans for Rauri's face or name, but as the sense of the daily
grind of combat in a jungle congeals, pegging Rauri among them
doesn't seem to matter—he could have been any of them. Alpo
downs a measure of whiskey, scrolling on.

The medics aided local villagers, and while there are fewer
written accounts concerning those patients, there are many pictures—of ill children, children hit by stray bullets, grandmothers
scorched by chemical burns, ginning old men on crutches, a dead-
eyed teen with most of her scalp and an ear seared. One, captioned *Medics treating landmine victims,* is of a small boy on a cot,
his eyes a world of pain, holding out the bandaged stumps of
his legs for the camera. Another shows a footless mother being
pushed in a cart by her two small sons.

The most surprising photograph is of a blue swimming pool
outside a villa called the French House, a hulk of European archi-
tecture left over from the French occupation. The pool, Alpo reads,
had been repaired and renovated by American soldiers. A number
of young men edge the pool, all wearing swimming trunks—not
army issue, but their own. With no uniforms to reveal their ranks
or positions, they could be freshmen at a pool party. The tops of

a few tropical trees blur in the distance. It could be Hollywood or Los Angeles, if not for the dog tags around their necks.

Alpo once believed that dog tags were notched to fit between the front teeth of a dead soldier, to be forcefully jammed into the gums, sometimes by kicking the corpse's jaw shut to embed them. He knows better now and unlearns something just about every day: thanks to the factual side of the Web, he now donates to Snopes.com.

A photo captioned *Ambush Alley* shows a rutted trail, scattered with wreckage and fuel tanks in the distance, the foreground dominated by a human skull half-sunk into the roadbed like a pale cobblestone. *Defoliating a rubber tree plantation* shows soldiers spraying in a chemical haze, kerchiefs as masks, gloveless. Likely dioxins, possibly TCDDs, Agent Orange. Not that an ingredients label would be a priority when trying to root snipers out of the undergrowth. *Dead cattle and Viet Cong* is a black-and-white composition Alpo quickly scrolls past.

Alpo had been deferred for having a skill needed by his government, a wife, and kids. His letter from the draft board had mentioned *production of the raw materials for the war effort. Vital civilian contribution.* And so he gratefully spent the war vitally contributing. He read the papers and watched the news and knew exactly how lucky he was to be working in a mine's machine shop while others mucked through jungles hunting humans while being hunted themselves. He worked himself hard. When it was over, he was dismayed by how returning soldiers were met with derision and by just how little their country gave in return for their service—what was evident back then still is today.

For years Alpo kept an eye out for men his age living rough: panhandlers and buskers with wild eyes. He still keeps a wad of tens in his glovebox for when he's down in the Cities, where it seems every off-ramp has a guy with a hand-drawn cardboard sign. Of veterans that fared better, he counts several as friends, schoolmates who came back functional if not a hundred percent. He affords Juri and Chim the occasional pass for their distrust in the system and Libertarian leanings, their each-man-for-himself attitudes, suspecting their suspicions are complex and jungle-dense. Juri's itchy Bic finger has landed him in legal scrapes with insurance companies after his garage, the family cabin, and a neighbor's boathouse all burnt. Not that anyone has proof. Chim is alone now, stewing in remorse over the kids who won't talk to him and the two ex-wives. He should just be thankful none had pressed charges.

No matter how many books he's read or films watched, Alpo can't know what those boys went through. He remembers stumbling out of the theater after seeing *The Deer Hunter,* Rose rushing after him with an empty popcorn container for him to vomit in. She said he should talk about it.

"It wasn't *my* war," he'd told her.

Only when he gets up to take his empty glass to the sink does he realize how drunk he is, that a quarter of the bottle has disappeared.

He clings to the rail going up the stairs. In the hallway he sways, shedding his clothes in a trail. After tossing for an hour, he gets up, feeling suddenly vulnerable in his nakedness. He puts on pajamas for the first time in months. Curling around a pillow as if around Sissy, he sinks into a series of fitful dreams.

7

ETE ROLLS TO A STOP AT HIS COUSIN'S BUNGALOW. Walking up the drive, he tries to remember the difference in their ages. Ten years, making Mackie only thirty-three, yet she's looking so matronly that the week before he'd barely recognized her in Red Owl. Hopefully she'll spring back from the latest loser boyfriend. Mackie cannot catch a break with men.

She's on her porch, still in her work blouse with her name badge on, wearing gray sweatpants, as if she'd run out of steam halfway through changing. Her feet are in one of those electric footbaths, burbling. Absorbed in the tractor beam of her iPhone she doesn't notice Pete. Molly is trying to wag her tail but only manages a slow sweep of porch dust. Her jaw is flat on the deck.

"Hi," he says.

Mackie starts. "Hey, Pete." She discreetly slides her bottle of Michelob behind a planter, reaching for a towel to dry her feet.

"How ya doing, Mackie?"

"Meh."

Leaning over the dog he can feel heat coming off her. "How long she been like this?"

"Since I cleaned the kennel and washed the puppy bedding. Now she won't look at me."

"Well, yeah. You bring her in to get spayed. Soon."

"I *will*." Mackie sniffs. "You think this footbath makes me look old?"

"Eighty. Don't tell me you have corns."

"I work in a bank, Pete. I gotta wear heels."

"No, you don't."

The chocolate lab looks up at him hopefully, as if aware Pete's there to help. He backs a few feet away, holding a treat from his pocket, saying, "Come."

When she doesn't get up, he gives her the treat anyway, but she only sniffs it. He crouches. "When were the pups whelped?"

"Last one sold a week ago."

"She's not dried up yet?"

"Not completely."

He gently rolls Molly to her side, smelling the infection before seeing it. "Jesus, Mackie, you should have called me."

"I didn't think it was . . . too bad." A flash of guilt flickers.

Pete swallows the urge to lecture. "Well, nothing that can't be fixed."

"Want a lemonade? I'm gonna have one."

"Sure, but you go ahead and finish your beer." He can't help his tone. He's giving away his time here; Mackie might at least spend some of hers taking better care of her dog. Pete opens his kit and sits on the top step, resting Molly's head in his lap. When Mackie lumbers past, the dog doesn't move.

"While you're in there, wet a bath towel, wring it out, and microwave it for forty-five seconds." Before she can lift the towel in her hand, he adds, "A clean one."

"Sure. Anything else?"

"A basin, something with hot water."

He works quickly, getting a rectal temp and filling a syringe before Mackie is back with a steaming towel. The dog's teats look like a pan of angry dinner rolls. "I'm gonna give her an injection that should dry her up."

"Thanks, Pete." She watches him work awhile before going back in for pie.

"And antibiotics," he says to himself, patiently pressing and massaging the teats until milk and pus begin to stain the towel. Molly looks up and Pete nuzzles the top of her head with his chin. "Atta girl."

Mackie crouches next to him. "You're so good with dogs."

"Meaning not so good with people?"

"You know what I mean."

"Molly is postpartum. You gotta spend more time with her. Wear flats at work so you still have some energy to walk her when you get home. Better yet, take her to the bank with you. Kyle won't mind: tell him I said."

"Oh, that'll go over well with the tellers."

"Tough. Walk her at lunchtime. Here." He reaches into his bag and pulls out a prescription pad and scribbles a few lines, adding his illegible signature, tears it out, and hands it over. "Give this to Kyle."

"Le'see: *Molly suffers mastitis and postpartum blues and Mackie is post-breakup.*" Mackie looks up. "*They are not to be separated.* Ha."

"What kind of pie is that?"

"Peach."

"Perfect."

"I didn't mean that you were crummy with people."

"It's true."

"Remember when we were kids and you freed that fox from the trap out at Hoodoo Point? You'll take risks for animals, is all I mean. That's brave."

"Consequences are different with animals, Mackie."

"Meaning?"

"There aren't any." His grin fades. He is a coward when it comes to people. As he tears open a pouch of antiseptic ointment with his teeth, he decides. He will do something approaching courageous. Tomorrow.

Thumbing a dab of ointment over each teat, he says, "Watch me here, Mack. I'm leaving you a full tube. You finish up like this after applying heat, *just* like this—twice a day, right?"

"For how long?"

"As long as the tube lasts." It's far more than what's needed, but some regular attention wouldn't hurt Mackie or Molly. He takes a second syringe and holds it up. "If the infection isn't cleared up in four days, you bring her in."

"Okay." She gets down on her knees next to him and they switch places. "You in some hurry?"

"I have to get up before five. I'm gonna wash up, eat this pie, and bolt."

At home Pete puts new batteries in his headlamp, stuffs a daypack, and expands his largest vet kit with items from his own supplies. He straps Alpo's canoe atop the Suburban; he'd sold his own to help pay off what insurance wouldn't cover for his second stint at Birchwood.

Alpo isn't answering his cell, so Pete tries the house. He gets the machine. "Dad, it's me. I'm heading out to Rauri's in the morning to see what's up. Just thought I'd let someone know." For the hell of it, he tries Rauri's number. *The mailbox you have reached is full.*

When the alarm sounds, Pete opens one eye to darkness and nearly rolls back to sleep. He feels for his phone and checks the forecast. According to NOAA, there's something rolling down from Ontario, due in the afternoon. Rain for sure, but at least it's too late in the year for snow. He'll grab thermals and raingear just in case. More awake now, Pete plants his feet on the cold floor. Of the many annoying mantras of recovery, one elbows in: *One step at a time.* The next one is simple enough, getting out of bed. As he unfolds to standing he mumbles, "Man up" to himself and asks Duke, "Double entendre?"

In the shower he sings loudly to wake himself up. The same Clash tune keeps him nodding through preparing coffee, filling a thermos, and washing down toast with peanut butter. *Should I stay or should I go?*

Letting Duke out, he notes the steps are slick with frost, the hedge along the porch is shivering as Duke lifts a leg on it, raising steam. Knowing something is up, the lab sniffs, circles the Suburban, and lets Pete know he's waiting for the tailgate to open.

Driving through empty intersections in the predawn, Pete sees only the paperboy and Mrs. Putzl guiding her blind daughter Wendy to six o'clock Mass. Joe Pavola is on the stoop of the restaurant, pulling *The Siren* and *The Observer* from their plastic sleeves, waving one at Pete.

No one would have expected to see Pete living in Hatchet Inlet again. Pals who went away to college didn't return. The old boys down at Pavola's blame the population drain on higher education. Staying isn't always an option, but if one were looking for reasons not to, there's the seven months of winter, black flies, and the fishbowl of gossip—knowing that if he gets a pimple on his ass Tuesday, the whole town will know by Wednesday.

Heading north on 88 he watches the length of the distant ridge where spruce tops sway against a backdrop of clouds pocked salmon by the rising sun. *Sailors take warning.* Not exactly a merry spring dawn, but in the pros column for Hatchet Inlet, Pete gets to witness a lot of spectacular sunrises. Occasionally one is awe inspiring—a near-spiritual experience, for lack of a better word.

There's the fishing, too, not that he does much.

He drums the Clash's back beat over the steering wheel, mumble-singing the lyrics, which could apply either to the folly of this paddle or his own tenure in town.

Should I stay or should I go now?

Frankly, Pete is in Hatchet Inlet because the place doesn't hold a fraction of the temptations the Cities do. He long ago cashed in his chips here, has no reserve of goodwill until he earns it, knows he will not be given any more passes. This scrap of near-nowhere he alternately loves and hates is the single place where he absolutely, positively, cannot afford to fuck up.

Pete's first job out of veterinary school was in Spring Valley, a town even smaller than Hatchet Inlet. He met Beth there when she was home visiting her father's farm. She'd just graduated and had taken a job in Rochester. In short order they married and Beth became pregnant. Before that dust even settled, she was pregnant again. He bought into a clinic near Rochester, where there was better housing and decent schools. Happy enough, if dazed, they bought a house beyond their means in a suburban cul-de-sac.

The Rochester clinic was a walk in the park compared to large animal veterinary. Instead of the hump and slog of barnyards and the straight talk of farmers, the price for easy hours was dealing with owners of fashionable breeds: accessory dogs, like Shih Tzus and Yorkies acquired because they are on Oprah's list of favorite things; an Aussie or Hungarian Vizsla because they were on the cover of *Hound*. Dog owners clueless that working breeds *need* work or they wreak havoc and grow neurotic. Such challenges at the clinic were hardly enough to drive a man to drink, so Pete couldn't blame his circumstances (though if one more owner of a Weimaraner mentioned William Wegman, he was pretty sure his head might pop off). The fortifications of vodka nipped in his truck or in the stockroom were merely in anticipation of the pressures at work and home, not because of them.

After the separation, Beth moved the girls to Duluth, where she quickly met Tom the cardiologist at Al-Anon, assuring the pair had one thing in common: both had been saddled with drunks. In the separation arrangement Beth was awarded full custody while he got two weekends a month. She filed for divorce while Pete was in treatment.

Since Hatchet Inlet was closer to Duluth, and since North Country Veterinary had been sitting empty and the retiring vet was willing to sell on a contract for deed, Pete is back in the chill bosom of Hatchet Inlet. At least for now.

Where the road parallels the shore, he slows. The surface of the water ruffles one way, then another. It would be best to cut down time on open water. He turns on the county spur so that he might put in at Crow Point and cut a water mile off the trip. It also gives him the excuse to drive through Naledi.

At the resort there are few signs of life save chimney smoke. He imagines Meg is probably still asleep. Jon Redleaf's truck is parked nearer to the lodge than to the cabin he rents on the point. Pete makes a conscious effort not to mull over any potential sleeping arrangements Jon and Meg may or may not have.

He swings the Suburban down to the landing. Rauri Lake is several portages away. Pete stands on the shore and assesses the clouds. If the wind were any stiffer, there would be whitecaps. Only a week has passed since these lakes broke up, and there's plenty of ice clinging to north faces of the cliffs—the lakes probably have floaters big enough to capsize a canoe. Pulling the canoe over smooth mud rimed with frost, he shoves it out into the surf and the surf shoves it right back in. He can't avoid getting his boots wet.

This time of morning Beth would be up, getting ready for her 7 a.m. shift, but the girls would likely still be asleep. It just seems he should tell someone where he's headed. There'll be no cell service where he's going.

He climbs back into the driver's seat, turns the blower to high, and aims the vents at his boots. After a full minute of staring at his phone, he calls, hoping the husband doesn't answer.

Allison had shown him pictures from Beth and Tom's wedding. Beth looked happy, Tom looked happy. It wouldn't kill Pete to make an effort, could start by thinking of his daughters' new stepfather by his name rather than Numb-Nuts or Needle Dick.

Beth doesn't seem surprised when she answers. "Pete. Did you get my message? Is that going to work for you?"

"Is *what* going to work? I'll pick them up at ten—that was the plan, right?"

"Pete." Beth pauses. She does that, pauses for emphasis. "You didn't play the message."

"When it's something important, you should *text*."

"There you go . . . never mind."

"Beth. You can't schedule how I spend my time with the girls when I only get them four days a month." Pete looks to the lake roughing itself to a froth yet suddenly looking like a better alternative to the conversation he's set himself up for.

"I wasn't scheduling anything."

"Okay. What was the message?"

"Sissy's invited us. To the wedding."

"*Us?*" For an instant he's confused. "Ah. You and Nee—*Tom?*"

"Yes, *us.*"

"Well, it's not my party . . . If Sissy wants you—"

"I wouldn't put Tom through it. But I'd like to come on my own with the girls, if you don't mind—it would save you the trip. I can drive them up."

"Oh. Okay. Not a problem for me. That it?"

"Pete. You called *me.*"

"Right." And just why had he thought informing Beth of his trip to Rauri's was a good idea? Probably because she, being the voice of reason, would talk him out of it. Maybe he *wanted* to be talked out of it. Another silence, which means she's about to change the subject.

"From what your dad says, it sounds like you're . . . good?"

Not knowing how to answer that, Pete doesn't. Since when does his father report on his behavior like some hall monitor?

"Pete, you *know* we talk. Alpo doesn't just pick up and drop off the girls and then bolt."

"Like I do?"

"Yes, in fact."

"If by *good* you mean sober, yup, I am. As a judge. Seven months."

"Yeah, so your dad says. He has . . . *positive* things to say. Anyway, I was thinking we could maybe revisit the terms."

"Terms. You mean . . . visitation?" Pete leans back.

"Yes, extending visitation."

He's squinting at the lake now. Something that looks a lot like a snowflake hits the windshield. Can she mean it? Or is it some sort of bait . . . ?

"Pete. You there?"

"Yeah." Pete inhales. "Should I be calling my lawyer?"

"No. I thought *we* could come up with something ourselves. Maybe talk about it after the wedding?" She sounds sincere.

He clears his throat. "Yeah. Yes, that would be . . . I'm fine with that."

"So, I'm driving the girls up on Saturday?"

"Great. Listen. Sorry. Sorry to bark."

"That's . . ." Her voice evens. "Thank you. Thanks for apologizing."

Pete sees the stern of the canoe swing hard, caught by the wind. "Listen, I gotta go. Some things need to be taken care of here this morning." He's out of the truck in seconds.

"Saturday, then."

"Great. Beth?" He grunts as he grabs for the bow rope.

"Yeah?"

"This means a lot."

Only after hanging up does it occur he hadn't gotten around to telling Beth why he'd called—that he's paddling into bad weather.

It doesn't seem nearly as cold as it had been minutes earlier. He peels his gloves and stuffs them in a pocket. As he pushes off, Duke whimpers with excitement. With the first dip of his paddle, Pete says aloud, "Extended visitation." That's a corner turned. Beth isn't above twisting the knife, but she is reasonable, and nothing if not a good mother. The girls are twelve and fourteen— Beth knows what he is painfully aware of every day—that soon Allison and Maddie will be off to college, that he has only so many years to make up for who he's been for the past five.

He's got a little timber-frame cabin on his lot at Hoodoo Point. It would be a place to bring the girls on weekends. The land was a launch point back when his great-grandfather owned an island, but it had fallen into forfeiture at the hands of Alpo's father. Alpo reclaimed it by paying a few decades of back taxes and gave the parcel to Pete and Beth as a wedding gift. The slope of old-growth pine had always held a hopeful "someday" ideal for Pete—a place where he might build a cabin, but Beth never warmed to the idea. Perhaps out of unconscious spite, Pete had tainted the place for himself by making it the scene of many benders, parking a crappy trailer and letting the timber-frame project slide. It wouldn't take much to finish up the electrical and put the trim up, clear out the lumber scraps and propane tanks, and haul away the Travel Mansion. Alpo has repeatedly volunteered to help with the cabin. That offer might still be good.

Could it be possible, if he plays his cards right, to have the girls for a chunk of the summer?

With his pack and Duke's weight keeping the bow low, Pete can paddle hard. The sunrise is indeed spectacular, dragging with it a skein of reddish clouds. He knows the old sailor's adage, but warning or not, paddles on, working against a headwind, arms chugging as if on autopilot. He's actually getting somewhere. As Granger says, sloughing off the self-loathing is one of the challenges.

Something wells from somewhere in his pit and Pete is surprised to feel a tear trace his cheek. He stops to float a moment and wipe his face. Despite the cold, he's worked up a good sweat, is out of breath.

"Fuck, Duke, am I over the hump?"

He's done everything he's capable of. Never misses a meeting unless there's a clinic emergency; keeps the house neat for the girls' weekends; is never late picking them up or dropping them off. Cooks decent food now, and not just when the girls are visiting. He took them shopping to a fancy Minneapolis kitchen store where, calculating the amount of money he was about to spend on a Vitamix against how many cases of booze it would buy, burst out laughing. He checks in regularly with Granger, runs every day, and works like a mule at the clinic. He studies new procedures, reads the journals, goes to conferences, and is an active member of his affiliations. He may have failed as a husband and fumbled as a father, but he can at least be a decent vet.

And every minute has been an uphill fucking slog, every day dying for a drink and every day not caving.

Had he thought his father wasn't paying attention? He's seemed so preoccupied with Sissy and moving on and closing out his old life. But that's Alpo, never missing a trick, no matter how busy, always observing, nobody noticing the wheels turning.

The brief conversation with Beth was the most civil Pete's had with his ex-wife in a year. Last fall, when he'd let her know he was going back to Birchwood and asked her to come to group family day, Beth's tone was flat and stone cold. "Good luck with that."

Angry couldn't begin to describe Beth's state in October. And who could blame her? She'd given him a chance, trusting him to take his daughters for the day of Kelly's and Jessica's funerals. To say he blew it would be an understatement.

From a morning meeting in a church basement where he'd been given his six months' sober medallion, Pete drove to Duluth to pick up his daughters and brought them back to Hatchet Inlet to the same church for the funeral. The pair of graduation photos on the closed caskets said it all. He milled near the coffins, keeping his distance from the families. Maddie and Allison took off with his cousin's kids, absorbed into the gaggle of girls hanging out up in the balcony.

At one point he went out for air and was waved to the parking lot where old classmates had gathered to listen to the first game of the season, boom box on the open tailgate. He was handed a beer in an NHL cozy and he did not refuse it. Without a thought, after six months of sobriety, he relapsed, just like that.

Drinking the second beer, he felt the weight of the medallion in his pocket. That beer was washed down with two more, and the medallion stopped its nagging. Drinking was one thing, but that he'd then driven the girls back to Duluth was another. That Beth might smell it on him at the door hadn't even occurred. She took one look at him on her front doorstep and ushered the girls in without a word, then rushed back out before he could reach his car. Pete was peeling Beth's hand off his arm and yelling when Tom came out to join in. The girls were glued to an upstairs window as he was banished.

Given that incident, Beth could have pulled the plug on visitation altogether.

You'd have thought that his slip would have been just that, a regrettable slip, but by evening he was wracked with enough regret to justify embarking on a real bender—the bender he was in the middle of when Rauri called about Scotty, and the last time he'd paddled this particular stretch of water.

From what he can recall, crossing the north arm of Little Hatchet will be the longest, hairiest paddle. After it, just two brief ones punctuated by three portages, the final and most difficult being up the Laurentian Crest. Even with a stiff headwind, it'll be three hours, tops. He can get out there, see what's up, and be back in time to get the girls' room ready for Saturday. Then he will go to his father's stag party.

Navigating the first portage in soupy mud, Pete suddenly feels less than equipped. Aside from packing morphine and splints, he hadn't thought ahead. What if something is seriously wrong? What if he finds Rauri badly injured?

Or dead.

The portage is mercifully short, only thirty rods. Just as he spies water ahead, one of his boots slides and he's down, smack on his coccyx. He loses his grip on the gunwales, the canoe flips sideways, and the thirty-pound Duluth pack slips off one shoulder. It takes a full minute of obscenities just to get back up. He shrugs back into his pack and resets the yoke.

"Nice start. *Nice* fucking start." His ass is wet now. He should take the time to shuck his jeans and put on his thermals, but it would mean unpacking them. The next stretch is easy enough.

At Copper Shore he puts in on sandy bottom, hearing the drone of a floatplane. Any aircraft in the Reserve requires emergency permission to fly or land, so he can assume that mission is no good news. The canoe bobs near the shore, and Pete waits for the plane to come into view to see what direction it's heading. It's one of the red-and-white DNR Beavers from the cribs at Hoodoo Point. As to who might be in it, Pete can guess it's either a ranger or a search-and-rescue team.

When the plane banks west instead of north, Pete wonders if the plane is circling its way in to approach or is searching. It's possible the plane isn't headed to Rauri's at all—Pete might not be the only fool out here. He's paddled around a number of low-floating ice chunks that could easily roll the canoe of a less experienced paddler.

As he humps across the portage, fragments of his evening with Rauri come back to fill in the blanks—blackouts, if he's honest.

That day in October it was late afternoon by the time he'd reached this same juncture in the trip. He'd packed stupidly light for that one: only his kit, two headlamps, and the quart he'd had the foresight to decant into a plastic Sprite bottle—supply-wise he hadn't begun to cover the basics. The first thing he had noticed upon landing was that Rauri looked very fit for a man his age. He had a small limbing axe strapped to his belt with a leather sheath that looked old. When Pete commented on it, Rauri told him about his found treasure.

"Out tapping birch, setting my sap buckets over on the Ontario side—you didn't hear that—when I tripped on that spike." He pointed to a spike lying on the dock boards.

"That? Looks nasty."

"Had some petrified rope around it. At first I thought the place was an old sugar camp, then I found the rubble of a few foundations."

It seemed like Rauri was delaying. No one relishes putting their dog down. Pete humored him. "So, what was it?"

"Follow me."

Walking behind, Pete was able to manage a few swigs from his Sprite bottle. Rauri's workshop looked different: whitewashed, cleaned up. Above the workbench was a wall of antique hand tools, polished and hung like a museum exhibit: saws, hand augers, planers, chisels, drawknives. Pete pointed to a pair of tools he didn't recognize.

"Hookaroons," Rauri explained. "And that's a pulp hook."

"Yeah? Ouch."

"The pretty ones there are diameter tapes. The calipers are brass, too."

A second wall held large tools: bow saws, mallets, sledges, axes, splitting mauls.

"You got all this where?"

"Old logging camp. Three barrels sunk in sand. Tools packed inside."

"Sand?"

"And mineral oil. They used to do that to keep 'em from rusting—store tools in sand and oil."

"Yeah?"

"These beauts were buried most of a century. 'Course some of the wood handles rotted, but see, I made replicas."

"Looks original."

"Carved from stunted oak."

Pete picked up a maul. "They gotta be valuable?" He was about to try lifting it over his head when Rauri eased it from his hands and rehung it.

"I thought at first I might give 'em to the Voyageur Homestead. But then I started trying them out."

To Pete's look he explained, "*Using* them."

"What, like some reenactor?"

Rauri shrugged. "Thought I'd spend a week in the boots of a logger. Took down a copse of maple, sawed and split it."

"And?"

"Sore? There's wasn't enough Bengay and aspirin."

Pete said, "I've never known a Finn to do things the easy way. Thank fuck I'm half-Irish." He tilts his bottle ceilingward, no longer trying to hide it. "Thanks, Mom."

Rauri gives him a look before showing him the parts to an antler chandelier he's making, demonstrating how he used the small hand auger to drill the holes. "Normally I'd use an electric drill, but this is smooth. Plus, no dust in the air."

Pete looked at the spirals of antler bone curled like rotini. "So . . ."

"No face mask, no ear protection. With all the electricity saved I can light this place up like a beach at noon, work till midnight if I want. I make toast in a *toaster* now."

"That's . . . great." Pete was hoping the tour was over.

"People have no idea how jarring the noise of machines really is. But when you have silence to compare it to, you can *hear* the work."

"Jesus, I'd think you got nothing *but* silence around here."

"I swear my hearing is growing back."

"Yeah?" He wished they'd get on with it.

Outside, Pete noticed Rauri's old four-wheeler was disused and puddled with pine needles, same with his snow machine—an alder sprouting from the Bombardier's torn upholstery. "These fixable?"

"They work. I just don't bother with them. Tooling around here I don't need more than a pair of skis or a sled for hauling. Old school, I guess you'd call it."

And then Rauri was saying something about birds.

". . . because I can hear them now, each bird. I can tell one from another."

"What, chickadee from sapsucker?"

"No, I mean the actual, *individual* birds. You can tell one gray jay from another if you listen long enough."

"Yeah?" Pete thought it best to agree.

"When it's quiet enough."

Was Rauri ever going to shut up about the quiet? Pete chuckled at his own joke and followed him into the cabin.

"With those motors running you never know what might sneak up behind."

"Like what? Like who?"

"There can be more in an echo than in a sound itself. Sometimes sound comes in color, sometimes in smell. You know the smell of jet fuel?"

Pete wasn't following but nodded anyway.

"It's a yellow smell, and the sound that comes with it is always the same."

"What kind of sound?"

"Sort of a *thip thip thip.*"

"Like a helicopter?"

"Exactly. Like a Huey Cobra. Except you don't just hear it—it gets inside, here." Rauri rapped a fist to his sternum.

Pete was on another run of open water. The wind had died to allow for the silence Rauri had gone on about, which Pete realizes is anything but, for it allows all manner of small sounds to surface: the lapping of water, branches dripping, paddle dipping, breeze in the shell of his ear. Rustlings. Pete has a clear view of his next portage now. Seeing the angle of the incline, he moans. The Laurentian Crest portage has footholds cut in stone along the hairpin zigs and zags. The slog ahead seems like adequate penance. The portage has many nicknames, *Witch's Tit* being the most apt in Pete's opinion. *Giishkadinaa* is the Native name, which Pete can assume means either *steep* or *Are you fucking kidding me?*

Sissy worried that Rauri might have intentionally walked off into some cold dawn to freeze to death, but Pete feels certain he wouldn't have gone that route. He hadn't been so drunk that day that he didn't understand Rauri was revealing something. That he was finding, in the quiet and the manual toil of his island, something akin to peace.

Pete has considered suicide himself.

One particularly bleak December day the year before, after Beth had taken the girls to Duluth and Pete had just found out about Dr. Tom. He'd been hopping foot to foot in his frigid backyard having a cigarette when it suddenly occurred to him he no longer needed to stand outside: he could smoke wherever he wanted—the entirety of his suburban home was his territory now. He chalked that into his mental column of reasons to live, woefully short as it was. He could smoke in Beth's closet if he wanted to, except there were only a few abandoned blouses left behind to foul.

In the kitchen he flicked on the range fan, pulled up a stool to the island where the girls used to do homework, where Beth had cooled a thousand cookies. How many warm cookies had he nabbed from behind her back? He usually got away with it—she'd swat his hand, pretend to be angry, laugh, and let it go. Then there came a time she'd catch him and her look made him back away, hands up. By then both knew he didn't want a cookie: he wanted a fucking drink. One of the small domestic dramas played across the stage of their flailing marriage.

He ashed into the sink and sniffed the air. Disgusted, he ran tap water over the butt. In the pros column of suicide, he would finally be kicking the habit.

There was a smorgasbord of methods: bullet, overdose, open a vein in a warm tub, hanging. He possessed enough horse tranquilizers to kill a few stallions. Despite Beth's opinions on guns, he had good reason to carry one, needing a weapon to put down a dying farm animal too injured to put down with a syringe. Shooting himself would be quickest, messiest, and the most distressing for Beth. The gun was locked in his glove compartment, the bullets kept in an Altoids tin under the seat. He loaded the pistol, poured a full glass of his best whiskey, and laid his phone between the glass and the pistol and considered all three. *Drink, Rehab,* or *Die.* Like that stupid game *Kill, Fuck, or Marry.*

Sitting at the counter with his hands clenched between his knees, two images kept butting in between his options: the faces of his children.

Simply, the choice wasn't his to make. Saying, "Final answer," he reached for his phone with a trembling hand. After making arrangements to check into treatment, he emptied the chamber, took his tin of bullets, and hurled them up on the roof, then dragged his new extension ladder to the curb with a FREE sign attached.

He called Alpo's cell. His father was silent as he explained—about the gun, about Birchwood—he didn't mention the glass of whiskey. He asked his father if he'd look after Duke.

"I'm in Minneapolis," said Alpo, "getting a new transmission for the Ford. I can be in Rochester by three. I'll take Duke on the condition I drive you up to the center myself."

Pete was grateful and angry at once. "You don't trust I'd get there on my own?"

"Something like that. Pack a bag." Alpo hung up before he could say more.

Pete drank his final drink, savoring each sip while waiting for his father. Finally—someone else was in charge.

He barely remembers the hazy drive to Birchwood, the intake process, doesn't recall much of his first day, though the second morning was full-on Technicolor and surround sound. He did not know you could puke yourself awake. That's when shit got real. Most mornings he felt as if he'd spent the night clamped into a paint shaker.

Pete hoists the canoe, takes a deep breath, and begins to climb the low section of the Witch's Tit, Duke weaving just ahead. Pete's lungs and thighs work the rhythm of the path, the tune in his temple still plaguing him. According to his mother, the best way to get rid of a song stuck in your head was to just give in, belt out the whole thing, get it out of your system. He starts singing, loudly, like a voyageur.

> *So if you want me off your back, well, come on and let me know: should I stay or should I go?*
> *Should I stay or should I go now?*

He's making good time. Three-quarters of the way up, chest thudding, he stops to prop the canoe against a cedar and steps out onto a rock shelf jutting over the treetops. Duke hangs back, with a single whine as if to say *"Humans,"* before lowering to the moss. The spear of rock he stands on has a view of pretty much everything. He sits and scoots to its edge to dangle his feet several stories above the canopy. Pete eats his breakfast of walnuts and apples while looking out over the vista—to the north are diagonal black lakes settled in glacial gouges, to the west stretch the great granite spines of the Divide in hues of rust and mold against a gunmetal sky.

A screech from above tears the air and Duke bolts upright. A red-tailed hawk circling overhead pumps its wings in three great efforts to build speed before aiming its weight in a downward trajectory so near to Pete that as it plummets he can see the mottled feathers compress with velocity, the body elongating as it missiles past to a patch of scrub far below. At the last nanosecond it sets its talons like landing gear and connects with something invisible to Pete. He dares not lean out but can hear a great upward *whoosh*. Less than a breath later the hawk reappears, dead grass ribboning from its talons along with a garter snake curling itself in the air as if to form an ampersand. Just ten feet below, the hawk touches down on a wide, scarred limb. It proceeds to dance quick purchase on the snake's head. Before the snake has a chance to lash, the hawk neatly dispatches it with a single blow to the base of its skull. The beak-to-bone *crack* is loud enough to echo across the valley.

Pete watches rapt as the hawk makes a meal of the snake: pulling tendons, tearing strips of pink flesh. It stops now and then to look out over the valley and twice it looks up to him as if to remind Pete just whose territory they are in. Its eyes are amber and obsidian, pitiless intelligence. Sinew and gore sway from its beak as its talons sink deeper into its prey.

The moment is at once a pinhole of focus yet fulsome in scope. Clouds above darken and flex as Pete's own muscles course with adrenaline. He feels as cracked open as the snake's skull.

He understands it is a privilege to witness such a scene. As the hawk dines, it kicks away viscera, sections of spine, the mangled head. Once finished, it plucks bloodied bits from its talons and shudders its feathers smooth. After setting its wings the hawk falls forward and away to soar out over the valley. All that is left behind is a stain on the bark and a few desiccated vertebrae. As the creature becomes a diminishing speck gliding away, the song comes back.

If I go there will be trouble, and if I stay it will be double . . .

He shouts the last line out over the valley and the question echoes back at him.

Should I stay or should I go?

8

S HE PEERS THROUGH THE HOLE IN THE MASSAGE TABLE at Veshko's immaculate sneakers. Sissy is half-covered by the sheet he's just repositioned, somehow tucking it between her thighs without getting anywhere near what Cora at Venus Waxing calls her "lady parts." Veshko kneads one oiled leg and exposed buttock, working Sissy's flesh as if it is something disembodied from her. She supposes such detachment is something massage therapists are trained to have.

Through the first quarter of her massage she's been thinking aloud about Rauri's disappearance and possible whereabouts. Veshko has been listening like a bartender, offering the occasional "yes" or "ah" or a polite-sounding mumble she can't make out between his accent and the padding around her ears.

She asks the floor, "Where would that little bugger even *go*?"

Veshko ventures, "Abroad? On holiday?"

"Hmm. I doubt that."

"Business?"

"Doubt that too."

"Away to see an . . . ah, lover?"

A small sound escapes Sissy.

The idea of Rauri having a lover requires more imagination than Sissy has. Not that he's a bad-looking man, but the grooming wouldn't exactly further his cause. He has all his teeth and most are straight, but they are the color of broth. He has a full head of ginger-gray hair, but when the watchman's cap comes off it stands like an oiled haystack. He's constantly thumbing the round glasses back into place on his sunburnt, windburnt nose.

Barely taller than Sissy, he wears cargo shorts three seasons of the year and from a distance is often mistaken for a Boy Scout. On the upside, while Rauri looks smelly, he isn't. Now that she thinks of it, Rauri usually smells like the pine chaff settled in the stitching of his quilted vest, or the clumps of mulchy cedar always falling from his boot treads as something good. He usually drags a forecast of what weather is following him: if rain or wind is what's in store, Rauri's *eau de jour* is the first hint. Smells aside, Rauri as a Romeo seems as likely to Sissy as Louise's loopy claim of having had intercourse (and tea!) with him. What had she said? *A thing like a core drill.* Good grief.

Veshko ponders, "Perhaps he travels to visit relatives in other provinces?"

Does Rauri even have family? Sissy can't image him bouncing a grandbaby on his knee or arguing politics over turkey, just as she can't image herself *not* having a family. As taxing as her sister and brothers can be and regardless of how much battier their mother grows by the day, she can't think what she'd have done without them these past months.

"I don't think he has family."

"Friends?" Veshko is on the wrong roll. "Maybe hosting guests to his lake home?"

"Guests" might include lost canoeists, some fisherman with a hook sunk in his thumb or a gash needing stitches. He must get some intentional visitors, but "lake home"—much less "home"—hardly describes the man-camp she's only been to once, a grungy collection of sheds and shacks as hobbity as Rauri is, weeds growing from the gutters like his unruly eyebrows. What garbage doesn't get burnt just gets added to the graveyard of old appliances, broken machinery, insulation, and unrecycled recycling. The islands are hardly a destination. Until now she hadn't much thought about Rauri's utter aloneness. A twinge of guilt stabs her for never having sat down with him to have a real talk or invited him to her home for a meal. She doesn't even know where he sleeps when in town.

Veshko gently pulls the sheet up to billow over her like a tent. "Time, please," Veshko says, "for you to flip."

"Like a pancake." Sissy laughs while turning onto her back. It's too dim to make out the exact color of his eyes; she can see they are not brown or dark but some shade of blue or hazel or green. Whatever color, they look puzzled. Rather than explain pancake, she offers another flippable food.

"An egg?"

"Ah. *Oui, un oeuf.*"

Thanks to her three years of high school French, she determines that Veshko's accent is very good. She's also heard him speak perfectly gargley-sounding German to Mrs. Weiner, which he pronounces *Viner,* which the old lady seems to appreciate.

"*Oui,*" she says dreamily. "*Un oeuf.*" As he tucks the sheet under her armpits, Sissy closes her eyes to savor the next bit.

His hands feel warmer than average hands as they massage upward from the plane of her breastbone to collarbones, then the fine muscles of her neck. There's no talking now, as Veshko pretty much has her by the vocal chords and those sinewy ropes you wouldn't think need massaging but do. His hands slowly plow toward a release point just at the junction of her ears and jawline. Then he begins again.

Heaven.

His hands, which feel so large along her spine, seem to shrink as they travel upward, so that by the time he's reached her face they feel delicate and small.

Veshko's fingertips mine her cheekbones for deposits of stress. He works along the dainty hollows of her eye sockets and the mazes of her ears. He somehow keeps a constant hand somewhere on her even when adding more massage oil to his hands. Sometimes his strokes match whatever music he's playing. Today, it's cello, just the saddest instrument in the world. She's heard this very music as a teen when Laurie used to drive her out to Naledi to swim. Mr. Machutova would play records in his office at the back of the lodge where you could buy ice cream or use the toilet.

Resort kids would track in sand, giggle, and finger all the items on the shelves until caught in the old man's crosshair-stare. Town kids knew better. Meg often minded the store, and even though she was younger than Sissy, always seemed older, especially when she and her grandfather spoke the Czech language like it was theirs alone.

Veshko's hands worm under her shoulder blades flat as spatulas; one hand then the other slip down as far as the dimples on her low back. Using the weight of her torso to do the work, he merely leans back, hands furling into fists as they travel to the base of her skull, where his fists morph into upturned rakes and the tines press, sending aching points of light like comets across her closed eyelids. This juncture always makes Sissy feel more exposed than her nakedness, because for whatever reason the pressure acts like a faucet and tears roll from her temples into the whorls of her ears.

It always happens. And he always says the same thing: "The crying is good. Cleansing. Tension and emotion get trapped in the body."

These tears fall silently, like they do after reading about a school shooting or seeing a post about children pulled from earthquakes or some violence like the little boy in Syria or wherever sitting in that ambulance.

"Crying is to be expected," he says. The tears dry on her skin so that some nights after a massage Alpo's lips find salt on her earlobes and neck.

Veshko cradles her skull, leans back, and begins to sway, as if gently harvesting a root vegetable—as if her head is a prize turnip.

He's gearing up to do that thing that makes Sissy uncomfortable for how much she anticipates it—something she wishes Alpo would do but is embarrassed to ask. After stretching her neck so that she feels taller even lying down, Veshko gathers hanks of her hair into his fists and gently, steadily tugs, releasing her scalp from its grip on her skull. The sensation sends an oozy-woozy rush down her spine to pelvis—a sensation that would feel more appropriate if it were Alpo at the wheel.

Conflicting emotions roll: gratitude for the dimness of the room; panic that something will happen down there; fear that Veshko will let go of her hair; hope that he doesn't.

He does, of course—*just* at the crucial second before. Sissy sinks into the table, realizing she'd been tense as a plank. Her eyes squeeze tight. When Veshko pulls the sheet up to her chin, tucking her in like a toddler, she loses the battle and trumpets out an awkward laugh, immediately failing at disguising it as a cough.

Is nearly, *accidentally* nearly, reaching climax by someone other than your partner cheating? She's not one bit attracted to Veshko. But what defines cheating? Some of her friends think just watching porn is, which seems harsh to Sissy. When flat-chested Patti Mudek found a link to BigTittyFuckers.com on her husband's PC, she packed herself and the kids off to her mom's cabin for a month. While Patti admitted that Brad wasn't actually cheating, she said it would have felt less like cheating "if he'd been choking the chicken over women with littler boobs." Her words.

Sissy, trying to understand, made the mistake of asking, "Does Brad know you have a vibrator?"

Patti went shrill. "How do *you* know I have a vibrator?"

"I didn't. I just assum—" Her second mistake was laughing. "That's different!"

They are still friendly, but Patti is a cooler friendly, back with Brad and probably embarrassed that Sissy knows what she does. Sometimes Sissy wishes people didn't tell her things at all, but she doesn't believe looking at videos of naked strangers counts as infidelity. She's seen Alpo notice other women—*appreciate* them, he's no letch, just a man. Her neighbor Kip has a maple tree in his yard that is more colorful than hers, so that each September she aims her lawn chair eastward; it doesn't mean she loves her own tree any less.

As a matter of fact, she *will* show Alpo Veshko's scalp-pulling move.

* * *

Veshko always saves her feet and calves for last. She's glad to have him move away from her head because even though the room's too dim to see, he might sense the heat toasting across her face.

Infidelity—*fidelity*. Surely neither is simply physical.

Living in Hatchet Inlet more than forty years she's seen a dozen ways to sour a marriage. Everyone knows Tony DeMagidio and Willa Roth have been in love since high school, even though they are married to other people. And while both have stuck to their original crummy marriages, it seems like martyrdom to Sissy. And that awful thing with Donny and Jill Zenenko after she got so jealous of him flirting with a younger woman at the Portage that she fooled around with his Facebook feed to make it look like he was stalking teens. And since people believe anything online, Donny lost his coaching job. Forget that he's innocent: there's still that seed of suspicion Jill planted on her husband, and how can she expect him to love her the same after that?

Veshko lifts her calf a few inches from the table and makes a snowplow of his thumbs to cleave a trench from the back of her knee to her ankle. Sissy holds her breath. He knows she's on her feet all hours because there are days she waits on him for both an early breakfast and late lunch. He digs, rooting around for cricks and knobs, sometimes triggering spasms, apologizing, "It must be done."

"Right," Sissy exhales. "No pain no gain?"

"Ah. Yes."

Sissy believes the body is like a relationship: for it to work right the small stuff needs as much attention as the big stuff. And all the small stuff is easy with Alpo—they put their heads together on things like planning an herb garden, or deciding how they'll split their data usage, or what to splurge on at Sam's Club. Sometimes there's big meaning in the smallest gesture, like the time she hit the fawn on 53 and even though they were late for something important, he gave her all the time in the world to cry it out. He didn't have a hankie so used his hands to wipe away tears *and* snot.

Or how he means it when he says he loves her.

She's confessed things to him she would never breathe to another soul, like how some nights she just wishes Louise would go to sleep and not wake up. Or about her Super Sissy fantasy, where she goes to Washington, D.C., and the White House and straps on a Wonderbra and high heels and finds a way to sidle up to the leader of the free world, tempting him to grab her by the *whatever,* only to have it all end with him looking at a grenade pin.

She tries not to think of the president—so awful to people like Veshko—and has quit Facebook. And she's asked that their bedroom be a safe zone with no television or radio, because she so often drags fragments of the news into her dreams, sometimes waking in a sweat for all the ways things might go wrong. Alpo will pet her back to sleep, always making a version of the same joke: "Nothing but rainbows and unicorns, Sisu." Or "Just kittens, boxes of kittens."

Forget that she is just so happy she will never have to go through starting another romantic relationship, ever. Of her five serious boyfriends—and the two casual ones—most were like skits in comparison to what she has with Alpo.

She's won the lottery.

Probably most of Veshko's clients just lie there quietly and leave him to his work, but the curiosity scratches at her. Without considering whether it might be too personal, Sissy asks.

"Veshko. Have you ever been married?"

His pause is awfully long. "No. I have not."

"Oh."

Has she upset him? She has wondered if Veshko might be gay, or if it's just his foreignness and nice manners that make him seem like he might be.

As if to head her off, he adds, "Almost. Once."

"Ah."

"She . . . *we* never got a chance to happen."

He rubs a muscle in her ankle as if trying to erase it. Of course, Veshko would have had his troubles living through those years in Sarajevo, dodging snipers just to get drinking water, losing swaths of loved ones to bombs or infections. *Never got a chance to happen.* "I see," Sissy says. "I'm so sorry."

She knows he's shrugged because the pressure of his hand eases for a second.

The one time Laurie came along to see the grief counselor, they were encouraged to talk about Kelly, especially to the rest of the family, who were too knocked back to do much of anything. "Tell Kelly's stories," he'd said. "Talk about her." Sissy thinks what he meant was, don't box the dead away, don't be afraid to remind yourself and others they existed. She thought the counselor nailed it. Laurie originally seemed eager to hear him out but lost interest after it became apparent he wouldn't prescribe the diazepam she was fishing for. She'd made a face on the way out, mimicking him, "Numbness isn't the answer, Miss Pavola."

Sissy took on the assignment to talk about their niece, to honor Kelly's existence—in the counselor's words, to validate the loss. Sissy raises her head and blinks at Veshko.

"So. Your girlfr—. Fiancée?"

"Fiancée, yes?"

"What was her name?"

Veshko hesitates. "Mia."

"That's a very pretty name."

When he adds nothing, she fishes. "Was she? Pretty, I mean?"

"Yes. Beautiful. Very beautiful."

"What was she like?"

"Ah. She was . . . sorry, it's not too nice word. A bitch?"

"What?" Sissy crabs up onto her elbows. "But. Not to *you*?"

"Sometimes yes."

"Oh." She collapses to her back. She will shut up now.

But Veshko suddenly seems fueled. "How do you say, like what I do now with your muscles? Mia, she did with emotion. Mine. Other men too, *manipulate*?"

"Oh, I see." She maybe sees.

"So, *bitch*, yes?"

"Sure." Sissy is glad he's reached her toes and is nearly finished. "*Bitch* works."

With a breath, he changes the subject. "You like work in the café? *At* it?" He often autocorrects like an iPhone, sometimes in midsentence. Probably asking questions to avoid answering more of hers. Maybe Laurie is right and she sometimes pries too deeply.

"It's all right. Not many career options, though."

"Hatchet Inlet is small, yes?"

"Yup," Sissy says. "I mean yes."

"And if it was bigger? Maybe a café of your own?"

"No way." Sissy surprises herself with how certainly she knows this. Not a café. What, then? There's SissyBrittle, but lately the more she considers it, the less certain she grows, maybe because making candy doesn't fill any real need, doesn't exactly contribute, doesn't improve the crummy state of the world or anything. Yet feeding people is all she's ever known. She knows working at the café is easy when compared to risking doing something real, starting something on her own.

Here she is, naked under a sheet talking to a foreign man she barely knows who is rolling each of her toes and then spreading them like wishbones, which could be comical in a dirty-joke sort of way if it didn't feel so necessary. She *will* do something different.

At the counter she lays down a twenty-five-dollar tip, which is only what she takes in during peak hours at the diner. Veshko looks up.

"Very generous. No need." In the daylight she can see his eyes are dark bluish-gray, set off by his olive skin. His lashes are long, like a child's. The whites of his eyes seem all the whiter for the blackness of his eyebrows. When he moves from beneath the fluorescent to the natural light near the door, his irises change to a lighter blue-green. She wonders if blue is a very Muslim color for eyes, then realizes she doesn't actually know if he is Muslim or not, only that people say he is.

"Thank you." In his measured way he says, "I am going to say I look very forward to your wedding."

Sissy grins. Veshko must be the "plus one" on Cathy's RSVP—the "date" she's been so cagey about. "And I look very forward to you being there."

As he walks her to the door, she turns. "Veshko?"

"Yes?"

"I . . . I'm really sorry for your loss."

"Loss?"

"Mia."

"Mia?" His head tilts like Jeff's. "Mia is not died."

"No?"

"No. She lives in Cleveland, Ohio." He smiles to show teeth that are crooked in a charming way. "With rich American husband number two."

Sissy laughs. "Oh. So, when you say . . ."

"*Bitch*? Is why. For sure."

"Got it."

Sissy's out the door. Halfway down the steps she realizes he's still holding the door and turns to see him looking at the sky, where the sun has poked through a mean-looking cloud. "Still . . . ," Veshko says, seemingly to himself. "Still. I hope for her some happiness."

9

THERE ARE TWENTY THINGS HE COULD BE DOING, *should* be doing to prepare for his move, his wedding, his next life. His stomach is sour from the whiskey. To think Pete used to face this every morning. . . . Alpo forgoes coffee, brews a cup of weak tea, and makes burnt toast, which is what Rose gave him on hungover mornings after his twice-monthly Suomi gatherings at Kalevala Hall. Suomi is basically a book club for men, except instead of wine there's Bud and Aquavit, and instead of books they watch adventure movies and documentaries or listen to talks put together by a former radio personality who owns a Scandinavian travel agency in Superior. Memberships and donations feed a scholarship that brings a Finnish exchange student to Hatchet Inlet each year. Even on nights Alpo doesn't feel like seeing *Kon-Tiki* a third time, hear an oboist from Helsinki, or watch slides on cod fishing, he always feels obliged to go because it is for a good cause and because the group is dwindling as members downshift into retirement and decrepitude. The new mission is to recruit members under fifty. Alpo believes changing the venue to the new Sasquatch Brewpub might help the cause.

Most of the Suomi group will show up at his stag party. As he dips black toast into scalding tea, he groans at the thought. The evening will commence—he looks at his watch—in fourteen hours.

Neighbor Perry doesn't know what he's in for. Alpo's pals tend to jab and joke or one-up their way through such social gatherings. If somebody mentions a cousin with an apple-sized tumor, then surely another's uncle had one the size of a boot. He's thinking of calling Perry to see if he's up for a sauna when he notices the kitchen phone blinking with a message.

He wipes charred crumbs from the counter as Pete's voice kicks in, "Dad. It's me . . ." When he says, "I'm going out there in the morning," Alpo drops the sponge to look out the window where fast-moving clouds are closing over the morning like a lid. Not a day to portage three lakes to the Lower Shield. After replaying the message to listen for any slurs in Pete's voice, Alpo sighs. He should have discouraged Pete the moment he mentioned chasing after Rauri. The lower basin will be riddled with residual ice from the thaw. He can only hope that Pete's checked the forecast and has changed his mind. He punches his home number. No answer. The clinic line rolls over to the emergency service, and Alpo hangs up before anyone can answer. He tunes the kitchen radio to the weather channel.

Given all Pete's put himself and everyone else through, it seems foolhardy to risk reclaimed life and limb to take stupid risks like a trip to Rauri's. Is he out to prove yet another something? It's admirable he's done the work to pick himself clean—Alpo has told Beth as much on Pete's behalf—but he seems to be repeating his twelve steps over and over, as if on some recovery treadmill.

Sissy suggests he might just try trusting his son.

He mindlessly retraces his earlier steps around the house, thinking. When he finds himself standing in Pete's old room, arms akimbo, he grins, thinking of the word Sissy uses for winding up somewhere but unsure why. *Destinesia.*

Not much has changed in this room. Tacked to the paneling are old posters of Patti Smith, Suzanne Vega, Journey, Blondie, and the Pretenders. The twin beds are covered with stained Hudson Bay blankets. The top bookshelf holds a cluster of hockey trophies and above the desk hangs a group of certificates and diplomas in cheap frames. He sometimes forgets how smart his son was—*is.* In the high recess of the glass-block windows is a collection of small animal skulls, towered over by the mounted skeleton of a bobcat cobbled together with pins and epoxy. Around its neck hangs a faded blue ribbon. When was that—fifth grade? Sixth?

There are two empty cardboard boxes on the bed. Alpo absently begins filling one with cassette tapes and textbooks from the shelves, items Pete can't possibly want to keep. An anatomy book bulges with notes. As he sets it aside, a few scribbled sheets fall out, along with an envelope. The papers aren't notes: they are letters, written in a vaguely familiar hand. He tucks them back quickly before he has a chance to give in to temptation. The envelope fallen to his feet appears empty and he's about to toss it when the light catches to reveal a shadow of a square within.

Rose used to raid Pete's room regularly to find speed and pot, and once, heroin. Inside the envelope is a square of waxed paper with something curled in it—a lock of coppery hair.

Of course. Meg. She was practically a drug to Pete. Alpo hasn't seen her since the unveiling of the painting he'd commissioned of the Hobby. She'd have been the only girl Pete wrote to during high school. Would he change things if he could go back in time?

Alpo couldn't have known what he was sparking when he took seven-year-old Pete out to Naledi to play with Tomas's newly orphaned daughter. He remembers her as an oddly poised seven-year-old with an air of authority over her patch of the bald-dirt playground. Alpo encouraged Meg and Pete, hovering some—he might have hovered overmuch.

One day Vac took him aside and said, "Sure, they play good, but best you be less . . . *present*. There is a newspaper in the bar, beer in the cooler, poles in the boathouse if you want to fish." He added, "No need to confuse her. I have to be both grandfather and father now." So Alpo stepped back, merely dropping Pete off at Naledi to visit his tomboy playmate. Years later, Pete got a summer job there as Vac's dock boy. It would have been around then that he picked up the torch he's still dragging for her. During the hormonal stew of adolescence, his son seemed imbalanced by Meg. At the close of each summer when she got shipped back to boarding school, a funk descended on Pete. He took no interest in other girls—just sealed himself in the dank of his bedroom with his stereo and books.

The summer before their last year of high school, Meg and Pete were suddenly going steady, and considering the boy's improved mood Alpo assumed the two were sleeping together and said as much to Rose.

"Goodness. I hope she doesn't get . . . I'll light a candle for her." Rose had her heart set on Pete getting through college. Alpo, keen to see him have more choices than he'd had, took a more proactive approach and left a box of condoms in his son's underwear drawer. No matter how tangled they got, both needed to make it out of Hatchet Inlet. When Meg went overseas to art school, Alpo assumed the distance would fizzle the wick.

Rose suffered the brunt of Pete's moods, which Alpo found impossible to read behind the fringe of his greasy bangs.

It was a relief when he first went away to college. Meg was barely mentioned. He was serious about his studies, though much of what he was hoovering up in electives were a lot of this-ism and that-ism, sociology, philosophy, Marxism. On weekends Alpo could look forward to Pete wringing his newly acquired smugness across the peace of the house. They could not get through a meal without Pete suggesting that Alpo was living his narrow life too cautiously, his horizons too near, his existence too dull.

Pete was a good-looking kid, well mannered (with strangers). He had a full-ride scholarship, had made the U hockey team, and finally met another girl, Angie. He should have been having the time of his life.

Still, he chided Alpo with names like Captain Sensible, as if there were worse things to be. Pete also had his nicknames for Hatchet Inlet: *Hatchet Incest. Batshit Inlet.* At the height of it, over Thanksgiving turkey Pete suggested Alpo possessed the intellectual and emotional life of soil, theorizing that for someone who lived through the sixties, he might have learned to relax, indulge, maybe even smoke some weed, do *something* to dislodge the bluecollar stick up his ass.

Even Rose balked at that, weak as she was by then, and asked him to leave the table. To make up for it, Pete gave him a dog-eared copy of *Siddhartha* for Christmas.

Between Rose's treatments and her not teaching, Alpo was working overtime to cover everything and was too tired to think. He threw up his hands, telling Rose, "My job is done."

"No," she countered. "It's just beginning."

Her final prognosis was just that, final. In weeks she was bedridden. Her absence was most keenly felt at the table—she'd have cut short the arguments and acted as a shield between Alpo and Pete as she always had. She'd have defended the valid points, dismissed the chaff. She was wasted as an English teacher, Alpo thought. Trial lawyer, more like.

"If we are so backward and mind-numbingly dull, why do you even come home?" Alpo asked.

"To see Mom."

Considering the amount of beer cans and tequila bottles he'd find in the recycle bins, Alpo knew Pete was drinking like a fish, which should have been the first flag.

Addiction, Alpo knows, is a disease. Pete's sponsor, Granger—a newcomer to Hatchet Inlet—can say such things without being sneered at. In Granger's vernacular, Pete's been diseased more than half his life. Alpo couldn't help but think of sobriety in the same uncertain terms as cancer, because given the odds recovery may as well be called remission. Having foot-jiggled his way through enough Al-Anon meetings, Alpo understands no one drives anyone to drink—the weakness is in them, whether acquired or genetic. Still, caving to either is an option, isn't it?

The hangover grinds along somewhere behind his left ear. He looks down to see he's still holding the lock of Meg's hair. The girl was never at fault. She's Pete's ghost to vanquish anyway, not his.

When Alpo was twenty, he had a summer job driving semi to pay his tuition at VoTech. His cargo was prefab homes—little houses made of ticky-tacky. His route took him from the Iron Range to the Twin Cities four times a week with another driver, each delivering half of a house to the site. He picked up a lot of hitchhikers on those runs—hippies headed up from the Cities, some going to the old Communist camp where a commune was forming; a few making pilgrimages to Bob Dylan's birthplace in Hibbing, perhaps expecting more inspiration than the unshaded pavements and the soaped storefront windows of a fading mining town. The girls smelled of patchouli and limes and did not shave their armpits and were wonderful. The boys offered or tried selling Alpo drugs. Alpo considered most of them deadbeats.

He'd become more selective after picking up a kid obviously doped with something.

"Acid, man. You should trip with me. Wanna tab?"

"Nah," Alpo held up his can of Tab. "Already got one."

That went over the kid's head. The actual trip went from bad to worse when a doe leapt directly into the truck's path. While Alpo pried the carcass from the Peterbilt's grill with the claw end of a hammer, the guy was doubled over on the roadside, announcing repeatedly to each of his bare toes that he was "fucking freaking the fuck *out*," then began swinging his head so forcefully a bead on one of his dreadlocks knocked one of his front teeth down his throat and Alpo had to perform the Heimlich maneuver on him.

Some of his stoner passengers were more amusing, assigning wonderment and new perspective to sights he sped past without seeing. *Tamarack trees. Who knew they were the color of a Push-Up? That heron walks just like John Cleese. What does a Red Pegasus have to do with gasoline?*

Most were dropouts from school or their families or work—seemingly proud of doing nothing as if it were some brave act. Their only plans as far as Alpo could tell were to chill and get their minds blown—concepts that he frankly could not get his own around. None ever seemed to have any money, so Alpo ended up buying a lot of coffee, which seemed a small price for the company. As for gas, Pine Homes (The Man) was footing that bill.

He listened to their circuitous ramblings and philosophies and rage against the Establishment. When that got old, he let them tune the radio. Alpo sang along with them to the ballads and rock tunes, failing to picture himself going to San Francisco with flowers in his hair, wondering if Mick Jagger was being literal about wanting to be bled on.

On his last run of the summer, he was pulling half of a two-bedroom ranch, poly-wrapped so you could see into it like a doll's house. His partner Rob hauled the other half, and since neither had any riders that day, they stopped for a long lunch. Each had a beer, then realizing they were on top of schedule, had one more. Then it was, *What the hell? One for the road,* possibly the most counterintuitive adage ever coined.

Rob pulled his rig ahead into lead position, which was out of order for the drop, but there were sixty miles yet for Alpo to overtake and make the switch. Coming up was the overpass they always diverted—a quick detour swing up the exit ramp and back down because the bridge height clearance was lower than their rigs' load heights. As he caught sight of it and let up on the gas, he noticed Rob's rig wasn't slowing. Alpo laid on the horn while easing to the shoulder, but Rob sped up. Watching the half-house sail on, he pressed the air horn so hard his thumb wrenched. When the rig met the underpass, each truss-peak of the prefab roof snapped, one after another in a shriek of *theek-theek-theek.* Shingles and splinters of two-by-eights and flags of Tyvek shot from under the bridge as if from a cannon. As Rob's brakes engaged, chunks of rigid insulation hung in the air and pirouetted in the back draft and fell to cartwheel along the pavement and float to the ditches in chunks of pink like a child's cake.

As the peak of someone's house settled across the roadbed, Alpo, mesmerized by bits of Styrofoam hanging in the air, found himself at a juncture. A question was posed—not in so many words, but the beam of self-interrogation was clear.

What might we learn from this?

He was cocky at twenty, with the attitude of work hard, play hard. He already knew most of what needed knowing. Or so he thought. He turned off the engine—nothing any real trucker would do—and slid down from the cab to make his way under the bridge and walk a hundred yards up the shoulder where Rob had pulled over. Toeing aside splintered pine, Alpo understood suddenly—and certainly—that in the bigger scheme of things he knew jack shit about anything of consequence.

The message he took from that underpass was simple: going forward it might be best to pay attention to the details and employ caution. Plenty of it.

Wind rattles the dryer vent in the room next to Pete's. Suddenly feeling the trespasser, Alpo stuffs the lock of hair back into the envelope and tucks it among the notes in the anatomy book. Pete may be a grown man, but his son is not the most cautious.

Who might he know who could easily get out to Rauri's besides Erv? Someone official on the Canadian side, maybe border patrol? The only Forest Service pilot he knows well enough is Chank Rivard, and he's grounded with diabetes and poor vision. He hefts his phone a moment before dialing. Erv is a DNR pilot (albeit retired) who has owed him a favor ever since last July when they winched his sauna back from the brink—a filthy weekend jacking up the structure and repairing the stone wall underneath. Temps had been in the nineties, humidity in the eighties. He dials.

"Erv. You got a plane going out this morning." It's not a question.

10

U NDER THE WEIGHT OF THE YOKE PETE HEELS HIS WAY down the north side of the Witch's Tit. Twice he's had to set the canoe down and let it slide ahead tethered like a dog, each thump or scrape going right through him, knowing one crack in the Kevlar and he's screwed. Going up the south slope of the Divide had been a hump, but making his way down on slick rocks and moss patches like banana peels, he wonders if his group health plan covers search-and-rescue. So preoccupied with looking down, he's barely noticed the sky until on a some- what level clearing. Above, clouds are curdled tight and dark, a nasty-looking front of cumulus congestus. He whistles. If he weren't already this far, now would be the time to turn around.

At the put-in he straps on the life vest he usually only employs as a seat cushion. He redistributes the weight of his pack and posi- tions Duke facing backward so they'll have eye contact in case things get hairy. Once settled and floating, he delays, testing the water, sticking close to the cliff where snowmelt drools from moss- lipped fissures. He swings his neck loose and plants his feet wide between the ribs. Zipping his anorak high, his hand automatically makes a sign of the cross on its descent. Grabbing the paddle, he aims for the single legible landmark—the flagpole on Rauri's dis- tant dock. The long stretch of open water between him and the islands is rippled and black.

He paddles against the wind. Once out in rougher water the waves seem to surge from multiple directions, splashing over the sides. Duke stirs as if about to stand and shake, but Pete hollers,

"No! No shake!" The dog sinks back down with an injured look.

During the thirty minutes it takes to reach Rauri's dock, Duke tries again and again to stand and Pete shouts him down until he's hoarse. Only when they've nearly made land does Duke finally lower chin to paws, resigned to the dripping eyebrows and wet snout.

When the canoe scrapes the dock, Pete is soaked from spray, his chest heaving and arms quaking. "No shake," he repeats to Duke in a gentler tone. Once the dog is hoisted to the dock he shakes a furious shower of rainwater from his ruff. Pete laughs. "Good boy." With barely any feeling in his fingers he manages to tie the canoe to a cleat, hands clenched as if still on the paddle.

Even as he stands, Pete senses that Rauri's tiny archipelago is uninhabited.

He follows Duke sniffing along here and there, investigating predictable places—the compost pile, and the fish house, where he roots for some disgusting morsel. If there is a body decomposing somewhere in the vicinity, Duke will find it. Shivering, Pete walks from building to building on paths banked on either side with blocky stone. He puts his own nose to the air, sniffing for anything human—wood smoke, pipe tobacco, cooking odors—but he catches only pine chaff and the foresmell of rain. Above, the stiff breeze sends boughs nodding in one direction then another, like gossips.

Doors to the workshop and icehouse are secured with padlocks. Pete peers through windowpanes to assure nothing is amiss. And nothing seems to be, save Rauri. At the unlocked boathouse he pauses at the soft thudding within. He whistles for Duke. Once inside, the door springs shut behind them and Duke growls at the moving shape producing the thud.

In the crib where Rauri's boat should be bobs a coffin.

"Jesus!" Pete nearly topples backward, hitting the door and sending it open with a horror-film groan. Light yawns in to reveal the floating thing for what it is, a block of lake ice melted down from the shape of the crib, rounded on top just like a real coffin. The seizing in Pete's chest is replaced with a trickling of sweat.

"Sur-fucking-real." He stumbles out, whacking Duke hard with his knee. Both stumble.

"Sorry, bud."

Having nearly pissed himself in the boathouse, Pete stops to take a preemptive leak. Watering the moss and looking around, he'd swear the place is neater than usual. Fewer piles of scrap, more order. His ears prick at every minute sound: the nylon *shoof* of his wet jacket against the branches; needles snapping softly underfoot; birds and creatures making their rounds in the under brush; the riled surf smacking the pebbled shore. Again, Rauri's "silence" is anything but.

Pete lifts tarps and circles piles of brush. Craning to peer into a shed, he feels a cold drip from the wet roof hit the top of his head like a bolt.

"Christ." The sound of his own voice booms. He bends to pat Duke, commanding "Easy," as if it's the dog that's on edge. When they near the main cabin, the lab bounds ahead up the steps and begins frantically sniffing near the door. Pete stops and stands long enough to feel himself sink into the spongy ground. He reaches for the handrail.

There's no death here, only an absence of life. Pete couldn't say how he knows this—maybe for how often he's been around dead or dying creatures. He'd been with his mother when she died. They'd all been—Candy, his father, his Aunt Sharon, and the hospice nurse who carefully combed his mother's hair before adjusting the drip to flood her veins with a final, whopping dose of morphine.

Long after the nice nurse recorded time of death, it still didn't register his mother was gone. There was life, still—in some form. That night, even in his room in the basement, Pete sensed some presence of her. When he opened his eyes he knew she was truly gone, knew that her body had been removed. He'd tiptoed upstairs to find his father at the kitchen table staring into a cup of cold coffee, struggling for words. "She's gone, Pete."

"I know. She's not here, Dad." Pete took the cup from Alpo's hands, emptied it, and poured a refill.

"They weren't supposed to come till afternoon."

"I know."

"I told them to be quiet. They woke you?"

"No."

"So how do you know . . . ?"

"Dunno." There was no explaining. "I just do."

Just as he now senses there is no Rauri. He rubs clear circles on the windows to see the cabin is neat, the bed stripped, and mattress tucked into plastic to protect it from leaks or crapping vermin. No indication of much of anything other than the place being obviously, intentionally, cleaned up and closed down. But for how long? Pete retraces his steps away from the cabin to various outbuildings. There are no footprints besides his own and those of small creatures. At thresholds, needles and leaves have accumulated against doors; bird feeders are empty. No one's been here for weeks, possibly months.

As far as Pete knows, Rauri can only leave his islands for limited stretches without risking his lease with the Feds. Two months?

"Three?" Pete asks Duke.

The surf, not too gentle when he arrived, has frothed into a manic clawing, as if trying to climb out of the lake. When a chill wind yanks the hood from his head, Pete is faced with a black front of rain. Checking his watch, he sees it's not yet ten. He'll have to wait it out—whatever's about to blow through.

He's not sure why he knows where to look, but he easily finds the cabin key in the outhouse, under an antique snus tin above the door frame. Taking a different path back to the cabin he encounters a small mound of earth edged with round stones. The head-stone is a moose antler with neatly carved letters, SCOTTY. The sight tears another opening in Pete's recall of his evening with Rauri and cold shame breaks across the back of his neck.

Rauri had fed him some meaty stew with potatoes and kept pushing bread on him. Pete frowned into his cup when he realized it contained coffee. After eating he was more sober than he cared to be. He gingerly stood to examine the bookshelves. Rauri was watching him, asking what he was reading these days and Pete was struggling to recall what was on his bedside table besides a few empty tumblers and vet journals. Rauri was mindlessly thumbing the fur on the dog's ears.

He'd stepped out of the pool of light he and Rauri had been sharing to go out for a nip—the plastic bottle was empty but he still had his hip flask. The air revived him some. Once back in the cabin he grabbed his bag and brought it to the table near where Rauri sat with Scotty in his lap. "Maybe now's the time, Rauri."

Rauri looked up. "Time for what, Pete?"

"To say good-bye . . ." Pete dug in his bag and nodded at the dog. ". . . to Scotty, my friend." But where were his syringes? He mumbled, "'Cept. I just need to find . . ."

"What?"

"Syringes."

"Pete. Christ. Sit down."

"Why?"

"Sit."

Pete did, coming down hard on the chair. "Sure. You're not ready."

The look Rauri had given him, his hand still on the dog, slowly stroking. "You already gave Scotty the shot." He shook his head. "He's been gone over an hour."

Pete said nothing. They sat in silence until Rauri got up, cradling the small body. "I dug the hole this morning. I won't be long."

He turned at the door. "You're on a slide, boy." He nudged the empty bottle with his toe and it rolled to Pete's feet. "You can do better for yourself than this. Your family deserves better." And then the kicker. "Your mother, God rest her."

Pete's sponsor emphasizes that he must look under every rock, see himself from the perspective of others and own it, no matter how hard.

There's a full cylinder of propane outside the kitchen. He turns on a stove burner to warm his hands and hangs his wet jacket from a rafter above to catch the heat. His pockets yield a bag of trail mix and a Slim Jim.

He rummages cupboards and finds a box of mac and cheese just past its date. As water boils, rain begins tapping the tin roof. At least there is instant coffee. Pete doesn't want to think of the return portage up the side of the Divide—which may not even be possible now, given the rain and mud. One option would be paddling a half-mile straight east and north to the marina at Lac Le Chien, where he can at least get a cell signal and find a place to stash the canoe. From there he could hitch to the border in one of the pulp trucks. Of course, he doesn't have his passport—which means asking Alpo to not only fetch that for him but drive an hour to pick him up at Fort Domain. The last thing Pete wants to do is call for help.

Goddamn Rauri.

Hungrier than he thought, Pete gulps macaroni, not terrible considering it was cooked with powdered milk and no butter. He puts more water on to boil and frowns at the woodstove—building a fire would seem like giving in. Instead, he turns up every burner on the range, sets the dial to bake, and opens the oven door.

The Lefty's Bait calendar is flipped to March, which is at least some hint. He lifts it off the wall and pages through previous months, scanning for any enlightening entries, any other clues to Rauri's whereabouts.

Each month features a vintage speedboat ad—fiberglass Crestliners and Sea Rays, Coronados. All have sunny scenes of perfect Beaver Cleaver families having fun: waterskiing, fishing, cruising. June features a '70s AquaCraft identical to the one they'd had when he was a kid, rotting in the pole barn now. The last trip he'd made in it was to Greenstone Point with his Uncle Peter. *Father* Peter, for whom he'd been named. Uncle Peter had insisted on piloting the boat back. He had a heavy push on the throttle and was no good at steering, so that when they finally pulled up to the Lahti dock, he'd rammed in sideways and Pete lost his balance.

Father Peter laughed, adding insult to injury. It was the last straw. Pete grabbed the bow rope and the single oar and hopped out onto the dock. But instead of twining the rope around a cleat, he held it up for his uncle to see before dropping it in the water, testing a bravado he did not feel. Of all the words he'd rehearsed on the trip back from Greenstone, none came out.

His uncle gave him a crooked half-smile and looked from the sinking rope and drifting bow to Pete. "You won't upset your mother over nothing." His voice was low and menacing, with an accent much thicker than his mother's.

"Over *noothin'*." Pete mimicked, glaring from under the fringe of his bangs. With the water between them Pete could dare to be mouthy. Out of reach of his meaty hands with their hairy knuckles. With the toe of his sneaker he gave the bow a hard shove so it veered to catch a wave, stranding his uncle without an oar. Pete's turn to laugh.

His uncle sputtered, "You little shite."

From nowhere his father was suddenly on the dock. "Pete? Give your uncle that oar. Now!"

Pete held it out as if to drop it in the water.

Alpo grabbed his arm. "What sort of nonsense is this? Apologize to your uncle."

Pete clutched the oar for a moment before letting it clatter to the dock. He wasn't going along. He was thirteen. At ten or eleven he wasn't so strong, but this time he'd fought back. He'd managed to bruise his uncle's shin and leave a bite mark on his upper arm.

He could have called him out right then.

Alpo gave him a blistering look before turning his attention to his brother-in-law. He uncoiled a rope and tossed it. "I was just thinking I'd better motor out to see if you'd run out of gas, Peter."

"We'd a bit of a delay. Hope you didn't hold supper."

Pete had begun sidling away.

"Hold it right there." His father pointed to the boat, then his uncle. "Apologize. Now."

"It's all right, Alpo." Peter's voice evened to the same oily resonance he used in the pulpit. "'Twas noothin'. The lad needed the toilet so we had to land on that island. Lord knows what he ate. That or too much sun is all. Feeling punk, I'd say."

"That's no reason . . ."

"Ach, leave him be."

In the kitchen his mother turned from the stove. "Where have you *been*? Your father was about to send for the Coast Guard."

"It's a lake, Mom. There's no fucking Coast Guard."

The wooden spoon in his mother's hand dripped spaghetti sauce onto the floor. "*What* did you say?"

He thudded down the stairs and slammed the door. Her footfalls clipped to the top of the stairwell just as the back door opened and his father's voice pulled her back. Pete cracked the door to listen.

He'd rarely even said the word *fuck,* certainly not around an adult, but to his mother? Now there was a new mark against him. Soon enough, his uncle banged into his mother's greeting, then the fridge door opened and Pete heard *phipp phipp* as beers were opened. His mother said something in her penitent tone, then he heard his uncle's voice, too low to make out, followed by his mother rising, "Oh, no." Pete could tell she was stifling a laugh. His father laughed too. Uncle Peter's voice, trained to travel, went up Pete's spine.

"Ah, sure now, probably embarrassed. Lord knows he was in those woods long enough. Probably could use some Pepto-Bismol about now. I wouldn't give him too much grief."

His father chuckled, then muttered something.

"Pay it no mind, Alpo, he's no worse than my punks at St. Bart's, certainly brighter."

An hour later his mother rapped on his door from inside the walk-through bathroom. When he didn't answer, she said, "I'm leaving an extra roll of tissue for you."

He could hear her picking up towels, the laundry basket creak-ing. "Goodness, have you taken *two* showers?" She rapped again. "Your uncle is leaving. Will you come up at least to say good-bye?"

"No."

Her sigh was audible through the door. "Sure you won't eat a little something? Toast, maybe rice?"

"No!"

"Right. We'll discuss your language later."

The next morning at breakfast when Candy made a joke about him having the trots, Pete punched the cereal box over, spilling its contents. His sister looked up from the Kix in her lap as though she'd been stabbed.

"Ah. *Dad.* You saw that, right?"

"It was an accident." Pete pivoted. His father took one step and his foot came down to crunch cereal. He turned to Pete. "Enough. You're cleaning out that boathouse today. You hear me?"

And that was that.

Pete rips the June page with the AquaCraft from the calendar. True to advertising it's a world removed from reality, depicting the perfect family: blonde mom and sister are seated in the back, naturally, while handsome dad stands tall at the helm with one hand on the wheel and the other about to alight on his all-American son, as if about to ruffle the kid's hair or pat him on the back. Father Peter took full advantage of his uncle status to tease Pete in a variety of similar moves: the macho shoulder grab, the fake gut punch, the particularly infuriating hair muss. Pete would squirm out from under as if greased, only to catch the disapproving eye of whatever parent was nearest. *Humor your uncle; don't be such a killjoy.*

Pete wonders at the depth of his hatred for the man, still.

He holds a corner of the page to the lit stove burner. Flames lick the glossy water and engulf the boat. The scene begins to buckle. Faces blister and the sky begins to yellow and curl upward. He can recall the drone of its motor—a sound he came to hate, its thirty-year-old echo rings in his ear. But when the droning grows louder Pete understands it's no memory but an actual motor, and a loud one.

Floatplane?

Through the window he can see the red-and-white Beaver approaching the channel, wings wobbling and body brilliant against the dark clouds. He opens the woodstove door as the flames threaten his fingertips and flings the page in. A trail of sooty flakes falls like black snow as he slams the door.

By the time Pete turns off the burners, grabs his things, and navigates the path, Erv Maki has taxied in and is standing on one of the Beaver's floats, holding a pole against the dock to keep the plane from bashing into it.

Erv shouts over the sound of the idling engine, "Pete! Empty that canoe. We'll lash it to the float. And throw me your pack!"

"I should lock the place up."

"No time! We got about three minutes before this wind changes."

They work at double speed, flipping the canoe, securing it to the float. Once Erv climbs aboard he shouts, "Get that dog in here!"

Wrangling Duke in, Pete nearly drops him, then gives an upward shove, twisting to keep his balance, wrenching his shoulder with the effort. Erv pulls the flailing dog into the cockpit by his collar and Pete catches a rear claw to his temple when Duke scrabbles for leverage.

While Erv crams Duke back into the cargo hold, Pete uses his canoe paddle to keep the plane from being driven back against the dock. He has one foot on the float and another on the boards, with the distance widening. When the paddle cracks, he lets it fall into the water and heaves himself around, groping for the wing support with the arm he's just wrenched. Grunting, he hoists himself up into the passenger seat.

Wrestling the door shut a bolt of white pain sears his shoulder. By the time he has his seatbelt on and looks up, the plane is roaring, pushing forward to the channel. They are gaining speed. Erv tosses him a headset, and Pete manages to position it with his left hand in time to hear Erv say, "This is gonna be rough. Plenty of chop."

Rain spatters the windscreen and pinwheels from the props. Erv checks instruments while Pete adjusts his headset. They aim into the wind.

The engine roars and the floats stutter through the waves, the nose of the plane canting up then down in sickening swells. Pete does not take a breath. He can hear Duke's whine vibrate as the shaking metal of the cabin floor rises through him.

"Christ," Erv mutters. "Here we go." His gaze triangulates continuously from the instruments to the waves to the far shore, assessing the distance and height of the treetops, counting seconds between waves under his breath like prayer, timing his lean on the throttle. With the next swell, the nose of the little plane points upward.

Pete knows jack shit about planes and flying, but instinct tells him to tighten his harness buckles. By the look of Erv, his blood pressure is about par with the instrument needles galloping along the dash. He presses the throttle as if it is an extension of his arm.

They tilt again at another gut-churning angle, laboring to get speed. Duke is sliding around, taking a bashing from the metal lockers. Suddenly they are up, a foot above the whitecaps, the floats bounce once, twice, then are cleared, airborne. No sooner does Pete take a breath than he sees the far shore coming at them like a plow. Along with Erv, he leans back as if hoping to affect the plane's angle. Their rise seems glacial compared to the approach of the trees.

For the second time in one day, the axis of Pete's world slows to stillness. They are speeding straight for the canopy of evergreens, many of the treetops already broken from lightning strikes and winds, a jagged green butte of veterans. When the plane hits, as it certainly will, they'll be finished. The Beaver will break many branches, crack, and splinter; cones will spew like buckshot. The trees will prevail. Pete can envision the plane rusting to pieces on the forest floor below, the heap of his own broken corpse. What of him that doesn't get eaten will break down into mulch to nourish the very trees about to kill them.

Makes sense, in a weird way.

He's almost amused. Life. It ends. It's all just biology anyway. Simple biology. Couldn't *be* simpler, really.

They have arrived at their destination. Pete clutches the seat as the plane sets to crash through the canopy, juddering side to side. Metallic screams tearing at the floats are felt as much as heard. But then the nose raises and the rasping lessens. They ascend by inches, then feet, then yards.

The laugh of a lunatic cackles through his headset, Erv booming, "Jaysuz Keeee-*rist*."

They are up, risen above the canopy, flying. Pete is abruptly pulled back into himself like a genie being sucked back into his bottle. The scene is surreal as bits of pinecones and pitchy needles skitter up the windscreen. He is speechless. Erv is anything but.

"Holy shit, boy. That's one for the grandkids. Wooo-eeeh. Got that canoe insured?"

"Huh?" He lets out the long breath he's been holding and shifts his sore arm, giddy with the affirmation of pain.

"That canoe. Is it insured?"

"Question is, are my underpants insured."

Erv bellows, then his laugh trails off. "What the hell were you thinking, college boy?"

"I was thinking I'd go check on Rauri."

"You could've just asked around. I already buzzed the place yesterday." He shakes his head and looks at Pete as if over the tops of imaginary glasses. "When there was flying weather."

Saving Pete the effort of a response, Duke vomits across the floor of the cargo hold.

"Shit. Sorry." Knots already tied in Pete's own stomach tighten at the smell. He wills himself not to follow suit. As they bank toward Hatchet Inlet under low clouds, Erv cracks a vent against the stink.

"You're bleeding there, son." Erv points to Pete's forehead, then thumbs toward the hold. "Your puking pal back there got his licks in, I'd say."

Pete had assumed sweat was pooling in his ear, but his fingers come away syrupy red. He tentatively touches the wound—a decent gash across his temple, a crescent of skin he presses back into place. He accepts a handful of grubby napkins Erv has pulled from somewhere.

His morning paddle seems a lifetime ago. As he applies pressure to the cut, Pete says, "I saw you fly over earlier. Heading north?"

"Thought I should check the marina up at Fort Domain and see if Rauri's runabout was there."

"Was it?"

"Might a been, but it was too windy to get low enough to tell."

Pete's so wired he's forgotten to ask how Erv knew to come for him. Just as he's about to, Erv cuts him off. "I'd say Alpo owes me one."

"Well, thanks."

"Don't thank me yet. We're not outta the woods." He shoots Pete a look. "Landing ain't gonna be any picnic either."

But it's not half as harrowing as takeoff, and less than an hour later Pete is standing in his exam room, attempting to adhere a butterfly closure to his wound with one hand. Once that is sloppily accomplished, he eases out of his sleeve, the cuff crusted with dog vomit and blood. He manages to wind himself into a clean shirt. Woozy from the effort, he considers 100 mg of carprofen.

Just until tomorrow.

It's already been a hell of a day and it's barely half over. He opens the packet with his teeth and runs water into a cup. The capsule is halfway to his mouth when he catches himself. He mutters, "Some wolf." As if summoned, Duke gets stiffly to his feet to lean against Pete's leg.

It does not get easier. It may never.

Pete considers his bruised old dog. Wincing, he kneels, gently forces open Duke's jaw, and presses the carprofen caplet far back into his gullet, whispering. "Attaboy."

11

S ISSY NOTICES HOW CAREFULLY PETE BUCKLES HIMSELF into the passenger side, as if his right arm is made of glass. He needs a lift to Naledi to pick up his Suburban because he's promised to be the designated driver for the stag party but hadn't wanted to bother Alpo for a ride—so he says. Sissy suspects he may be avoiding his father.

She takes in the raw knuckles, the crookedly applied bandage. Pete looks like he's just lost a bar fight.

He's oddly talkative. She listens and nods as he reconstructs his adventure from the beginning—early morning and his trepidation over the weather: the decent, actually fruitful conversation with Beth. The hawk's visitation like an intermission between his roughest portages. He seems a bit wired to Sissy, laughing as he tells how the chunk of ice he mistook for a coffin in the boathouse made him yelp like a little girl. How relieved he was to not find Rauri. And finally, the incredible takeoff in the Beaver and his awe at Erv's steely nerves.

"Dude's gotta be sixty-five."

"Seventy. I made the cake for his party at the Elks. Alpo must have been in a state to call the DNR."

"Well, I *was* paddling his canoe."

"Pete."

He winds down and goes still, watching out the window for several miles.

Sissy slows at the curve by the railroad bridge and asks, "Mind if we stop?"

"'Course not." He smiles but is pale as dough. "Mind if I stay in the car?"

Sissy leaves the engine running so Pete has heat. Reaching for something in her purse, she promises, "I'll be quick."

Pete yawns. "Take your time."

Released from the back seat, Jeff bounds ahead, pinballing along to smell what there is to smell. Sissy notices the trail of reedy yellow grass has been pounded flat by a wintering herd. The path is marbled with fresh scat and rain and has settled into hoofprints like so many servings of cold tea. The hill, carpeted with shed cedar, is bright and the air is clean-scrubbed. Sissy crosses under the power lines through thickets of lowbush blueberries, trying not to trod on them—this spot was known as a particularly good patch before the accident, but it's not a place she'll come picking anymore—berries from here would only fill a pie too sad to enjoy.

At the trestle, last autumn's offerings lie scattered and fallen from the natural altar of the concrete base. Two candles from the Mexican market are broken; the college graduation portrait of Kelly is facedown on the ground. Sissy wipes the glass with her sleeve. Moisture has seeped into the frame to distort Kelly's face. After propping it back into place, she wraps her scarf tight against the chill and tidies things—the sodden Beanie Babies, a tipped jar of Lake Superior stones, the ceramic German shepherd linked to three puppies with a thin tarnished chain, a smiley face squeeze ball—everyday things people have assigned meaning to. She dumps the muck of long-dead flowers and a disc of ice from the mug with Kelly's sorority emblem. Once everything is back in place, she eases the paper rose from her pocket, beginning to flake like a real dried flower would.

After positioning the rose, she sits on the bench someone has made with two treated boards and concrete blocks—her brother Dan, she suspects. She's eye level with Kelly's face now and sees she's not only distorted but is fading behind the glass.

"I'm worried about your mom, Kel. Your dad is coming around, but they're still missing you. We all . . . we're *all* missing you. I'm sad you won't be here Saturday to see your spinster aunt finally get hitched."

It's never felt silly to talk to Kelly, exactly. But it's beginning to feel less normal.

"Thing is," Sissy wipes her nose, "I think I'm done coming out here. I'll go to the cemetery . . . on your birthday." She's not been to the grave, not since the funeral, not yet ready to face the name and the dates so chiseled and final. But by August and Kelly's twenty-fourth, she'll put on a dress, lay real fresh flowers, and act like a proper aunt.

"You'll be glad to know, after the wedding I'm quitting the diner. You always said I should. I'm not going to make brittle, either. I'm taking the advice I used to dish out to you—I'm deciding what I *don't* want to do before figuring out the rest. And something my mom—your gran—always told us: that if you *really* want to do something, just say it aloud to someone who will hold you to it. People break promises to themselves all the time, but it's harder to back down on a thing when you've let a person you love in on it." She doesn't say the rest out loud—that she knows everything *will* be all right.

Repositioning the paper rose—already rolling to the edge—she lays a hand on the cold concrete and says, "Alpo doesn't believe in anything like an afterlife. He says if the dead are anything, they are understanding and kind, and don't want those of us left behind to suffer." Sissy cocks her head. "That seems good enough."

Jeff nudges his snout under Sissy's wrist and looks up with a faint sniff, as if to say, *It's time.*

Pete straightens with a jerk when she opens the door.

"Oh jeez. Were you asleep?"

"Maybe a little." He blinks. "You say hi to Kelly for me?"

"I said hi from everyone."

Pete notices she's steady and dry-eyed. "You okay?"

"I am, actually." She puts the car in reverse and backs onto the road, glancing at him.

"You?"

"Great. Never better." Pete laughs. "I just realized."

"What?"

"You're going to be my stepmother."

"Oh, cripes, I guess I am." They both crack up.

Fact is, she's always felt a bit maternal toward him. In her senior year, she was on the Wolverines hockey cheerleading squad, and Pete was a freshman coming up through the lines as a promising center known for his ferocious slapshot and short fuse. He was often in the penalty box, ready to spring. He never started a throw-down himself but was always the second kid to shuck his gloves. She laughs. "Oh Lord, I just thought of Mally the Mallard."

"God, imagine having to skate in that costume."

"Remember how mad that one ref got if Mally dropped a feather on the ice?"

"Odegard." Pete laughs. "Mally lost his shit on that guy one day—you'd have graduated by then. Full-on moult, feathers and blood everywhere. The Zamboni just went right over it all."

"No. Really?"

"I shit you not, we skated pink ice for a week." Pete laughs. "The fuzz was hell on our blades."

"Can't say I miss those days."

"Weren't you always being flipped in the air or flung somewhere or topping some pyramid?"

"'Cuz I was smallest. Jeez, the things they let us do in those days."

Even back then, Pete struck her as the sort of kid who couldn't get out of Hatchet Inlet fast enough. He'd been recruited for the U hockey team but turned it down after being offered a full academic scholarship. She wonders if he regrets being back here now.

For many, the accident had been a wake-up call—she believes it was for Pete, too—he just didn't wake up immediately. First, he had to fall back into the hole he'd dug for himself and climb out a second time. Maybe he's still climbing. But he's a more solid presence these days, even reliable. More like his dad than himself. Even runs the AA meetings now and has become a sponsor.

A smoky room at Sokol Hall full of old farts telling drinking stories is not a place Sissy can picture her sister-in-law Janine, but still, Pete might be able to help. Nobody in the family, least of all Janine, needs the drama of some intervention when a better solution could be found right at her feet, needing to be let out to pee, begging to be walked and fed and loved. *Needing,* period.

Sometimes you don't know what's going to kick-start a stalled heart until it pees in your lap, which is nearly word for word what Alpo said after he'd proposed to her.

"Pete."

"Yeah?"

"Kelly's mom."

"Janine."

"You'll help me help her?"

"Absolutely." Pete considers her before adding, "Whatever she needs."

"Janine needs a dog. A rescue, maybe. For now, let's just start with a dog."

They are five miles from Naledi. Sissy wonders if Pete's aware that Meg is with Jon Redleaf now—he has moved into the lodge, according to Cathy. Just when she's thinking she'd rather not be the person to break it to him, they see the buck, half in the road, half in the ditch. Points of its rack are broken and a faint steam rising from its fur. "Oh," Sissy says, pulling over. "Do you suppose . . . ?"

Pete's voice sounds thin. "It's dead, Sissy."

But she has already pulled over and is out of the car, around the front bumper, and kneeling before he can even open his door.

The bottomless eyes are still clear, its impossibly long lashes blue-black. Pete grunts when lowing to one knee next to her and points at the jagged wound on the neck.

"It would have been quick, snapped vertebrae."

"Gosh, people don't even stop, do they?"

Pete shakes his head. Sounding less than enthusiastic he offers, "I can probably drag him off the road with some help."

"Hang on."

"What?"

"Gimme a minute, Pete."

One minute becomes three, her hand on the animal's neck, still warm. Finally looking up, she says, "It's bad enough they're killed, but then to just go to waste like this?"

"I hear you."

"You know Jon Redleaf and his nephew Bear have built a smokehouse out at the reservation."

Pete says, "Yeah?"

"Did you know you can process about every bit of a deer?"

"You mean besides the venison? Yeah. I guess I knew that."

Sissy gets up. "S'pose anyone at the Highway Department has any figures on how many deer get road-killed around here?"

"I suppose they might have a guess. I drive a lot so I see maybe a dozen a week, more during fall. What are you thinking?"

She looks down at the carcass. "Just thinking."

Back on the road, Sissy catches him wincing a third time. "Maybe you should take it easy tonight, Pete. The guys can always call an Uber."

Pete scoffs. "In Hatchet Inlet?"

"Yes, Pete, right here in Batshit Inlet. You've been away a long time. We've got flush toilets now, too."

"Ha."

She applies the brakes, hard. Pete's right arm shoots out to the dashboard to protect himself—his left remains cradled tight to his chest.

"Jesus! What was that for?"

"I knew it." Sissy grinds into reverse and swales into a wide spot, then faces him. "You're not driving anything. I'm taking you to the ER. What did you do to yourself out there?"

Pete deflates into his seat. "Not sure, probably tore my rotator cuff."

"Right." Sissy eases back onto the road to turn in the opposite direction.

At the hospital lot, she starts to walk Pete into the ER when he stops and grins.

"Hey, uh, *Stepmom*. That's nice, but I got this."

"Oh. You'll need a ride home, though?"

"Sissy, don't you have about a hundred things to do?"

"Actually." Sissy shrugs. "Not much. Between me and Laurie, everything's done, believe it or not."

"Well, thanks anyway, but by the time I'm outta here it's only a block to Pasta Portage."

"*That's* where the stag is?"

"That's where the fun starts." He winks. "Who knows, we could end up at the White Tail."

"You will not."

"Ha." With his good arm he gives her a quick a hug. "I'll see you at the church."

To her surprise he plants a kiss on her forehead. "So," she looks up, "you're okay with this?"

"This?"

"Your dad and me getting married?"

"Okay with it?" Pete laughs, letting her go. "You're a kook, you know that, Sissy?"

"You're in a good mood," she says, "considering what a sight you are."

He shrugs the one shoulder. "Well, I am in one piece. So there's that."

"Right. Pete. You must be wrecked . . ."

"The opposite, actually." Pete, suddenly light on his feet, does a slow twirl, face up and one arm out like Julie Andrews on the mountain, barely a grimace of pain. "I'm great. The hills are alive."

"Oh, boy. Please don't sing." She backs away. "I'll see you at the church."

They are heading their separate ways, Pete to the ER and Sissy to Memory Care, when an ambulance whips past both of them slow and turn. Its lights are turning but there's no siren. They watch, expecting it to turn in the next driveway, into Senior Cedars as it so regularly does. When the vehicle gains speed instead, they exchange a look. *Rauri?*

The worrying is beginning to wear. Sissy turns into the diagonal park, the long way around to her mother's wing, not exactly delaying, more like not rushing. Rain has soaked the sleeping grasses, lime green peeking from beneath pantyhose-colored schmutz webbing across the lawn. Sissy puts the ambulance out of her mind, noticing the signs of spring. Buds plump on the flowering crabs, tulips and iris spear from the beds along the walkway. Under the no-nonsense aroma of cedar, the captive smells of winter have broken out: mud, lake water, bark, wet gravel—things you don't realize smell until they start up again.

At the base of the broad stairs Sissy's shoes turn to cement. She dreads the odors within: plastic chair pads, an iron-tinged vitamin smell, wool, old breath. Cooking smells stabbing up from the kitchen like crimes in progress. The facility is surrounded by the trees it's named for; most are older than the residents within— grandpa trees with arthritic-looking roots and trunks, twisted as if growing had been painful. It occurs to her that just because she's passing by Senior Cedars doesn't mean she has to go in. She turns and squelches across the lawn without looking back. It won't matter a whit to Louise whether she's there or not. So she won't. And Sissy isn't going to torture herself over it.

12

AT THE FIRST RING ALPO BOLTS FOR THE KITCHEN.
He flings newspaper and bubble wrap from counters, but
by the time he's found the phone Erv's call has gone to
message so he has to wait before he can replay it.

Just landed. Pete's hunky-dory.

Alpo chokes back a sort of laugh.

He tackles more packing, cheerfully spending his afternoon
mindlessly putting boxes together, winnowing, making piles.
Only when he's gone through an entire roll of tape does he allow
the thought, and the scissors drift to his sides: *What if he hadn't
been hunky-dory?* How ironic would that be—forty years of ups and
downs (and way downs) finally leveling into something decent,
only to have Pete drown, fall off some ledge, or disappear like
goddamn Rauri?

As Rose would have it, time spent on what-ifs is time wasted.
He shakes himself to, realizing he's been staring at the carpet. He
shouldn't have skipped lunch. He stands in front of the fridge and
wraps a slice of deli turkey and some swiss around a pickle, eating it with the door still open. Same for the half-container of cot-
tage cheese and the dregs of orange juice. One way to cut down
on dirty dishes, at least.

Dishes. The cupboard doors open onto a marriage-worth of
platters, glassware, souvenir mugs, pottery bought at craft fairs
too heavy to eat or drink from. What is left of the Scandinavian
stoneware set—*Arabia,* top of the line at Dayton's Bridal registry
circa 1969. Rose would sometimes open the cupboards just to bask

in the satisfaction. The dozen dinner plates are down seven. Only a few cups remain, six cereal bowls. All twelve of the useless coffee saucers have survived. Alpo packs fast, bypassing memories by quickly wrapping them in newspaper.

He pulls small appliances from low cupboards—some gadget that seals food into plastic wrap, and a malt maker, Father's Day gift probably used twice. He places them in a box with baking dishes and CorningWare. In an awkward low cupboard he finds dozens of containers marked with initials of neighbors and friends on curled masking tape. So many meals were delivered to the house toward the end, and afterward. Somehow, he'd never returned the casseroles, pans, and Tupperware containers. He stacks them in grocery bags to take to the truck. Twenty years may be a bit late to return many of them, but the gesture would matter to Rose.

Several are marked L.P. for Louise Pavola. Sissy's mother and Rose had been close friends during the dozen years they both taught at the school. As well, Rose was Sissy's high school English teacher, which is how Sissy came to be the family's summer helper. Alpo barely remembers her as a girl. If he had any impression back then, it might have been that Sissy was bright but perpetually chatty. More than once Rose had observed it was a shame that Sissy wasn't Pete's age—a few years younger and they'd have made a good match. Now that Alpo knows Sissy, he understands Rose was thinking of her as a sort of antidote to Pete, as if the mixture of sunny and stormy would equate calm.

And here he is about to marry Sissy himself. What Rose might make of that isn't something he's pondered much but likes to imagine she'd approve. He's weighed the pros and cons of marrying a woman twenty years his junior, has tried to picture himself down the road at eighty when Sissy is only sixty. What burdens might he pose for her? On the other hand, now is now, and the next years could be the best each of them ever get. Sissy tries joking about the age difference, saying, "You'll outlive *me*, you old fart."

Doubtful.

She's still upset by the results of her genetic testing. For a few hundred dollars in a Groupon deal she'd swapped a vial of spit and some hair for a readout of what diseases and weaknesses she might look forward to. Their last visit to the memory center Sissy had warned, "Watch, now. Ninety minutes with my mother could be a movie of your future."

Louise has been in care for years now. She greets every person with surprise even if having just stepped out the door for the toilet and returned—in her crossed wiring it might as well have been years, each visit a scene from *Groundhog Day*.

A shame such tests weren't around before Rose was diagnosed. If they'd known about the seed of her cancer, they might have traveled more, worked less. Alpo could have built that pergola she hinted at every year around Mother's Day. He tells this to Sissy, the only person he has ever spoken to about the remorse he's only now shedding.

"Don't misunderstand," he told Sissy. "I wouldn't change a thing." One of the sort of white lies that paves the path of any romantic relationship, though Alpo thinks such well-intentioned slights deserve a less accusatory descriptor than *lie*. He would change one thing.

The beauty of Sissy is—what you see is what you get. There is no testing the waters, no agreeing to terms of service before engaging. She falls into that rare category of a woman who is as she seems. Which is not to say she is simple, far from it. But easy, surely. Easier than Rose.

Louise had still been sharp and articulate when she spoke at Rose's funeral, remembering her friend as "a complicated piece of work," which got nods and knowing chuckles. Louise went on to bemoan the fact that her friend had not lived long enough to realize her dream of becoming a writer. For a moment Alpo was released from his grief into a state of puzzlement. He dared not look at either of his children. Had they known? That their mother wanted to be a writer? What else did he not know? He stared at the framed portrait propped next to the urn. What else of her beside that secret desire was about to get scattered like ash?

A shower, he thinks, running a hand through his sweaty scalp. *A shower, and I'll be raring to go.*

Leaving the house, Alpo drives slowly through the canopy of trees, window down and arm out, his fingers able to reach the new growth—that's how shaggy the Hobby has gotten. The coniferous needles are still in the soft stages of new bud, some not completely free of their papery casings and sticky to the touch.

He arrives early at Pasta Portage. Rather than sit conspicuously alone at the big booth with the RESERVED sign, he chooses a stool at the end of the bar near the door. Shelly is about to lay a dish of cashews in front of his neighbors, but when she sees Alpo she pivots and plunks it in front of him, switching out the bowl of peanuts. Two fishermen lean to see who their usurper is.

"Aw, Shel, we hardly knew ya." Their Down Under accents seem not to be impressing Shelly.

"What's your poison, Alp?"

"How about a ginger ale?"

"Living large?"

"You bet."

He assesses the lineup at the bar, acknowledging those he knows with a nod, like Mary and Tim from the hardware store. He gives a thumbs-up to the Northern Power crew who are laying high-speed cable up the Pioneer Trail, still in their neon work vests. As Alpo might guess by the number of empty shot glasses, they've already carved good-sized dents in their paychecks. It would have been a particularly tough day out there.

There's a clutch of tourists milling with drinks while waiting for tables, wearing the telltale garb of Filson and quick-dry khaki with multiple zip-off options. Next to Alpo the cashewless fishermen look windblown and done in, both wolfing the spaghetti special. Five stools down sits Gimp Wuuri. Alpo takes the Grisham paperback from his pocket in case he needs a shield. Sheer escapism, no different from Sissy's novels with covers featuring shopping bags and champagne glasses or cartoon high heels.

Gimp looks about a beer away from either belligerence or tears—never easy to predict. Fortunately, the crowd looks tame enough, no one likely to tangle with a hunchback the size of a granny. Alpo knew Gimp long before he'd curled and stiffened, back when they were the same height, when Gimp was still Gerry and his arrival guaranteed trouble. Poor bastard is less ignitable these days.

He's avoided Gimp since February. He'd been about to attack a porketta platter at Czarniekie's. Granted he'd been a sitting duck in his booth by the window, pinking and unpinking under the neon sign. And there was Gimp, swaying along the length of the bar mooching drinks.

"Check this out, Alpo." He was lugging along his latest X-ray, not the first time for that ploy.

"Nope," he told Gimp, "don't want to see it."

But before he knew it, there was the X-ray in the personal space between Alpo and the dinner he badly wanted. He decided on the spot that this would be his last transaction with Gimp—he'd indulged him, *enabled* him, along with a dozen others—for decades. He took out his wallet and slapped down every bill he had, about ninety dollars.

A conflicted look passed over Gimp. "I'm not a charity case."

Alpo looked at him. "No?"

Gimp folded the bills into his palm. "So, what'll you have? Since it looks like I'm buying."

"Please, just go."

But even after Gimp had gone, he couldn't unsee Gimp's X-ray, the vertebrae twisted in the impossible shape of a question mark.

Alpo cannot assume all drunks are equal or know the first thing about their addiction or their sources of pain. His father had been a drunk; his son was a drunk. True enough, there is some fault line the Lahti men have a propensity to cross. He'd had two uncles who, when alive, were only spoken of in past tense, both *died in Superior,* as if that said it all. There but for the grace of God, etc.

Shelly sets his drink down with a flourish, a twist of orange and a paper umbrella, topped with three filberts like deer scat.

"Shel. You've outdone yourself."

"Only the best for the groom-to-be." She winks. The two fishermen turn and Alpo sees they are about Pete's age. Friendly looking.

One raises his beer. "Cheers."

The other follows suit. "Groom, hey? First go?"

Alpo twirls his little umbrella, avoiding a full look. "Nah. First one . . . didn't last." Which is one way to put it. He'd hated the label *widower* and only considered himself one for as long as the real pain lasted, back when waking in an empty bed and taking the first breath of the day felt herculean. They say time heals all wounds, which is bullshit. Staying busy helps.

The fisherman nearest him winks. "Well, good on ya."

If not for the accents these two could be locals—sturdy and road-grubby, both with several days' stubble. Their serious fishing vests have seen time. The red, ore-rich clay on their boots suggests they've portaged north of the Divide. Destination fishers that travel half the globe—Alpo has to wonder if they did their homework. Fishing in northern Minnesota in May is a crapshoot, can feel more like survival than vacation.

Before they can comment further he asks, "What lake you boys on today?"

"Upper Shield."

"Rough?"

The closer one shrugs. "Rough enough. I wouldn't go it alone."

"Australian?" he asks.

"So close." One spreads his hands wide. "Kiwi."

"Ah, pardon."

"No worries. You Canadians must get the same treatment all the time."

"But I'm not—"

"My brother is having you on, mate. Sorry."

He sees the resemblance now. "Any luck?"

"Not a bloody nibble."

"Fish don't go out in this weather," Alpo says.

"Right." The taller one shakes his head. "Weather wasn't having us either. The portage out was a real cunt."

Alpo looks to Shelly refilling their pints, but she doesn't blink. He offers his hand. "I'm Alpo."

The nearest reaches. "Pleasure. I'm Conner."

The other wipes his palm on his pants. "Adam."

"You have any trouble out there?"

"Besides losing a pack and having to paddle our hams off just to make it out of there?"

"Entire day bollixed, and we've only three more to go."

Alpo slides the cashews nearer. "Sorry you got skunked."

"We were lucky to get out." Conner turns and opens his vest so Alpo can read his *I Survived the Divide* T-shirt. "I've earned this—we just found out some bloke had to get airlifted out."

"Yeah?"

"Poor bastard broke his neck. Might never walk again." Adam shakes his head.

"Is that so?" Alpo raises a brow toward Gimp. "What else did you hear?"

"His canoe got torn up." Adam shrugs.

"And did you hear where that happened?"

"An island where some hermit is supposed to be murdered and buried."

"This guy was out there trying to dig him up, right? But only found a bunch of buried dogs."

"That's terrible." Alpo tosses a cashew and catches it in his teeth.

A group of young women in heels trip in, dresses barely longer than their parkas. One is crowned with a cheap tiara.

Conner singsongs, "Hen par-tay." He looks from the girl in the tiara to Alpo. "Oh, hey mate, not *yours* . . . ?"

"Ah no. My intended . . . can vote—and drive."

The brothers crack up. As the girls pass, Conner's stool swivels like a compass needle. His brother snaps his fingers to bring him around, then plays the bar like a piano, yawning into a nasal Dylan impression:

Well, if you're traveling in the north country fair,
Where the winds hit heavy on the borderline.

Conner picks up an air guitar, twanging with a harmony:

Please say hello to one who lives there.
She once was a true love of miiine.

"That brunette." Conner turns to see where the girls have settled. "Is particularly fit."

Adam sighs. "Forgive my brother. He's an ass."

Alpo smiles. Most tourists are dull. "Where you fishing tomorrow?"

"After today? Streams. Know any where we might snag a trout?"

"Staying nearby?"

"Just there by the church, The Rectory." Adam wipes his mouth and points out the window to the B&B between the church and cemetery. "I wouldn't have expected a pair of nancies running a holiday lodge this far north. Class act, but those lads know jack about fishing."

Pete walks in, carrying himself stiffly, one sleeve empty, jacket unzipped to reveal his arm in a sling. A square bandage is plastered above one eye.

"Speak of the devil," says Alpo. "Here he comes now, the fella got lifted out this morning."

"That's him?"

Adam laughs. "Neck doesn't look too broken."

"Well, the night's still young." Alpo winks and slides off the stool. "Good to meet you boys."

"Same. By the way . . ." Adam points to the specials board. "Does *meatball* mean something different in Minnesota? We ordered the spaghetti, but got spaghetti and something-else-balls. Don't get me wrong, they were tasty, but when you're expecting one thing and you get another, you know?"

"Ah." Alpo claps each brother on the back. "Fish balls. Must be Friday."

Pete recites a droll list: "Rotator cuff torn; occipital ridge whacked; melon sliced. This," he points to his temple, "is courtesy of Duke."

Alpo wasn't going to ask but does anyway. "They give you any painkillers?"

"Nope." Pete shook his head. "But they offered."

"Hurt much?"

"Like a mother. But I'm alive to feel it, so there's that." Pete folds himself into the booth in sections. He orders a soda, and after it arrives he silently hands over a small gift bag.

"Oh, nuts," Alpo sighs. "Don't tell me there's gonna be presents?"

"Nah, just this. Open it before the guys show."

It's a tiny birchbark canoe, with a glossy page rolled like a cigarette inside. Alpo fishes it out and smooths it flat on the table. It's half a catalog page for a twenty-foot Kevlar Wenonah, the *Minnesota Three*. The price is torn away but Alpo knows this is not a cheap item.

"So it's true? My canoe got wrecked?" He immediately regrets his tone.

"What?" Pete pulls a face. "No. Just a few scrapes. Dad, I ordered this a month ago. I thought, since yours barely holds one guy and a pack, it won't be enough now with Sissy. Hell, Jeff weighs as much as you."

"That's a spendy wedding present." Again, the tone. He smiles too late.

"Yeah." Pete is as cautious as his father. "I wanted to get something nice you could both use together."

LAURENTIAN DIVIDE ~ *165*

For a moment they sit.

"It's beautiful, Pete. Sissy's gonna be thrilled. You'll keep that Old Town then. It's the right size for you."

"Now, hang on, that's not why—"

"I know. You keep it. My solo days are over." Alpo's gaze drifts to the bar. "Goddamn, you gave me a scare today, Pete."

"Yeah? Scared myself, actually. Hadn't exactly thought it through. Sorry."

Sorry is a recent addition to his son's vocabulary. Each time Alpo hears it, his wariness depletes some. "You're doing great, son. You really are."

"Okay. All good?" Their eyes meet.

"Yup. All good."

The guys begin to trickle in: Juri and Alpo's brother-in-law to be, Joe. Veshko and Granger arrive together. Pitchers of beer appear on the table. Alpo asks for water for everyone. Erv arrives and gives Pete the once-over before nodding approval.

When Perry shows, Alpo makes a point of a formal introduction, though they all know who he is.

"City mouse," Juri fake-coughs.

"Juri," Joe says. "You cannot whisper for shit."

Perry is unfazed.

Alpo crosses his arms. "City mouse with a state Golden Gloves title."

"Bantam weight. Obviously." Perry is a full foot shorter than Juri. "Way back."

Juri makes room in the booth and grabs a beer glass for Perry. "Yeah? I boxed. Navy, '71." He nods to the space next to him. "Sit down."

"I am sitting." Perry gets a big laugh before sliding in.

When Sissy's brother Dan comes in, Alpo, who is not a hugger, makes an exception, steers Dan to a chair in the middle of the fray, and gets him a beer, saying aloud what everyone is thinking, "Really good to see you out, Dan."

"Yeah? We'll see. Sorry-ass crew of miscreants you got here."

"Dan," Erv takes on a serious tone. "Are you here to see to it Alpo keeps your sister in the manner to which she's accustomed?"

"Hell, he's gotta do a lot better than *that.*" Dan stops laughing when he sees Pete in the corner. "Christ, Alpo, what's happened to your boy there?"

The story gets told.

A bottle of aquavit appears with a tray of shot glasses. A good-enough start, Alpo thinks, as lettuce wedge salads are plunked down with a trough of lasagna and baskets of fried mozzarella sticks.

Toasts erupt, though not everyone has alcohol to tip: Jon Redleaf sits apart on a barstool, nursing a Coke; Granger sips iced tea as if it's old Scotch; and Pete hugs a glass of crushed ice against his shoulder. They lift their glasses, Pete using his left hand.

Veshko politely convinces Pete to take off his jacket, asks him to clench his fist, then holds up fingers for Pete to squeeze as hard as he can. Pete flinches when Veshko first lays his hands on him but relaxes once the probing commences. They all watch.

"I do sports massage. For injury." He tells them, "Was masseur for Bosnian national swim team." He looks around as if expecting someone might challenge him. His thumbs test Pete's upper back and neck while the rest chew, shoveling lasagna.

Pete moans but not in a bad way.

"See?" Veshko says. "You come and see me, no?"

"Hey, thanks, man." Pete's eyes glaze. "But I got a referral for a surgeon in Duluth."

Veshko shakes his head sadly. "Americans. Always wanting the . . . quick fix? You come see me. For free, three times—*then* go get cut like a roast."

Chim, Ray, and Bibb Esko come in, still wearing their bowling shirts. They number too many for the table now, so another is dragged over and stray chairs are commandeered. Erv's second telling of the story of his search-and-rescue mission to save Pete is more colorful than the first.

Bibb tells a series of lewd and forgettable Ole & Lena jokes. Alpo is given a sample packet of Viagra with an expiration date of

2009. Gimp, having smelled free rounds, hovers near whichever side of the booth has either a fresh pitcher or stray shot. When pours of aquavit and tequila get set before Alpo, he furtively slides them to others. By nine o'clock most everyone is jolly, as Sissy would say.

Alpo hadn't noticed when his new Kiwi pals slipped into the party, but they soon have everyone in stiches with their attempts at American accents.

Conner asks, "Whatdya call someone who speaks two languages?"

Erv grunts, "Bilingual?"

"Dead-on." Adam gives a thumbs-up. "What do you call somebody who speaks a dozen languages?"

Once Veshko realizes no one is going to answer, he pipes up. "Polyglot?"

"Ding-ding!" Adam says as everyone blinks at Veshko.

Then Conner asks, "And someone that speaks one?"

Veshko answers again, quickly, "An American."

Alpo spits a little beer. Jon Redlcaf, leaning against the pool table, asks Conner, "How many languages *you* speak?"

The brothers look to each other before sputtering, "One!"

"Just sayin'," says Jon.

"Fair enough!" Conner sidles next to Jon, as if to compare heights. "You look just like the dude in that film, what's-it . . . help me out, mate."

Jon humors him, raising to his full height, a dead ringer for the actor. He crosses his arms and mutters, "Juicy Fruit."

"That's *it!*" Without the accent and smile, Conner would've been punched by now.

"Really? Never heard that one before." Jon rolls his eyes but submits to a high five.

Bertie Kangas shows up front and center, still in uniform. "I can't stay," he announces. "Just wanted to let you boys know the latest . . ." Bertie seems distracted by activity in the far booth where the hen party is squealing, waving raunchy party favors.

"Yeah, Bertie?"

"Here's the thing." Thumbs hook on his holster to emphasize. "Something's been spotted in the Basin."

When glasses are set down Bertie knows he has their attention.

"Some*thing*?" Alpo asks.

"Well, we don't know fer sure yet, but a hiker claims it's a body."

"But you're not sure?"

"We got a climber on his way up from the Cities. At first light he's gonna rappel down to see if anything's washed up or jammed on the ledges."

"You think it's Rauri?"

"We're not even sure it's a body. If it is, the ID might take some time—you know the Basin, how it bashes anything around like a rock tumbler."

Chim considers the half-eaten mess on his plate.

"So," Bertie's voice drops a few octaves as it does for police business. "I gotta pick up the climber from the airstrip and run him out to the lodge tonight."

As Bertie walks away, one of the Kiwis says, "Well, that's a heap of heavy."

"Isn't it." Alpo agrees.

They watch Bertie's zagging progress as he detours to square his shoulders in the vicinity of the hen party. As he edges nearer, the bride-to-be looks up, takes one look at Bertie, and squeals at her friends, "You hired a *stripper*?!"

Guffawing and hooting erupts. It takes Bertie a beat to get it, but once he does, he cannot reach the door fast enough, his neck six shades of red. Once the door closes and the laughter finally dies down, a thicker atmosphere settles.

"Aw, crap." Erv leans back in the booth. "Let it not be Rauri."

Alpo is struck, for no logical reason, by a bolt of conviction that whatever *is* churning around in the Basin, it's not Rauri.

"So, this missing guy?" Adam asks. "What's his story?"

Everyone looks at everyone else before facing the brothers like deer.

"Well," says Erv.

"That's just the thing," Alpo adds.

Chim elbows Erv. "You probably saw more of him than any of us."

"On my route?" He swivels to explain to the brothers. "I used to drop and pick up for winterers back when my Otter was on skis."

"Right," Conner says.

"Not much to tell. One thing I thought was funny—Rauri never knew what day or time I'd land—hell, I didn't know. Yet every single time I put down in his channel something had just come out of the oven and a fresh cup of coffee was on the table. I'd kid him that he was setting bait for company like some trapper."

They all lean, waiting, but Erv only shrugs. "That's all. Just made me wonder if he didn't have some sixth sense or something."

"But wasn't he the last on your route?" Alpo asks.

"Sure, but . . ."

"Erv," Dan says. "Pal, he'd have heard you coming. All that landing and taking off all day?"

Erv smacks his forehead. "Oh. *Oh.*"

"That's the thing about obvious." Jon shrugs. "It isn't, always."

After that sinks in, Alpo ventures, "What I can't figure is what he does with himself all winter."

"Chop wood? Haul water?" Erv offers. "Plus, he works like some migrant in that little shop of horrors."

"Well, he reads a lot," Chim says. "One time I delivered him a box, heavy as shit, and it was like Christmas out there. He kept repeating some weird thing about a book being *an ox to break up souls* . . . ?"

"Close," Pete says. "'*A book must be an ice-axe to break the seas frozen inside our souls.*' It's a quote.'"

Veshko mutters, "Kafka," and gets a thumbs-up from Pete.

"Anyway," Erv continues, "Rauri's never said much. Sometimes he'd talk about his customers, and when we loaded the hold with his outgoing orders, he'd describe what was in each package, who it was going to, the price. Like an inventory list—and that was on a talkative day."

"Toast!" Alpo stands and sways, and they all follow suit, raising glasses, aiming in the direction they all think of when they think of Rauri. North.

13

ERTIE'S BIT OF NON-NEWS HAS PETE WONDERING WHY he'd bothered reporting it at all. Whatever's up there in the Basin, Pete hopes it isn't Rauri. As bad as that would be, the timing would be just as tragic. But if it were the worst news, what would be the harm keeping it under wraps a measly while so Sissy doesn't catch wind and have her wedding day ruined?

Before Bertie's arrival the party had actually been fun—not something Pete has had in a while. The Kiwi brothers were a gas, and as usual when new faces pop up, everyone puts their best foot forward—that wonder-of-me thing people do when bending a fresh ear to tell their best stories and jokes.

As usual, a night out for Pete includes making the sorts of observations one does being sober in the midst of those who aren't. For instance, he's deduced that none of Alpo's pals have serious drinking problems, excluding Gimp. They are hobbyists who do not order another drink until the one in front of them is finished; they tend to lose track of or even walk away from their drinks without a second glance. A drunk always knows the exact coordinates of his alcohol. Jon Redleaf never drinks more than one beer in an evening, but he's lost a sister to addiction and has a stake in sobriety as a team leader at his native youth program One Sky.

Early on in his recovery, Pete would go to his old local, drink Coke, and play designated driver, toughing it out just to prove he could. But being sober around drunks only reminded him what a horse's ass he'd likely been himself. Besides, he'd found that short of a scene there was no stopping someone convinced they're sober enough to get themselves home. His father is tonight's exception, happy to leave his Bronco in the lot and walk to Pete's to spend the night.

They are only blocks away from bed and sweet relief. His shoulder feels better since Veshko got his mitts on it—he hadn't realized how the rigid muscles in his neck were making the whole thing worse until they were pried free. The long day and the energy spent have left him a little weak when faced with the hill to his house. He could cry actually, looking forward to putting the day behind him. *That time I was so fucking tired I could not see straight.*

His father is whistling, cheerful.

He turns. "You have a good time, Dad?"

"I did, yeah. It coulda been worse."

Alpo has no idea. For one thing, Juri, who was footing the bill for the stag, had been set on chartering a party bus. When he'd slid the brochure for BusTAss across the counter, Pete nearly choked on muffin crumbs. He'd only ever encountered one party bus, and it had been the worst sort of memorable. After a hockey game in Minneapolis on a freezing January night, he'd been stuck in traffic next to a repurposed school bus painted black. The interior was harshly lit, with a carpeted ceiling. Curtains would have been an improvement. An exotic dancer was working her way down the aisle of rowdy partiers, folded bills poking from her thong. Pete nudged the gas hoping to pull ahead but only managed to align his grill with the bus at the red light. There, three feet to his left behind the folding glass doors was a second dancer, this one gyrating the bus pole, the kind he used to swing his backpacked self around the instant the driver cranked the door open to disgorge him at the Lahti mailbox. The girl—because she *was* a girl, really—was arched in a kind of backbend so that her face was inches from the upright chrome door-opener, an object you never realize is as phallic as it gets until you see a dancer aiming an open-mouthed *O* at one. Just beyond her in a surreal juxtaposition, the driver scowled in concentration at the traffic ahead. A second before the light turned green, a partier inside launched a red plastic beer cup, which missed the dancer and hit the windshield, its contents splattering her face. Her head snapped up and she was blinking beer from her eyes, staring right at Pete as hoots of laughter roiled from mid-bus. Their eyes locked for three seconds, during which Pete was more profoundly humiliated by his gender than at any other moment in his life. He rammed the car into park, ready to climb aboard to locate the prick who threw the red cup and make him eat the goddamn thing. Then honking commenced behind him, and instead of doing the right thing he pulled ahead. As he put it to his AA group, such moments were the sort that at once justified his drinking and posed a perfect example of why not to.

Pete told Juri, "No bus. Dad would be mortified."

"Jaysus." Juri gave him that look. "Just say embarrassed."

Pete shook his head. His father *would* be mortified.

Still, he and Juri had to find a place for a dozen gray foxes to "party hearty." Thankfully, the paintball field was no longer an option. Years ago, Pete went to a stag there. The groom, Rob Perla, was outfitted in a white rabbit costume, bunny ears, and pompom tail. Poor bastard was given a brief head start before being set after by good friends wearing camo, paint rifles cocked. It had been a blast, actually. After the accident, Tony Schulte bought the paintball property for boat and RV storage. There were scant places in Hatchet Inlet in which to host a stag; most were either too touristy, or loud, or too shithole. Driving out to one of the nicer lodges or supper clubs just meant too many cars on the roads after dark. Pasta Portage had done nicely.

They walk on, passing Old Lady Husom's house, its FOR SALE sign freshly sunk. He wonders if Alpo will regret selling the family home—there's a century of Lahti history there.

"Dad, you gonna miss the place?"

"Nah. Yeah." Alpo looks up. "Some. It was a good place to live."

"Not every kid gets to grow up on a lake."

"Yeah." Alpo brightens. "Yeah. We *both* had that, didn't we?" He lightly punches Pete's good arm. "You sure you don't want it? Family discount?"

"No, thanks."

"At least take your doghouse for Duke?"

Pete had built the doghouse as his senior shop class project for the family's retriever, Mick. Long after Mick was gone, when he and Beth would visit, the girls would play in it. By the time they grew too big for it, Pete's habit had grown to the point he was hiding bottles in the doghouse. He warned the girls that snakes had taken up residence in it, just in case. The back of his neck tightens with the thought. His arm aches anew.

"Duke sleeps inside, Dad." Will there come a time when the lies don't come so easily? Honesty has its price. He could be honest with Alpo right now—in fact this may be his last chance—speak now or forever hold his peace. After his mother died, Father Peter quickly followed with an aneurysm, though by rights his uncle should have been the one to die a slow and painful death. Would spilling now, after so many years, assuage Pete's guilt at never having spoken up?

On most counts, it's too late. Too late for any other boys who might have been spared had he brought his uncle's abuse to light back then (and Pete is certain there were others). At this stage, getting it off his own chest would just mean foisting it onto Alpo's. Send his father off on his honeymoon with that kind of baggage? It's his mother he should have told, but he didn't when he had the chance. How many times had she looked him in the eye and begged, *What is it?*

At ten p.m. in Hatchet Inlet the only sounds are their footfalls and the occasional car. The stillness under the greening elms is not so different from that on Rauri's island—was that really just this morning?

"Son, there's . . ." Alpo clears his throat. ". . . something I've been meaning to—"

Pete stops. "Nothing you're gonna regret later when you're sober, Dad?" It would be laughable if Alpo chose this very moment to rouse what he's just put to bed.

Alpo faces him. "It's in the past now, so . . ."

"Which past? Recent or ancient?"

Alpo gives him a look. "A few years ago."

"Okay." Pete lets out a breath. "Hit me."

"I should have been more straight with you."

"About what?"

"Beth. It's about Beth."

"Beth? What about her?"

"It wasn't just Beth who decided to move the girls to Duluth."

Pete turns slowly. "What do you mean?"

"I mean, Beth couldn't cope. You were at your worst. I suggested she take the girls and go. I found her a place. It was best . . . at the time."

"What?"

"As I said: you were at your worst."

"What do you mean *my worst*?" Pete stiffens. "Did you think I'd *harm* them?"

"Harm? No. No, Pete . . . but home was a lot more stable when you weren't in it."

Pete shakes his head, opens his mouth, closes it.

"There." Alpo swallows. "There was probably a better way, but at least it got you into Birchwood that first time. We assumed it was all temporary—I sure didn't anticipate that Beth would file or that she'd—"

"Meet someone else? Who is now raising *my* daughters?"

"Yeah." Alpo meets his eye and squares his shoulders. "But they are my granddaughters, remember."

Pete cannot trust himself to respond. He doesn't trust himself to be standing on this sidewalk within hitting distance of his father. He fishes the keys from his pocket and concentrates mightily on removing one from the ring.

"Here's the house key." His voice is flat.

"Where you going?"

After a few strides he spits the answer over his shoulder. "A walk. A long one."

14

CATHY HAD EXPLAINED THE CONCEPT OF PERSONAL coaching, had shown Sissy samples of the worksheets she gives clients, even performed a brief mock interview. But when pressed about what her passions actually were, Sissy first drew a blank and then grew uncharacteristically defensive.

"I *work*. And this coaching stuff seems like it's for yoga moms, or 612ers who do archery and Reiki or whatever—women with time to play bridge."

Since Cathy's own passions include rooting around in other people's personal business and the sound of her own voice, personal coaching is the perfect career for her: she glows when dishing out advice, and Sissy would too for seventy-five dollars an hour. But Cathy had been patient and Sissy came away with questions to ponder. Four pages with all the blanks still blank sitting on her desk. She sees now that what Cathy does is simple—makes a person step back far enough to take aim at themselves from different angles. Basically, Cathy encourages women to hunt themselves down.

Where and when are you happiest?

Fine. She can answer that. Either in the company of dogs, or whipping up something in the kitchen. She would never say aloud that she loves dogs more than people, but they are more predictable and don't keep score. And she agrees that sometimes you can't see your own forest for the trees, but it is dawning on her that her forest is one where a lot of deer get killed by cars.

One online search leads to another. Sissy is so absorbed by the screen she is shocked to look up and discover it's after midnight.

If someone had told her a month ago that on the official eve of her wedding she'd be browsing online for bone saws and watching YouTube tutorials on how to field-dress a buck, she'd have laughed.

Joe claims that butchery is in the Pavolas' genes. Maybe. If she can break down a hindquarter of beef, she can dismantle a deer. She knows what's involved in getting meat from hoof to plate—a process most people are willfully ignorant of, as if hamburgers are something you just gather, like eggs. That old Smiths song is right: meat *is* murder. Since the accident, Sissy catches herself making disturbing comparisons between meat in the butcher case and human flesh, because, really, wrap either in plastic and who would know?

How frail our bodies are, she thinks—skin barely thicker than a sausage casing, a fork prick away from tragedy.

Eventually she'd asked one of the EMTs, a newcomer to Hatchet Inlet who barely knew the girls, to share details of the accident so she might stop concocting her own. Evan was straightforward, explaining how the impact had thrown both with such force that their deaths would have been instantaneous, assuring Sissy it was one of those cases in which seatbelts would not have saved them and would in fact have made for a grislier scene, given the compaction of the van's front end and the cab. Sissy had not asked for that level of detail, but there you have it. Alpo had been among the volunteer firefighters arriving to help, to cordon off and search the scene. Evan described encountering Alpo holding Kelly's arm, cradling it, rocking lightly, and mumbling the line about sugar and spice and everything nice. Sissy halted the conversation there. Certain griefs are unrelatable. She walked away a little less miserable but with her heart cracking anew for Alpo.

Scanning her to-do list, she decides there are wedding preparations she can get away with not double- or triple-checking. Her laptop is open to a blank document titled HONEYMOON, just another list of things to do, sights to see, and activities near their resort. But what if they let the honeymoon play itself out, just plop down on the beach and see what unfolds?

When her brother Dan claimed that Finns leave nothing to chance, she'd made air quotes, replying, "But 'we' haven't been Finns for three generations."

"Trust me," he said. "We're Finns."

Sissy sends HONEYMOON to the trash and creates a new document typing MISSION, a term Cathy encourages clients to embrace. A new file, UNNAMED, stares at her. She sits back. Sits forward. Stands up and walks a circle route through the dining room and kitchen and back to her desk in the alcove before repeating the sequence. Jeff follows, knowing a second round equals restlessness and might result in a walk.

Finally plunking down, she taps out *Road Kibble* and stares at it. Treats and chews and bones aren't really kibble, so that's misleading. The Finnish word for food is *ruoka*. Road or street is *katu*. But saying *katu ruoka* aloud feels like mouth aerobics and likely isn't the right translation anyway. For now she'll just call it what it is, *Roadkill*. Besides, a name is a pretty low priority considering she'll need to find space and equipment and a refrigerated truck. The rest is a matter of girding up for a bit of debt and a lot of carcasses.

It's all means to one end. "Happy dogs." When she says it, Jeff's ears prick. She has *his* attention.

She recalls an odd encounter with Rauri years back, just before he'd begun making his fancy cabin accessories from dead things. It was a week or so into big game season when all the motels in town were jammed, the only time of year Pavola's opens for supper, serving a limited rotation of Joe's booyah, pot roast, and pasties (hungry hunters will eat woodchips if smothered in gravy). Hunting season is always a hump at the diner, with the testosterone levels off the charts. Sissy and the hired girls work their butts off while deflecting or ignoring comments about them, only putting up with it because the tips add up to a nice Christmas and a

March escape to whatever warm beach can be reached by what-ever charter is cheap.

The gas station where she and Rauri were both filling up and getting coffee was a DNR weigh-in point. At a buzz of noise they each looked up to see a pickup approach, flanked by a swarm of four-wheelers zagging around it like Shriner cars in a parade. The pickup bed was stacked with deer—hooves bound and sticking up like fencing. Two big stags were tied to the hood, tongues out. The hunters seemed high on the carnage. With much horsing around, each man dragged his kill out of the truck to the winch fitted with a scale for the season. Each deer had to be hoisted, weighed, and designated: Adult Female, Adult Male, Fawn Female, Fawn Male. She noticed that many oozed blood, a sign they'd not been prop-erly dressed.

The loud banter was heavily salted with *fuck, fucking, fucker, fucked,* or *motherfucker.* Rauri looked at her with an apologetic shrug, being of the generation that watched their language around a female. Sissy smiled. If the "ladies" of Hatchet Inlet were offended by cursing, they'd be cringing 'round the clock.

As another hunter posed for a picture with his kill, she reached to her passenger seat for the coffee tote with six to-go cups meant for the Senior Cedars breakroom, famous for its dumpster drip. They both watched, drinking their coffees until every deer had been pulled up, weighed, and photographed.

Natives will thank their kill and give the animal a respectful send-off. No hunter she knew would swear at the dead animals or dance around them like Rocky throwing punches or pretend to hump one while a buddy shoots video on his iPhone. Sissy memorized the faces of the men in case any might come into the diner. When Laurie has a particularly horrible customer, she's been known to mutter "Spit happens" when snatching their orders from under the heat lamps.

Who knows why she'd stood that morning shivering so long. As for Rauri, maybe all those antlers and hooves sent visions of chandeliers dancing through his head, the inspiration for his future craft? Or maybe like her he just couldn't look away.

When it was over, Rauri and Sissy climbed into their cars—not a word had passed between them. These days a pair of his antler sconces with tanned-hide shades and wolf-fang pulls costs nearly a grand—nothing he could afford himself, just like other locals whose own work is priced beyond their means. Stone masons, canoe builders, cabinet makers—what's the saying? The cobbler's children have no shoes. She thinks of the high-end pet stores she'd never shop in, where a forty-pound bag of kibble costs a day's wages, the kind of store where Roadkill would sell like hotcakes.

Her mission? She supposes it would be to make some sense of the senseless. There's no way of going back in time to change any accident. Why not at least make an animal's death mean something? Since a lovely young woman's never will.

After texting a string of good-night emoticons to Alpo, she yawns all the way up the stairs, hitting the pillow hard, dragging an entire herd along into her dreams.

15

HIS SON HAD BEEN AN AVERAGE KID, IF A LITTLE ON THE
serious side: smart, a good-enough sport. He endured
his sister, shared his toys. Most of the mischief he got up
to bordered on amusing—flinging a pair of Sunday shoes to snag
irretrievably on a high power line; feeding half a bin of dog bis-
cuits to the fishers plaguing Rose's garden—misdemeanors that
Pete would blame on his imaginary twin. According to Pete, *Jack*
was a mean blond boy with yellow teeth who lived in the attic.
Jack had many food allergies and would *blow up like dynamite* if
he even smelled carrots or raw tomatoes. It was Jack who peed
down the laundry chute when Candy took too long in the bathroom. Jack deflated the tires on the station wagon the morning
Alpo was to drive Rose to the airport to visit cousins in Dublin.

And then, as if all his hormones began raging at once, Pete
ceased to amuse and turned inward, surly. Alpo and Rose never
knew if they'd be having breakfast with Jekyll or Hyde. He still
skated through school at the top of his class, even with marks
for poor attitude and lack of participation. He stank, his room
stank. Rose pointed out that the word *adolescent* contains *scent*. He
excelled at arguing and was the worst sort of smart-ass—a smart
one. They expected he'd grow out of it, wouldn't have guessed it
would take thirty years.

Alpo reached his tipping point with Pete during his first stint
at Birchwood. Near the end of the twenty-eight days, he'd driven
down for Family Day to sit in a circle with a dozen strangers
and listen to each recite the damage and wrongs done by their
addicted loved ones, one sad laundry list after another. After

being lambasted, each shamed addict was given a chance to repent, grovel, apologize, or in some cases simply bawl.

While he had bones to pick, Alpo didn't think Family Day was a place to air dirty laundry. He suggested as much to the group, saying Pete's ruined marriage and whatever harms he'd saddled his girls with were his to deal with.

"Not liking your own son isn't much fun. I didn't keep a tally of the times he shamed us—didn't make a list." He looked Pete in the eye. "I imagine he's stewing in his own juices now that he's had time to figure out how he got where he is."

"Well. I *am* an alcoholic. Which runs in the Lahti family, right?"

Pete still wasn't owning up?

"I've got Mom's Irish genes to boot . . ." He was about to say more when Alpo stood so fast the chair clattered out from behind him.

"Blame your mother? Blame *genetics* rather than admit you're a fuckup?" He retrieved his chair, begged pardon of the woman next to him, and sat back down, shocked for how badly he wanted to bloody his own son's mouth. Other than a smack to the bottom, Alpo had never struck either of his children. There'd been a short stretch when sixteen-year-old Candy made some slappable comment with every pass of the salt or pepper, but Pete seemed to be always asking for it.

Still, Alpo shouldn't have colluded with Beth behind Pete's back. At the time it had felt more than justified, given his concern for her and the girls. In hindsight, they should have confronted him.

Best intentions paving the road to hell and all that.

He settles in the girls' room. Discovering he still has the crime novel, he props himself up against one of Maddie's *Frozen* pillows and opens the book, planning to read until Pete comes home. But the sentences won't stay in straight lines and the lock doesn't turn.

* * *

Waking at four-thirty he's bone-dry, tongue like a hairbrush. Padding from bathroom to kitchen and back, he drinks three glasses of water. As feared, the house is empty, Pete's bed not slept in. Alpo fills the dog's water dish and lets Duke out, looking both ways down the dark alley. He could drive the streets looking for his son—hardly a first—or he could go fishing. While coffee brews he helps himself to the contents of Pete's fridge, building a pair of ham sandwiches to toss in a bag with a few oranges. The cooler in his Bronco has a few beers, apples, and a jar of peanuts. He fills a water jug and sets out to walk to the parking lot at Pasta Portage.

Fishing seems a fine way to spend the day before his wedding.

The road on the north arm of Lake Eve runs out of pavement after seven miles. The gravel goes on for a few more before it peters out and the Bronco thunks into the ruts of the old logging road. Crawling along in low gear Alpo watches for the break in the tree line, and when he finds it carefully rocks the Bronco off-road into a tunnel of pine. At the USGS marker, he's greeted with last year's waist-high weeds. To cross beyond and into the Reserve is to risk a fine to the tune of five grand, possible jail time, and certain confiscation of his vehicle. Not that any ranger would bother venturing where he has.

After an incline as steep as his nose, the hard clay gives way to a slope of granite. Shifting into four-wheel, loose stones and moss spew from the tires. Just as he feels the front end lose purchase, the Bronco's rear locks down, still weighted with bags of winter salt and sand. He guns it, practically launching up the bald dome of rock.

And he's there. The massive ledge of stone is the size and shape of a baseball diamond and nearly as flat. His headlights barely reach the far edge, where predawn hangs gray and edgeless. He parks under the cover of a few lodge pines in case any aircraft decides to skim the no-fly perimeter. Once out of the cab, he plants both fists on the saddle of his lower back—the night hadn't been exactly restful, listening even in his dreams for footfalls or the flush of a toilet.

One thing he knows for certain: he can no longer fret over the boy. A man now.

He lays his fly case on the open tailgate and snaps on his headlamp. His most recent creations—and therefore his favorites—are the iridescent Lefty's Deceivers tied with peacock feathers. He's tied an array of Wooly Buggers, Damsel Nymphs, Muddler Minnows, and Bunny Leeches. A single Parachute Adams. Each fly resting on its felted bed is a testament to patience. He makes his choices for the morning and sets the hooks into the square of sheepskin sewn onto his fishing vest.

Pete is his own responsibility now. As a parent you have to call it a day at some point.

The coffee from his thermos raises a column of steam. Leaning against the bumper he gnaws a granola bar, watching as the last of the stars blink off like workers punching out. Due northwest, the smokestacks of Fort Domain slowly reveal their outlines like photos coming to in their chemical baths. To the south the distant smudge of Hatchet Inlet becomes less smudge-like. A faroff semi downshifts and growls its way up the south side of the Trans-Divide. He walks to where the ledge narrows to a cantilevered point—a stone prow cutting over swells of wild spruce—and looks out over the slowly lightening landscape.

The Reserve somehow feels different to him, knowing Rauri's not in it. And if Rauri is gone for good, the seasons will quickly reclaim his islands, rot the buildings, and knit moss over the rubble. Roofs will cave under the weight of winters. Rauri's mark on the place will scab over and heal.

Framed like that, the notion gives Alpo pause. If you think about it, each human is an assault on the Earth: the populace forms the worst sort of army. The scrap of land spread out below Alpo has been fought over since he can remember. Copper mining interests will never stop lobbying for permission to harvest its riches. Locals hoodwinked by empty promises of jobs will go right along, ears firmly shut. Everyone wants their cell phones, their microwaves, their iPads. But without fresh water, what good will those be? Even a dog knows not to shit in its own backyard. Alpo's not naïve. Greed—if not eventually need—will likely get its grubby hands on the place.

For now, the Reserve churns on, bursting out in miraculous life after six months of banjaxing cold. In only three or four months the place will throttle down again—go to seed, burrow, hibernate. Alpo looks back at the plateau, now washed in light, the sort of impossible place that gets featured in truck ads, where by dint of reaching a place the driver has conquered it. There's your irony.

He looks down, nearly giving in to vertigo. A chorus of birds starts warming up, stating the obvious: daylight! He squints, feels the heft of his breath lessen with the waning humidity. In the valley below, shawls of mist unravel to reveal the grooves of long, black lakes in the distance. In an hour or so the sun will be high enough to set them glinting like the shards of some great mirror busted across the Reserve.

The sun cracks the horizon, staining the low clouds yolk-yellow and sending beams spoking up through the gaps. Alpo suspects the words for such moments don't even exist. He has read a hundred attempts to describe instances of awe, usually paralleled with the writer admitting his insignificance when perched on the rim of a canyon, adrift on an ocean, or staring down an avalanche. How often the forces of nature are attributed to one god or another, whether a striking sunrise or a plague of locusts. Alpo's feet are planted at the cusp of day on the Divide's great spine, roiled up from volcanos and ridden in on the backs of glaciers when the planet was young and God was a boy, if there is a God and he ever was a boy. Alpo has his doubts.

He's gone to his share of Al-Anon meetings where so much dependence and hope get foisted at some all-forgiving Higher Power. He sees the damage caused by those drunks just across the hall in the AA meetings, heads bowed and praying away their pasts—having lied, cheated, stolen, neglected, aggrieved (fill in the verb)—yet accepting things they did *but cannot change.* Asking for a pass in all they wrecked along the relay from one quart and the next.

Yes, he does think too much, thank you.

16

"**G**OING FOR A *DRIVE* . . . ?" LAURIE GIVES HER THAT LOOK.
"I have things to do." Sissy squats to pry off Lou's muddy tennis shoes. The three have just walked one of their Habitrail routes around the grounds and back to the Memory Wing. There's been no talking with Lou this morning—she's clamped into her headphones, just headphones, no music. It disturbs Sissy that their mother rocks to a beat no one can hear, looking crazy.

Trying to stuff one of her mother's feet into a scuffed loafer (on its second resole), Sissy gets zero cooperation. She sits back on her heels. "Dammit, Mom!"

Laurie turns. "Are we testy?"

"I'm not *testy*," sounding all the more so for denying it. Laurie has struck a nerve, because she *has* been moody these past weeks, ups and downs triggered by seemingly nothing.

"Oh. Getting your period, then?"

Sissy would hurl the shoe at her sister if not for the sudden dawning. She's lost track, again? Lately, her periods have been annoyingly irregular. During her last annual, when Dr. Cindy had been kneading around her abdomen, she'd mentioned early menopause. Menopause. Minnow-paws. *Change of life,* the mothers and aunts always whispered.

Of course. The recent half-awake sweaty nighttime episodes; the intermittent road rage; the sudden billows of heat as if a burner's been cranked at her very core. And now, holding her mother's foot, inert as a loaf and refusing its shoe, Sissy fights the urge to twist the ankle. Getting to her feet she hands the loafer to Laurie. She *is* going for a drive—that much is true.

At the DNR, Gladys Esko leans over the counter, listening as if she gets asked such questions every day.

"Oh, sure. Three or maybe five a week get killed on the roads, but that's just what gets seen or reported. Then there's the ones hit maybe on purpose to take home for dinner—Lord knows how many of those. Gladys writes down a few phone numbers. "These two guys pick up carcasses for us. They'll know more."

She loads Sissy with charts, zone maps, regulations, and dates for all three deer seasons, harvest stats, and location surveys. She also hands over sheets of regulations for badger, snowshoe hare, muskrat, mink and pine marten, elk, bobcat, and caribou. Birds, too. Sissy frowns. "Sandhill cranes? Mourning doves?"

"Oh, sure." Gladys shrugs. "If it moves, you can pretty much kill it. 'Cept these." She hands over a Suspended Hunts Notice: moose, cougar, wolverine. "Not like you could find one to shoot these days." Gladys fingers a bristle on her chin. "Sissy, hon, aren't you getting married tomorrow?"

Sissy drives to the deer farm in Gilbert River and meets the owner, Per Orjala. She drops Alpo's name, knowing Per was a manager for OreTac.

"Fiancé?" He gives her a second look. "Alp . . . well, good for him. Skol."

After swigging the sample of doe's milk, she must ask for water, unable to get the too-milky bitterness off her tongue.

Per laughs. "That's what nineteen percent fat tastes like. Whole cows' milk is *three*. We made some cheese just for fun, but factor in the labor and it's eighty bucks a pound to produce—we couldn't even charge our New York customers that."

He gives the tour himself. They bounce along the two hundred acres in an open jeep. The only place Sissy has seen taller fencing is at the driving range. Herds are sectioned into twenty-acre plots to graze; they also have the run of the large garden plots and fields.

"We got twenty acres of alfalfa on the hillsides, and in the rocky flats we're sowing sweetgrass, clover, and buckwheat."

Sissy swats at black flies, the surest sign of spring. Pointing to a fenced muddy field of rows tented with plastic she asks, "And that?"

"Experiment. Yams, sugar beets, and yellow potatoes—to see if increasing the starch might sweeten the tallow. Season's too short to grow corn, and root crops keep longer."

In the calving sheds, about twenty does are nursing, nudging, or licking clean their wobbly fawns. A few pace around in labor, drum-bellies stretched and occasionally rippling with visible movement. One doe stops and blinks as an obvious hoof budges against her side. A new mother lets go a stream of pee on one of her twins as it tussles for position at a teat.

At a low building Per leads her to an anteroom where they put on jackets and paper booties. He hands her a hairnet and opens the door to the refrigerated processing room.

"Pretty quiet on a Friday," Per explains. "We hang the carcasses here to cool for a few days before we butcher, usually on Wednesdays and Thursdays."

"Ah." There are questions she might not like the answers to. "And how do you, you know . . . ?"

"Captive bolt stunning."

"Oh dear. Like that movie *No Country*—"

"*—for Old Men.* Exactly."

The room has three stainless butcher stations, each with an overhead pull-down sprayer, floor drain, and a hard acrylic cutting surface. Everything is on casters, including the central meat saw and a rotating caddy of knives. All the electricity dangles from above in shiny Slinkyish cords.

"Once the cuts are wrapped, they get run to the airport in

Duluth in the cold rig. From there it's overnighted to our three restaurant regions, New York, Chicago, and D.C."

"Huh. So deer that were running around on Monday are already . . . ?"

"Headed for a plate in Manhattan or D.C." Per looks at his watch. "Probably delivered by now. If not, the phone'll start ringing—those chefs that get bent out of shape on the reality TV shows? We got a few like that."

They pass the stainless steel bins at the foot of each station. Per pats one and says, "Most of what you'd be interested in goes in these—bones, organs, offal."

"And from there . . . ?"

"Incinerator. So, actually, you'd be saving us a step by taking it."

"Really?" Sissy grins at the prospect of free bloody bones and guts. "And the black dumpster?"

"Hides. About half are tanning grade—those go to the mukluk maker over in Greenstone. The seconds I could sell you cheap."

Hide chews are high on her list. "Oh. I *would* want those." She also covets what she sees on the way out, a heap of clear plastic bags stuffed with antlers.

"What do you do with those?"

"Fella up on Lower Shield Lake usually comes in once a month in season to get them."

"Rauri?" Sissy says. "Rauri Paar."

"Chandelier man. You know him?"

"Kind of. Actually, we're all sort of worried. You haven't seen him?"

"Not yet. He's usually come and gone by now."

She's about to ask more, but he is steering her into a walk-in freezer fogged with such deep cold her words seize on the inhale.

Oh, yes, she thinks. A *"minnow paws"* heaven.

Per points to shelves of frozen stock. "This is for the local market." He hands her two long white packages the size of baguettes marked BACKSTRAP. "These are from yearlings, fed on acorns and alfalfa."

She hefts them politely before trying to hand them back.

"No. You take those. Wedding present." Before she can thank him, he adds, "Now don't go feeding *those* to any dogs."

From the deer farm she drives north to the reservation. Parking at the community center she can see Bear Redleaf working near the communal gardens. The casino has funded a greenhouse, a brick oven, and a smokehouse for the indigenous gardening program,

The smokehouse is wooden, the size of a steeple set atop a stone foundation. "Tamarack," Bear tells her, showing off one of the carved doors that slide to reveal smoking racks within. The foundation is waist high, made of greenstone. Set into each corner is a smoke vent screened with copper mesh.

"Keeps vermin out." He opens one of the iron stove doors at knee height and invites Sissy to stick her head in.

The chamber is lined with creamy stove brick, unfired. "Wow." Sissy's voice echoes around her as if she's somehow in her own mouth. She backs out, "Nice."

"Overkill, right? But you know Jon."

She walks around, looking up to the peak where iron rods jut out and cross each other like teepee poles.

"Is this a traditional design?"

"Nah," Bear chuckles. "That's Jon having a laugh."

"It looks pretty expensive?"

"About ten grand."

"*Ten?* Oh jeez."

"Hang on." Bear disappears to his truck and returns with a clipboard, easing a page from it. "I dug this up for you." It's an ad for stainless steel smokers, no bigger than refrigerators. "I know a supplier in Superior can get you a used one of these for about eight hundred. Good for what you're talking about, and propane isn't near as messy as wood-fired. Till you get your own setup, you're welcome to smoke out here."

She asks him about the job he'd recently quit at a Minneapolis bistro where reservations run a month out.

Bear shakes his head. "Six or seven hundred bucks for a table of four? I wouldn't want to have dinner with anyone spends that kind of money on a meal, so why cook for them, right?"

Bear asks Sissy to sit at the picnic table overlooking the Reserve and proceeds to lay out the lunch he's packed: smoked lake trout; wild ramp chevre with watercress on crusty bread; a beet and carrot slaw with fennel; yam and maple popovers; sweet Labrador tea.

"Oh, my."

He shrugs. "I was goofing around with recipes this morning when you called."

"To the first picnic of the year." She clinks her bottle of tea with his and they dig in, chewing thoughtfully as the meal deserves. It's warm enough to shed jackets, with a breeze flapping the wax paper and sending Tupperware skidding. Neither mind, since it keeps the flies away.

They are perched on high ground with a long view into the Reserve across the lake where reservation land meets federal. Halfway through lunch Bear looks up.

"Besides, you know? Kel and Jessie. Something like that happens, you stop and think, hey, is what I'm doing right now what I *wanna* be doing?"

For a second she's confused. "So you quit. I totally get it."

"'Cuz when your time comes, it can be *any* time, right?"

"Right."

Compared to his uncle, Bear is chatty. What he's chosen to spend his time doing impresses Sissy—a young guy coming home to go to bat for his people. "I imagine Jon's thrilled you've moved back, Bear."

"Moved? Fuck no. This is just a pit stop."

"Oh?"

"I'm outta here come July."

"Where to?"

"Work my way south. Brazil for starters. Maybe Down Under after that. I met a couple Kiwis a few days ago. Promised to teach me how to surf if I show up in Auckland."

"For real?" Sissy sees he's serious.

"Well, it's summer there when it's thirty below here, right? I'll be on black sand beaches in January when you guys are going snow-blind. I'd be stupid not to go."

Sissy can't disagree with that. When they finish lunch, he gives her a ring binder of smoking formulas and techniques before walking her to the car.

"They find that old dude yet?"

"Rauri." She stops. "No."

"I wonder it Jon's tried flashing him?"

Sissy turns. "Pardon?"

He points to the decommissioned fire tower on the next bluff. "You can see Rauri's islands from there. Jon says back in the '70s, him and my grandpa would climb that and flash messages, not just to Rauri's island but his other places, like his woodlot or his sugar camp where he had another little cabin. Even across the border."

"Messages?"

"Coded ones." Bear shrugs. "Jon thought it might be Morse or some code they learned from being in the war. He thinks they didn't just smuggle draft dodgers across the border—that other things got smuggled back."

"*Smuggled*? What the heck would you smuggle from Canada, syrup?"

Bear gives her a look. "Weed."

"Ah."

Leaving the reservation Sissy thinks on that. The Rauri she knows might be anything but who he seems. Had he been a criminal once, a fugitive? She doubts it, but when you think of it, anybody could be anything.

A T YOUR WORST COULD REFER TO A DOZEN INSTANCES
during the two years of his final descent. He is well aware
of the dates; it's the details that are fuzzy.

Despite his battered state Pete makes good time, concluding
that adrenaline must be a by-product of fury. Balls. It takes balls
to elbow into someone else's business like his father had. He'd
encountered Beth and Alpo together a dozen times, nodding over
coffee, going quiet when he walked into the room. Talking about
him, of course.

Plotting, as it happens.

An easterly wind deposits him at The Rectory where he takes
the outdoor flight of stairs down to Ravens, an establishment not
patronized by locals and precisely why Pete has chosen it.

By definition, his *worst* suggests memories of it that will likely
be unreliable, since actual chunks of time went missing at the
height of it. Like the morning he woke in his car on the wrong
side of the North Dakota border wearing someone else's parka.
There was the piano he did not recall buying, though he clearly
remembers the argument with the deliverymen that resulted in
them abandoning it in the driveway. An hour later Beth pulled
in to find Maddie and Allison under a tarp in the rain, playing
"Chopsticks" on "Daddy's big surprise," while Daddy was on the
other side of the garage door pacing and getting shit-faced.

Those are right up there. Near the end, there had been weeks
he could count his sober waking hours on one hand.

* * *

The bar was once the laundry of St. Gummarus convent and school. Ravens is popular with cabin owners and visitors to the resorts. The name has less to do with the bird than the nickname given the Carmelite nuns who once ran the place. Pete remembers when the school building was demolished in the eighties after enrollment had shrunk to six or eight kids per grade. Late on a Friday the place is full. Pete recognizes the music as the sound-track to *The King and I*.

James and Jim are working the bar, making drinks and fetch-ing small plates from the kitchen. James has a handlebar mustache with waxed ends like Dali's and wears tweed vests over linen shirts with no collars. Jim is plaid-clad, gym-ripped with a chest like a boulder and a jaw like Dudley Do-Right. Both are the picture of Up North masculinity—until they pick up one of their tricolored papillons and start cooing. Audrey and Cher, he remembers. Pete never forgets the names of his clients' dogs.

Jim and James don't really know Pete outside the clinic. They might know he's in recovery.

They might not.

"Hiya, Doc." Jim slaps down the drinks menu.

Apparently not.

Registering the bandage on Pete's forehead and the sling, Jim tactfully ignores both, "Any food tonight?"

"Nope." Pete shakes his head.

"I'll be back for your order toot sweet."

"Take your time, Jim." He holds up the multipage menu. "I've got reading to do."

After Jim bustles off, Pete nods a cursory hello to the couple next to him, a fit-looking pair of sixtysomethings dressed as if for an expedition. He's glad they're playing cribbage and otherwise occupied.

The frosted-glass wall behind the bar shelves is backlit, cast-ing the glow of spirits like stained glass. The brands read like a roster of long-lost companions: Jack, Walker, Phillips, Hendrick's. His best pal from college, Smirnoff. Gone but hardly forgotten, they wink cordially in amber, sapphire, and emerald hues. He can recall the comfort of Jim Beam like the arm of a pal slung over his shoulder. The physical memories of alcohol are still lodged. Scotch's full embrace, the clean nudge of gin, the fatherly clasp of bourbon.

The embossed menu stares up at him. *Imbibements* pretty much says it all. The martini list includes Dirty Linen, Crown of Thorns, and Vicky's Knickers. Under *Sullied* are mojitos muddled with basil, blueberry, and lavender. Gimlets and juleps are named for each of the seven deadly sins and Sloth alone has as many ingredients. Some novelty drinks arrive in flames. Venal Sin and Father Confessor have warnings about their high-octane content. A highball with bitters and absinthe is named The Kneeler.

Amateur hour, nothing for a real drinker. He swivels away from the tractor beam of booze to admire the renovation. The original green tile walls shine; the maze of copper plumbing crisscrossing the ceiling is brightly polished. Rugs soften the worn flagstones; low-slung upholstered loveseats and moose-hide beanbag chairs make it nearly cozy. Old boilers have been fitted with gas fires. Jim and James have spent a mint and the menu prices concur.

Jim slows in mid-scurry to set down a glass of water. "Decide yet?"

Pete shrugs. "I'm torn."

On the wall opposite the bar hang two large waterscapes, unmistakably Meg's. She has always painted water, what it reflects and what it refracts. Pete suspects somewhere along the line she was told water was too difficult or even impossible to paint (which is only true when you think about it), but challenge Meg Machutova and she'll go to lengths to prove a point, even make a career of it.

The first canvas is of sandy shallows: water softly stirred to mirror a lazy summer sky. Half of the painting is shadowed to reveal the bottom, pebbles warping, milfoil swaying over a half-buried rusted can of beer, a brand no longer brewed. The other painting is a gilded trail of the moonlit wake of a boat, its trajectory veered off the canvas; the troughs and eddies hatching the black surface are quickened by colors only moonlight can muster.

Each canvas is as wide as Pete is tall. He can guess their value.
James looks up from shaving lime zest.

"Fabulous, aren't they?" he says. "The artist is from Hatchet
Inlet, if you can believe."

"Gotta be from somewhere, right?"

"You know her?"

He thumbs the condensation on his glass. "As well as you can
know anybody here." He peers at the water, realizing the ice cubes
encase tiny sprigs of herbs like bugs in amber.

James stacks three cubes into a tumbler, strains the contents of
a shaker over them, and drops in a garnish of lime skin. He holds
the cocktail to the light. It is the color of the ocean. "Tempt you
with one of these, Pete? It's mostly gin."

He stands suddenly. "Where's the toilet?"

James nods. "Just down there."

The steps descend to a tiled tunnel strung with vintage-
looking bare bulbs. The tunnel once connected the school to the
church and the convent to the rectory, a convenience so the priest
and nuns could avoid flapping across the commons like winter
birds. It now dead-ends at twenty feet in a pair of unisex WCs,
each with a vintage sink hung from its curved wall.

Pete has heard about this tunnel from Old Kate, an ex-nun
living out a happy retirement as proprietress of the single known
gay bar north of Duluth. Bucksaw Sisters had been one of Pete's
favorite watering holes back in the day—no one bothered him
there because no one would think to look. Kate had arrived at
Gummarus as a novice just after Father Merkle had the tunnel
bricked off in the seventies, ostensibly over safety issues.

"The older nuns obviously thought differently," Kate mused.
"I gathered from them that he closed the tunnel to block his own
route to temptations on the other side."

"Temptations?" Pete asked.

"They wouldn't say what kind. I was only there a few years,"
Kate said. "I don't know if it was the nuns, girls, or the boys he
wanted to get at. Maybe the pantry, for all I know," Kate laughed.
"Fat bastard."

"What do *you* suppose?"

"Probably boys." She sighed, suddenly looking her age. "Isn't it usually boys?"

Pete washes his hands and drip-dries over the sink rather than use one of the little hand towels. The bruising on his temple has turned mottled. His barber appointment had come and gone at noon, around the time he and Erv were defying death and snapping spruce tops. He touches the prickly hairs near the bandage and rubs dried blood from his scalp with wet fingers. His daughters tease him about his hairline, dare him to grow a comb-over. He's adopted a buzz cut because you are what you are and he is balding. For a stretch there he'd scraped his thinning hair into a ponytail and grew muttonchops. At his worst, he was definitely looking the part, thirty pounds heavier and jowled, with capillaries clearly mapping the decline across his nose. A year ago a glance in the mirror reflected a barely recognizable fuckhead. Pete no longer recoils at his reflection. The running has paid off. His skin is no longer pasty and he looks like he feels—decent. His gaze is clear, bluer now that the whites aren't red.

It's how his daughters see him that matters. And if that plane *had* gone down? He wonders what they might take from his life, what memories might be lobbed across the lid of his casket. The best and truest times with his children are history. Back when the three of them were a pack, their den a tent under a backyard maple, the lawn their territory. They spent hours on all fours, green-kneed, pawing and clawing; they growled while eating their apple slices, grew ferocious over baby carrots. Pete let them lick his ears and nearly deafen him with yips and squeals. They paw-fought, tumbled, played tug-of-war with fruit roll-ups stretched between their Chiclet teeth. They tracked their prey, pounced, and killed the Beanie Babies, carrying them off in their little wolf-mouths to feed their own dolls. They snuffled and licked each other and dug cool bowls in the sandbox to nap in. Beth had not approved, but seeing their animal joy had to indulge them.

They were his pups, too, and rousing them warm from their beds on full moons to go howling was his right. He taught them to sniff out dangers; without their even knowing, he groomed them to be wary. Stranger danger wasn't enough: you had to know who the bad wolves were in any pack, not least your own.

Did his father have any right to interfere? Does he expect to be forgiven for breaking up his pack, moving them hundreds of miles away?

If he's honest.

If he's really honest, the question is, *did* he—at his worst—deserve his own children? The person in the mirror—the person he is now—does not offer an answer.

Pete mounts his barstool to discover a pewter ice bucket and pair of tongs have been placed there. He's about to ask when James sets aside the bottle he's been wiping—twenty-one-year-old Balvenie.

"Jim guessed you'd be a Scotch man." He sets the half-full tumbler in front of Pete with some ceremony. "A little thank-you for seeing Audrey through her kidney woes."

The Scotch looks and smells like Indian summer, earthy and sunshot. About to rattle together some excuse, he makes to slide it back. His mouth opens and shuts like a flap. As his palm connects, the glass practically vibrates, as if the few inches of booze within has a life of its own. Pete shakes his head too late—James has turned to the kitchen cubby where a minimalist plate of something has appeared. Before darting off, he tosses Pete a conspiring wink.

THE PATH BELOW THE LIP OF GRANITE NARROWS FROM yards to only a few feet wide. Footholds get trickier the farther Alpo descends, but the rock face is pocked with natural handholds and there are sturdy saplings and alder to grab in case. Halfway down is a vertical fissure the width of a closet door. He listens for the sound of water before slipping in. The deep shadows make each step tentative and his eyes are slow to adjust. The path curves and narrows, holding sound, as if he's navigating the shell of a whelk. The dull source of light ahead is his beacon. A dozen more yards the light is no brighter but there's more of it. Here the path suddenly grows steeper, stones scrabble underfoot.

Gravity deposits him into a cavern. A half-shell opening the size of an amphitheater—one tiny divot in the foundation of the Divide. Much of the cavern is taken up by a clear, bottomless pool.

There are times he thinks this place is a dream and is relieved to find it still here, its greenstone walls wet and tangible to the touch, the presence of mold and guano affirmed by his sneezes. He's not been since October—a lifetime ago. High above, crevices ruffle with bats tucking in, a few latecomers swooping up to jostle for space. Sunlight aligns with an open fissure in the eastern wall and lays a sliver of morning light at his feet.

The origin of the pool is a mystery, likely fed from multiple sources since no single one is obvious: aquifers deep in the stone, a spring or some underground river beneath.

The cavern opens to a dank bowl of low wetland anchored

with hooked cedars. One end of the pool spills down into it, a sheet of water the width of a door. It foams upon impact but settles smooth a few yards into its course. Where the stream meets a boulder, it splits neatly in two to flow in opposite directions.

Certainly, this spot is unknown and uncharted—otherwise it would be plugged with tourists on boardwalks, plaques explaining how at this weird rent in the Divide water makes the decision of whether to flow north or south. There would be an interpretive center, a parking lot, and the mother of all handicap ramps. And roads leading to it all.

For the moment it's untouched. Who knows for how long. He hitches his waders and steps into the south-forking channel. The streambed makes for safer footing than the banks, where sphagnum conceals slick boulders and dangerous pockets of nothing. As he ploughs along, he notes rivulets and rills, narrow as a ribbon to wide as tinfoil, each adding volume to the flow. As the stream broadens, it finds its voice, burbling over stones and muttering along banks shagged with leatherleaf and rushes.

At the landmark of an upright boulder Alpo stops to check the sky, hoping to get a read on the sun. Twice he's failed to find his way back up to the plateau from here, assuming that if he simply climbed it would be there somewhere. Both times he ended up backtracking. A compass needle will not settle here; his Garmin cannot pull a coordinate. Lesson learned, he now sticks to the stream.

Several hundred yards to the south is a pool where treetops part to provide a platter of sky in which to cast. His spot. There are two sizable flat rocks for sitting on or cleaning a fish, should he decide to eat one.

The zing of his reel parallels the white noise of water. There is something about the repetition and rhythm of casting that is nearly hypnotic. But that's fishing—some say it can cure what ails you. Every year Dale at Bordertown Outfitters donates a dozen fishing trips to vets with PTSD. Alpo has been a volunteer guide on such paddles, has seen firsthand the leveling effects of being in the wild, on water. As to how helpful the fishing is, it's hard to say. There's a story from his own family in which it did work for one such damaged man—until it didn't.

Back in Finland Alpo's Great-Uncle Einar fought in the Revolution as a Bolshevik. During the battle of the town of Lahti, the family seat, he was dug in with several hundred other Reds in a three-day siege. Entrenched and under fire, they held out against the Whites but suffered many casualties—more than thirty of their own lay dead among them. At times it was necessary to use the corpses as shields. He later wrote to his wife describing how he'd seen comrades killed two and three times over. After being captured along with eight hundred others, Einar was held for months in a concentration camp where half the prisoners starved to death, died of disease, or were shot, mostly at the hands of other Finns. By all accounts his own countrymen killed each other with more vengeance and brutality than the Germans or Swedes ever roused. Alpo supposes no hatred can rival the sort borne of living back-to-back among those you disagree with.

Einar's widow, Karan, told Alpo how his great-uncle had emerged from the camp having lost a third of his body weight, his left eye, and much of his will. He might have lived long enough to forget a war, but not a civil war, however short. Great-Aunt Karan visited Hatchet Inlet in the sixties when Alpo was just a teen. She had wanted to see where her brother had settled, meet his family. She brought photocopies of journals, clippings, letters from Einar, medals, photos—ancient documents to Alpo, but Karan wanted her American relations to remember the bloody legacy of the Lahti name. The topic interested few but Alpo, whose curiosity was sparked enough to investigate the family tree. He read what he could about the battles, nagged the librarian to order books.

After that summer, Alpo wrote Aunt Karan regularly, an odd set of pen pals—an American teen into sci-fi novels and Chuck Berry, and a Finnish octogenarian who was once a courier for the Resistance delivering coded messages sewn into her brassiere.

Karan nursed Einar as best she could. He was claustrophobic

and jittery. Only when she could lure him to the lake or river did he seem himself. One day she brought his fly rod and steered him to a stream where he quietly fished. The spot was downstream of a pig farm where runoff and manure tainted the water. It had scant few fish, but Einar didn't mind. After that first afternoon of casting he joked about nothing biting and kissed his wife for the first time in a year. Over the next few Saturdays he fished by himself, coming home calm and with an appetite. He was coming around, had come around. One Saturday when he didn't arrive home for lunch, Karan found him at the stream, curled on the bank, pole frozen in his fist. One of the nibbles on his line had finally materialized into an actual bite. The trout struggling on his line had sent Einar into freefall.

He later he tried hanging himself but failed. With his claustrophobia, hygiene became a problem—the outhouse proved too cell-like, so he took to using the garden as his toilet. Any sauna, even one with a window, incited panic. A bathtub was dragged to the garden near the grapevines where Einar could bathe in the light of the moon. For the rest of his days Einar was a poor version of himself, dying of liver failure in his thirties. Karan lived another fifty years into her nineties. When she died, Alpo seriously considered traveling to Finland for her memorial. But he and Rose had two young children then and between them worked three jobs. The house was being rewired, they'd just bought a newer car. Any trip would have been an extravagance; an overseas trip was out of the question.

One day he will go to Finland, explore the town he shares a name with, visit Karan's grave and the family home, meet distant cousins. He had nearly asked Sissy if she'd consider going on their honeymoon and may yet surprise her with the idea of an anniversary trip—he might like to fish in Finnish streams.

Alpo pulls focus to take in the current flowing around his knees. The cutthroat are spawning just as hoped—he must tread lightly not to disturb their shallow redds of buried eggs. This nameless place is perfect trout habitat: undercut banks, overhanging vegetation, a maze of underwater root systems. The water is pristine—every drop filtered through miles of glacial moraine. Any colder and it would be ice.

He's thought of bringing Pete here to see if it might lighten whatever weight still slouches him. *Some* old battle continues waging there.

There had been valid reasons for his interfering—his granddaughters, Maddie and Allison. He shouldn't have to explain, and he won't. Nor will he apologize: his actions need no defense. Pete's not coming home last night was an emphatic *Fuck you.*

Alpo sniffs the hard air. Time will tell.

19

O F COURSE, SHE HAS A DOZEN THINGS TO DO. PROBABLY
two dozen, but as Sissy nears the Aurora Trail and the
sign for Jasper Mushers, it occurs to her that the twins
might know something.

About Rauri.

Other than to say hello, she doesn't know either twin well.
They're rarely in town.

Alpo had gone to school with them back when they were identical. "Before your time," Alpo ribbed her. "As most things are."

"Fiddlesticks," she'd said. "I remember Princess phones!"

Alpo grunted. Sissy's glad he doesn't laugh at any little thing.
He's no cheap date.

He'd told her what he knew about Ronny and Donny Jasper,
how they were tied for handsomest in the Wolverines yearbook,
had co-captained the hockey team. They married sisters Helen
and Mary Knutson in a double ceremony. Bright, they could've
gone anywhere but stayed here—that old saw. They ran their
father's Dodge dealership and built houses across the road from
each other like mirrors. Ronny and Mary had three girls; Donny
and Helen had three boys. When the fourth set of babies was
born, it looked like nobody could break the gender run, so they
swapped girl for boy and each brother raised the other's youngest, no questions asked.

Until opening day of the '85 grouse season, you couldn't tell
one from the other. After the accident Ronny's days on the show-
room floor were over. Donny ran the dealership until the recession

hit. Ronny did the books. Surgeries to rebuild his face nearly bankrupted them.

"Must have been awful for everyone," said Sissy.

"Mary gained a hundred pounds," said Alpo. "Helen had an affair with the IGA produce driver. Each blamed their woes on the other's husband and quit speaking. Everybody got a divorce and the swapped kids got swapped back. The boy ended up in juvie at Red Wing, and when the girl wound up pregnant at fourteen Donny had a heart attack."

Inseparable throughout, Ronny had forgiven his brother for shooting him even before the paramedics had him loaded into the ambulance holding a handful of his own teeth. Donny vowed he'd spend the rest of his life trying to make it up to Ronny, and he had. The heart attack gave Ronny a chance to take care of Donny for a change. They sold the Dodge dealership, bought a ramshackle resort at the hind end of Aurora Trail, and trained a brace of sled dogs. When that worked, they trained another.

These days Jasper Mushers get featured in magazines like *Outside* and *GQ,* and their twelve-day yurt-to-yurt luxury sled-dog adventures make all the lists of things to do before you can't.

If anyone would have seen Rauri over the winter, it would have been these closest neighbors. Since she's this far north, what's another few miles? She need only follow the sound. Huskies sing pretty and look pretty, but their bark is anything but. High-pitched and sharp, the sound multiplied like a serrated blade.

"Goodness." Her own voice barely registers. She slams her car door in hopes of announcing herself. Something's up. Donny has isolated a single dog in a side pen. It's muzzled, one foreleg bloody. So are Donny's hands.

"Oh, Donny, that doesn't look good. What happened?"

"Wolf. Broad daylight. Three young ones thought they'd go play with it. Their mama—in that next pen there—went after them. She's worse."

"Jeez. You called Pete?"

"Only about twenty times."

"I'll try." She digs for her phone.

Whatever he says is drowned out, but he points to the piney slope, flipping his thumb and pinky in the universal phone sign. He hollers, "Reception!"

She nods, heads back up the hill. Once her screen shows three bars, the call goes through fine but the automated message reports, *The mailbox you've reached is full.*

Sissy finds Ronny in a pen sitting in the dirt, pinning a young male onto its back with his legs. The dog is kicking to get purchase, and Ronny is pressing gauze to the underpocket of the hind leg. He looks up. He's not hideous, despite Joe's claim that looking at him makes a person want to chew their own cheek. Ronny doesn't seem surprised to see her but maybe surprise isn't in the range of his expressions.

"Well, thank God. Can you hand me that white tube?" The dog is trying to squirm free. "Oh no, you don't." His tone softens when talking to the dog. "We could use Dr. Pete 'bout now, couldn't we, pal?"

He says it in a way that would do Pete good to hear.

Sissy frowns over the open kit—a tray of grubby jars and first aid items—grabbing the first tube she sees, and says. "This one? Looks like Super Glue?"

"More or less. Still gonna need stitches, but it'll do for now." The dog is wagging its tail. "He's not in real pain—I numbed his belly—he thinks this is a game."

She crouches and tilts. "What can I do?"

"Hold this together while I glue?" His one eyebrow works fine. "You up for that?"

Her jacket's already off and she's plowing her sweater sleeves. He lifts the gauze to reveal a seven- or eight-inch tear beginning near the dog's inner thigh. Superficial but nasty looking. The wound veers to the furred middle where the tear travels the penis casing to its very tip.

"Whoa," says Sissy.

Ronny nods. "This guy's gonna be pitching left from now on." He shows her where to hold and how hard. Once the glue is applied, his hands join hers. For a full minute she barely breathes.

Ronny is muttering something like *shu shu shu* in a calming tone: for as long as he repeats it, the dog stays still. Her hands look small budged in between Ronny's. She is nodding along to his *shu shu shu*. The belly flesh is warm, reminding her of something—a physical memory in her hands—the feeling of something similarly soft and aching for how distant it is, so near yet so far out of reach.

"Good work." Ronny's voice brings her back. He eases his own hands away and hers trail after. "That'll hold for now."

"What else can I do?"

He nods to the pen across and a spilled bucket just outside the chain link with frozen fish tails sticking out. The penned dogs are going crazy over the smells of fish and blood. "They'll settle once they're fed."

She picks up fish, paddle stiff, and hurls them one by one into the pens. After the initial frenzy, the dogs do calm some. When she reaches the pen with the lamed bitch, Ronny rubs his face and walks over. "Don't bother feeding her. She'll be put down."

"*Oh?*"

Oh, she thinks, *Pete could save this dog.* She looks Ronny in the eye, saying quickly, "Should I try calling again?"

"Sure." Though most of Ronny's mouth is scarred into a smile, he looks sad.

Still no Pete. She leaves a message on the emergency line and tries the vet in Greenstone, who says he'll drive out.

On the way back to the pens, she stops at her car to grab anything that might be useful. Ronny and Donny have gathered tools and gone off to fix the fence so the dogs might be let out again.

She edges into the pen with the injured bitch. Only the lead dogs wear red collars. This girl is tawny and thin, one eye gray, one half-blue. Her tag says Mensa. The break on her back leg looks clean, not so bad, but the ligament that holds all together, the cruciate, has been torn through. Surgery for such an injury is complicated and expensive. There's amputation, but for a sled dog? This business is the Jasper brothers' livelihood and these dogs aren't pets. This girl will be put down. The dog bares its teeth, but only half-heartedly.

She is not going to cry. "Mensa, huh? You must be a smart one?" Pulling the white package out of the bag she waits for the dog to react, to sniff. Mensa's eyes fasten on the paper as it's torn away in a spiral, Sissy saying, "I don't know about you, but when I'm not feeling good, some cold treat like ice cream or a Popsicle always makes me feel better." The venison has started to thaw. When Sissy holds it out to Mensa, her black nose twitches and her ears prick.

20

LIQUID CALM. THE AROMA MAKES HIM THINK OF CARTOON characters dragged aloft by their nostrils, sniffing toward whatever ambrosia awaits. Not any old glass of booze. Before this Scotch reached Pete's glass it spent its youth maturing in a cask on some boggy Aran isle. Come of age and bottled and shipped across an ocean to land here in front of him. He'd seen the label, hand-numbered by the distiller. Distiller—now there's a job requiring more patience than he'll ever have—knowing your labors might not see the light of day in your own lifetime? That's the sort of thankless endeavor his father would sign up for.

"You letting that breathe?" The guy next to him has laid down his cribbage hand and advanced his peg.

His wife smiles. "He's about to wipe the floor with me."

"Yeah?" Pete looks at the board. "You *are* in for a skunk."

She nods at his glass. "I should be a good loser and buy Mark a pour of that. He's a Scotch man."

Mark nods, agreeing. "This is Lily, I'm Mark."

"Pete." With one arm in a sling, a nod suffices for a handshake. Pete taps the glass with the silver tongs. "So . . . *Scotch man,* how long would *you* let this breathe?"

"Twenty-one-year? I couldn't help noticing earlier. Lily gave me a Macallan the same vintage for Father's Day—now *that* was a good Father's Day. If it was mine, I'd let it air one minute for every year it's been casked—I mean, if you have that kind of patience?"

"I'll give it a go." Pete looks squarely at Mark, slaps the bar, slips from his stool, and goes to stand in front of Meg's paintings on the premise of examining them.

A Scotch man. Normal drinkers can make such claims. How would he classify himself? *I'm an anything man.* He almost laughs but then remembers the look Beth had given him when waving an empty bottle from the pantry at him. "Really? The *cooking* wine?"

A moment solidly in the category of *worst.* He blinks, concentrating on the paintings.

Part of appreciating Meg's pieces is identifying how and where her signature has been incorporated. Twined, sunk, wavering, reflected backward or inverse, the letters of her name can be found in some ripple, tucked into rushes, in an air bubble, spelled in froth. The quirk has been speculated over in glossy art magazines and interviews, but Meg only shrugs it off. Some have called it a gimmick. Pete smiles. If they knew her inspiration, they'd spew their white wine.

Of their many childhood competitions, one was to see who could beat the other at the *Find the hidden things* page in *Highlights* magazine. They'd been ferocious then in the way young children are. Before they were old enough to understand they were not the center of the universe, he and Meg could simultaneously be monstrous and tender with each other. Instinctively, Pete knew not to return her slaps or hair-grabs, trip her the way she had him—but did engage in name calling. Her fits were full-on but short-lived, her grief acted out in spurts. There were times it took both him and the old man to quell her sobs and staunch the tears and snot. In ten minutes they'd be playing again as if nothing had happened, back to their sandwiches and milk—or the magazine, tugging the pages, pointing and shouting out all the hidden things.

Pete likes to imagine her signature is a nod to their shared past.

As children do, they wanted to discover the workings of their small corner of the world. Both grew up half-drenched on lakes, in boats, on rafts, on docks, their playgrounds edged in surf. They lived on the opposite shores of the same lake with a whole underwater world between them. By nature, children are dowsers (naturally, he supposes, having swum into existence then floated into their world on amniotic seas). Around the northern arm of Little

Hatchet were streams and bogs and ditches and ponds. They followed each shimmering to its source, then the source's source. They traced their routes from the squelch and flow of tiny capillaries to tricklets of snowmelt to rain chunnels and burbled creeks, to waterfalls and racing streams—the flow invariably leading them to the same conclusion every time—big water. They intrinsically understood every drop of the place was part of some whole but only learned the name for it later in school, *watershed.*

Meg's paintings are inspired by the relationship of light, the surface of water, and the eye. Water to light, light to water, and all that reflects and refracts above, between, and beneath.

At least that's what the artist statement on her Website says.

Pete occasionally browses the site to see new work. Lately it's louder and more colorful, more political: Meg now paints plein air at holding ponds; drainage ditches; seepage sites and spills—usually while trespassing on company property. She's been arrested at OreTac and Mesabi Copper and will be again if she's going after sources of sick water.

He'd heard her on a call-in radio show, mentioning how the waters feel out of sorts these days, sometimes smelling wrong, looking opaque in places. Pete's heard others mirror this concern, mostly out at the rez. After her arrest, Meg's tires got slashed and the Naledi signs leading to the resort gates were all knocked down. Afterward, she wrote a letter to the editor in *The Siren,* stating, "I've watched the fish act differently around Crow Point. When things are off-kilter, affected species usually modify their behaviors to align with the limitations of their environments. Even what you might consider the dumbest of creatures know to do this. Humans, not so much."

Sitting back down in front of his glass of Scotch, Pete is nearly convinced it could be just a drink, a salve to soothe his woes, or, conversely, a celebration for having survived one hell of an airplane ride. Around him people are drinking for all the reasons people do: to relax after a long hike or hard week, celebrate catching a trophy fish; or skunking the wife at cribbage. Occasional occasions. He should be able to sit here and have this one drink. He should. He's a grown man.

He's a big lad now.

The voice would come from behind, *Ah, you're a big lad now,* damp in his ear, even the panting thick with the accent. The incoherent breath, the sensation of the words being etched onto Pete's neck as if his uncle's spittle were acid. *A big lad now*—he felt it there on his skin no matter how he scrubbed with Lava soap and once even with Brillo.

Of course the bastard had only been talking to himself, needing to assure himself his prey *was* a big lad. Not a little kid.

Pete picks up the tongs, chooses a chunk of ice, faceted and pale blue, as if calved from some small glacier. He lowers it into the glass so as not to spill a drop of Scotch. The words of that sick priest are only shadows now, *palimpsest.*

The ice floats heavily, not quite submerged.

An iceberg.

And he's its fucking Titanic.

21

O N THE PLATEAU ALPO EATS HIS LUNCH STANDING AT the open tailgate. He's tempted to skid back down the spiral path to catch more fish, but he's already shucked the weight of his waders and feels almost buoyant for it. And why push his luck after a perfect morning of fishing? Fifteen catches— but who's counting?—all cutthroats, all fighters. Wrestling bouts as well matched as you can get, man-to-fish-wise. During the frenzy of nibbles and bites and rallies he'd found himself laughing aloud, reeling and tussling, laughing like a kid.

Fifteen releases, holding each trout under the surface to take a good look at its markings before letting it go. Waiting a few minutes before casting again to lower the odds of snagging the same fish. In the course of the morning he's lost only one jig and one fly—its replacement, a battered wooly bugger, has now survived six sets of jaws, frayed but still on his rig.

This place shouldn't be kept secret. He's been tight as a knot about it but is beginning to think a select few could be entrusted to enjoy it, leave it as they find it, and keep their mouths shut. A few come to mind. On a grocery bag he maps the route, starting at The Rectory—he'll assume the Kiwi brothers will know to use miles and not kilometers. Bright guys, sincere enough despite the default joking. For some reason the thought budges in and he wonders if they are good sons. He imagines they are. Wonders what their own father might be like . . .

Poor schmucks traveling all this way to fish for nothing.

Of one thing, Alpo is certain—one can be proprietary without greed. *Stewardship* is the word he's looking for. He will show this place to Pete—though he's not sure if he fishes anymore— somewhere along the line Pete took a dislike to going out in the boat. Still, he'd appreciate the place for what it is, and he'd keep mum.

Has it come to that now? That he trusts his son?

Alpo taps his pen. Now that he sets to the task it's hard to describe the plateau, the exact spot in which to commence the descent looks just like every other edge of the place

There are a few dozen moraine stones scattered across the sur- face, some probably still where they were dumped an eon ago. Each is about the size of a curling stone, awkward but not too heavy to carry. He weaves around them, thinking up and sum- marily dismissing patterns to lay. He's not about to stack a cairn or lay a trail or arrow, announcing *look here!*

Testing the radius of his neck left to right, Alpo aims his chin skyward like a coyote, and there hangs the answer—invisible in daylight but there just the same. A constellation is as good as a map; in fact, *stars were maps before maps were maps*—something a teacher had said ages ago. Alpo knows most constellations by heart, etched in memory after a life of stargazing. Or perhaps cer- tain features of the universe get branded onto our lizard brains?

It's crazy to think that he can aim his phone at the universe and its stars and planets can appear on a screen—in a sky map. His phone has NASA schedules and reminders to watch for meteor showers, notifications for when the Hubble Space Telescope will be visible overhead. Not that his phone works here—he must rely on his memory, old school. Alpo considers the number of scattered stones against his memory. Closing his eyes, he employs the old- school trick of visualizing a chalkboard—and isn't a chalkboard just the earliest computer screen? Perseus, Orion, Scorpius, Ursa Major. The constellation he remembers most accurately consists of as many stars as there are stones on the plateau. It doesn't take long to position two dozen of them, but then he decides place- ment isn't enough—size matters. He repositions biggest stones for biggest stars and small for small. He locates a large light-colored stone to represent Kornephoros, the brightest of all the stars of Hercules, representing the strongman's knee at the exact point the path leads down. Unlike curling stones, these have no handles. His back will be roaring tomorrow.

He folds the map corners inward to a solid square, then repeats the process. There's nothing akin to tape or string in his tackle-box, so he takes the tired wooly bugger from his line and pierces the folds of paper together. Hopefully the brothers won't bloody themselves opening it.

At The Rectory, Jim says he'll deliver the map to their room when he brings up towels. Alpo hems a moment. "Would you much mind doing it now? While I wait?" He wouldn't want the map to be forgotten on the desk. "If you don't mind. It's, uh, sensitive."

Jim looks at him over imaginary glasses. "Oh?"

"*Time* sensitive."

"You say this is for *both* of them? Oh, my." He uses the map to fan himself. "Consider it done."

"Thank you."

"Those accents, right?" Jim mimes locking his mouth and toss-ing the key and clips to the stairs, his longshoreman looks not cor-responding with his gait.

"Jim. *Jim.*"

"Kidding." Jim turns. "Alpo, I'm just messing with you."

When Jim ticks back down the stairs, one of their little dogs is draped over his arm. Not exactly Alpo's idea of a pet, but oddly the incongruous pairing of large man and tiny dog somehow works.

"Delivered."

"Thank you."

"You gonna be seeing Pete today?"

"Maybe, why? Your little dog okay?"

"Audrey? Audrey is perfect. Aren't you, pumpkin?" He lifts a set of keys. "Pete left these last night. I've called, but his voicemail box is full. They *are* his?"

The ring holds his front door key, a sturdier key Alpo recognizes from the clinic, and his six-months' medallion. "Oh?" Alpo nods, holds out his palm. "So he stayed *here* last night."

"No. Just popped into the bar."

"The bar." Alpo's voice goes flat. "Was he there long?"

"Mmm. Less than an hour."

"Did he drink?"

"Drink? Um . . ." It's Jim's turn to hem. "James was waiting on him, actually."

"But he was at the bar?"

"Well, yes . . ." Before he can say more, Alpo has pocketed the keys and is shouldering out the door.

22

I T'S UNLIKE ALPO TO NOT CALL OR TEXT, BUT EVEN LESS
like him to send a string of heart emojis. Sissy knows he's
okay because Laurie saw him come out of The Rectory after
lunch. Unusual, but nothing she's going to think about because
she trusts Alpo without question.

But since Joe passes Alpo's on his way home, she's asked her
brother to see what he might see. A drive-by.

"What I see," Joe reports over the phone, "is Alpo's car is in
the driveway. It looks like the sauna's fired up. The recycling is
dragged to the road. You want me to go in there and take his
pulse?"

"I just want to know he's home and not out on some crazy
quest to find Rauri, like Pete."

"Wait, I can see him now, he's *raking.*"

"In the dark?"

"Yard light's on."

"Yeah, that's Alpo."

"You sure? 'Cuz I can take a picture, Sis—"

"Stop it."

An hour later Sissy's phone dings with another notification.
"Hmm . . ." She asks Jeff, "Who is this Alpo that sends smiley
faces and hearts to me?"

Another two hours and she's in the bathroom asking herself
through a mouthful of toothpaste, "Whath's *up,* mithster?" Now

he's sent a load of red roses, a kiss, a wink, and the *Zzz* emoticon. He'll be in bed by now. Maybe.

She spits mint foam into the sink. "Well, two can play at that." She sends about a hundred Zzzs and one red rose. Then she texts Janine to triple-check the arrangements for Jeff's transfer. Sissy has lied outright to her sister-in-law, telling her the dog sitter from Rover has backed out and that she's desperate. *Janine, you're an angel. He'll be zero bother, and you've got that huge fenced yard.*

Her wedding dress hangs facing the bed, the pearl necklace around the hanger. Underpants, strapless bra, and earrings on the dresser. The gorgeous little purse is her something new, the hankie within is her something borrowed from Louise. The little suede pumps the color of a robin's egg rest pigeon-toed on the carpet under the dress.

That's her in sixteen hours.

Everything set out, the packed things packed. She smacks the bedcovers and Jeff leaps. "Get it while you can, kiddo—tomorrow Momma gets a new bed buddy."

Just why her future bed buddy is being so cagey is unclear: maybe he's confused not *talking* to the bride before the wedding with not *seeing* the bride. Silly. She has things to tell him. Like how she's just realized *The Change* (her mother's term) may be upon her. Alpo might also like to know she's decided to quit her job and spend her savings on an enterprise she knows nothing about (emphasizing that while it might seem rash, it has zero to do with the hot flashes).

Her husband-to-be might just have an opinion about all this, might like to think things over and gird himself before saying *I do*. If he tried to talk her out of Roadkill, well, he just wouldn't. And if he did, she'd do it anyway. "It's nice . . . ," she tells Jeff, sinking her chin in his ruff, "to be certain about some things for a change."

23

P ETE WAKES ON HIS COUSIN'S COUCH UNDER A QUILT, his shoulder howling.

Mackie is making something in the kitchen. *Please let it be coffee.* Molly's head is on his knee. She already looks better, the panting has subsided—the eye movements less pronounced than they'd been the night before.

Canine vestibular syndrome. Mackie assumed Molly was having a stroke, as most anyone would, and freaked out accordingly. The syndrome often comes on suddenly: the animal will plow to one side, stumble, bash into things and become disoriented. Most disturbing are the eye movements, pupils juddering side to side as if frantic to find focus. The distress of the owner is usually disproportionate to that of the animal. In older, weaker dogs it's a longer recovery, but Molly is in her prime and will be just fine. He, on the other hand, needs Tylenol and coffee, in that order.

He dreamt he drank.

Staying sober in a place where every social event (including church functions) involves alcohol is a challenge. Invariably someone will offer Pete a bottle or pint, as if beer doesn't count. Days like the fishing opener, the Super Bowl, and Labor Day are hard enough—but walking into a bar is a game of Whac-A-Mole. A grateful, well-meaning pet owner will pour you a Scotch and wipe six months of progress off the board.

A cup is placed in his hands. An ice pack set over his shoulder. "Thanks, Mackie."

Mackie sinks to the carpet and pets Molly's head. "Poor girl."

"She's better. It's good you called, though."

"I thought she was *dying*."

"I know. It's scary as hell. But in her case, temporary. She'll be better in a few days."

Mackie frowns. "Could my cleaning her ears have triggered it?"

Pete considers. "Maybe." Then shakes his head. "Even if, not your fault."

"I wanted her all groomed before bringing her in Monday."

"You taking her to the bank?"

"Kyle's fine with it." Mackie brightens. "The tellers are thrilled, actually. Better to give some bratty kid a chance to pet a dog than hand them a sucker, right?"

"Right."

She'd been a wreck when he arrived. This morning she's her old self, wearing sneakers and dressed in a sweat suit that actually smells like sweat. She's quite pink.

"Have you been *running*?"

"Ha! Speed-walking. You and Molly were both dead to the world, and I can't sleep past six. I have to get in shape if I'm gonna be walking this girl, right?"

"Good." He wobbles to his feet, and she helps him on with his jacket. "Mack, that coffee was the best."

The phone in his pocket is dead, his keys are missing—hopefully somewhere on his way home or in the two blocks between Mackie's and The Rectory he'll find them.

"Retrace your steps?"

"Or maybe just go home and break into my own house so I can go back to sleep."

She walks him to the door. "I mean it, Pete, thanks for coming last night."

"Actually, I should be thanking you."

He should. He'd been three seconds away from crashing when she called, having managed to convince himself he could be just like everyone else, have one really nice drink and go home. The

Scotch had indeed breathed one minute for every year it had been sleeping in its cask, just as the Scotch man had recommended.

His hand had been wrapped around the glass. As he lifted it to his mouth, the side of his chest thrummed, making him jerk, which sent a bolt of pain down his arm. Naturally, he thought he was having a heart attack. Then *stroke?* Then he remembered the phone in his shirt pocket, set to vibrate. Jarred, he set the glass down none too gently, drops of Scotch sloshing onto his knuckles. He answered.

"Pete Lahti here?"

As Pete listened to a nearly hysterical Mackie, he felt indescribable relief and gratitude that she'd called, and thankful to Molly for needing him at that exact moment. After hanging up he feigned reluctance while sliding the Scotch to his neighbor. "Duty calls," he told him. *Mark.* "Any chance you could see this doesn't go to waste?"

"You kidding me?" Mark lit up like a Christmas tree.

"Please, Pete, at least let me drive you home."

"It's okay, Mackie. Really." He pulls her into a one-armed hug. "See you at the wedding, cousin?"

"With bells on."

24

"HAND DELIVERED?"

"The countdown begins." Laurie gives Alpo the boutonniere in a clamshell, like a flower salad. "Not too late to back out."

"Why would I—"

"Kidding." Seeing his look, she repeats, "*Alp.* I'm kidding."

He nods a few beats. "How's the bride?"

"You haven't talked to her?" Laurie gives him a look.

"Well, you know the old tradition, superstition. Whatever."

"Right, 'cuz you're just the guy to cave to superstition."

"You got me there." He repeats, "How's the bride?"

"Mmm. A bit squirrelly, a little ditzy. The usual. Other than that, fine." Having literally swung by, Laurie's standing behind her car door, leaning.

"Don't . . ." He doesn't intend the tone. "Don't underestimate your sister."

Laurie opens her mouth, closes it, and looks him in the eye. "And how are *you* this morning?"

"I didn't mean it like that." He straightens. "I've been better."

He *hasn't* called Sissy, has only sent silly texts, uncertain what excuse he'll use if Pete doesn't show up at the church. A veterinary emergency is the most plausible; a *canine* emergency might be one Sissy would not question.

He sees how things will be with his new sister-in-law: straightforward. With Sissy balanced between them, hopefully both will forgo judgment and do their best. And because he trusts Laurie, he dares ask, "See or hear anything from Pete today?"

"Oh, Alpo, tell me he's not . . ."

"Dunno," he shrugs, "I do not know."

Laurie sinks to the bucket seat and puts the car in gear without breaking his gaze.

"Pete better not fuck this up for Sissy."

He knows the crack in Laurie's armor is her sister. For all her steely judgments, Laurie's not as hard as she seems. For the moment they are in complete agreement.

"Let him try."

His suitcase and laptop lean at the door. There's nothing for him to do but read the last paper delivered to him here. A truck will come Tuesday for the furniture, and the next people in will be the stagers hired by his realtor to clean and decorate, bringing their own everything. He'd been a little stung that his perfectly good furniture, nice enough for his family, wasn't good enough for his *house*. He lays the newspaper in the fireplace grate because there's not so much as a recycling bin left in the kitchen.

Getting out the door is a negotiation with his bags and the lockbox hanging from the knob. Not until he's loaded the car does it occur that this *is* rather a momentous departure. Alpo folds his suit coat across the passenger seat, careful not to crush the boutonniere. Through the windshield he considers the home he has lived in all his life, save his two years away at VoTech and the year he and Rose rented that cracker box in town.

His grandfather had homesteaded the place—had felled the pines and hewed the logs to build the house. His scribe marks are on the notches and his initials carved into the living room mantel. The square log structure has been added to a few times, not always taking the original roof pitch into consideration. A second story was built in the thirties, adding two dormered bedrooms. Alpo's father had tacked on the back porch, along with a bumpout for the kitchen. His own early contributions were redoing his father's handiwork and bringing the place up to code. In '75 he jacked up the house and had it winched thirty feet over onto a new cinderblock basement with a walkout and sliding doors on the lake side. He added the family room and long glass porch a few years later. When Rose got sick, he tore the upstairs apart and remodeled it into a master suite in four weeks, which Karl at the lumberyard claims must be some record.

Most recently, he'd sandblasted the exterior walls and stained them all the same smoky gray, then he clad the disparate roofs in dark red steel. Now the place looks like one decent house instead of three huddled under different hats.

And isn't that the way? You finally finish a thing to your liking just when it's finished of you.

He drives slowly through the shaggy boughs of the Hobby—two acres of nonnative ornamentals he once groomed like poodles. Topiary had been something to keep his hands busy after Rose died. Looking back, he understands the Hobby was something under his control when little else was. People made more of it than they should have. It became a landmark when giving directions. Something could be two fire numbers after Lahti's Hobby, or if you got to the Hobby, you've gone too far. Lou Pavola asked to bring her kindergartners out on a field trip for Arbor Day, and he could hardly say no to that, and wouldn't have guessed it would turn into a tradition. The older kids called him Alpo Scissorhands, which frankly went over his head until he saw the film on Netflix and laughed until his back hurt (and, admittedly, cried).

His trees are well out of control now, free-range, au naturel. At the height of it, Pete tried to be the comedian, calling it Alpo's *grief grove,* his *angst orchard.* He likened Alpo's pruning to Scandinavian keening.

The county spur at the bottom of his forty was renamed Lahti's Hobby and a sign slapped up, ironically the same year he abandoned his hobby. So many of the trees had gotten sick with some virus. It hadn't killed many, and most rallied back, but he'd had enough of disease.

* * *

At the cemetery gates he takes the bouquet of iris picked from the protected corner of Rose's garden that thinks it's in a warmer zone. Down a needle-orange path, the oldest part of the cemetery is shaded under the largest pines where time has softened the names on gravestones to whispers. Many tiny slabs mark infants and children lost during stretches of hardship, outbreaks of this or that, long winters. Now there's grief for you, Alpo thinks. Hatchet Inlet was a raw place once, and this plot of headstones with vowel-laden Finnish names attests to its ragged history. Many of the dead under Alpo's feet had fled starvation back in Finland, where bread made from pine bark was actually a thing.

Most of this cemetery was once a farm. The grave diggers often pull up bits of it—the caretaker's shed has a corner shelf with broken pots, milk bottles, the jaw of a draft horse, square nails, a wooden ladle.

Up the hill in the newest section, a spate of fresh graves has been dug now that the ground has thawed, and those stacked in the cooler over the winter have finally been interred. Unbundling the iris from the cone of waxed paper, he meanders the rows, laying a flower on each new mound, knowing he'll run out by the time he reaches Rose, knowing she'd like that.

Flashing his empty palms at her headstone, Alpo shrugs, finding that for once he has nothing to say. The old regrets have worn themselves out. It used to gnaw that he didn't do things differently with Pete, but he sees now nothing would have changed. He used to regret accommodating Rose's superstitions and blind faith, believing he should have fought them harder. Her Irish menace of a mother had done a real job on Rose, so that by the time she came into his life her shame was ingrained. He knew what he was in for before signing on. Her body seemed her great regret. She undressed every night in the bathroom. There was the birth control issue: he wasn't interested in raising a litter and wanted the children they would have to eat, wear new clothes, go to college. *You can ask me to take the Pill. You can't ask me to feel good about it.* Occasions of sex with the lights on had been doled out like sacraments.

Agreeing to have the kids baptized was enough of a compromise without mention of renouncing Satan. Of course he challenged Rose, but such arguments were unwinnable. *Tell me again how a newborn is saddled with sin the minute it's born?* Usually Rose simply went silent, leaving him to duke it out with himself. *Never argue with an angry colleen* was her own advice.

Early on she told him about the time the nuns forbade installing a tampon machine in her junior high school. When she mentioned it to her mother, she had her mouth soaped for relaying such filthy news. She was shamed for developing before the other girls, and for the sin of having a figure her uniforms were ordered two sizes too large so that she barely filled them.

Rose became further dispossessed of her body when the mechanics of it stalled, when her organs gave over to corrosion and her skin became something she was trapped in. *Putrefying* was a word she used repeatedly. *Festering.* The vocabulary was like an arsenal.

ROSE CORRIGAN LAHTI 1953–1996.

Born in Cork (on St. Patrick's Day). *Erin go bragh blah blah,* she would say. For marrying a Lutheran, a lapsed one at that, Rose was shunned by the ginger-haired knot of her family. Only years later did her brother Peter start coming around in summers. Rose hadn't seen him since he'd been ordained. She joked, "What am I supposed to call you? *Brother Father,* or *Father Brother?*" Silently, Alpo called him Pious Pete.

By the nineties Rose's parents were dead and the grip of the church eased some. For a while there Rose pulled him into her fray, even developed a mild appetite for intimacy, just in time for her to get cancer.

One Sunday toward the end—Alpo remembers it was the day before the hospital bed was to be delivered, the last night they would ever share a bed—the book in Rose's hand dropped and she looked at him. She had been particularly lovely those days, as if cancer suited her; the lack of pallor brought out the green in her eyes.

"It's quit," she said. *It* being the disease. She laid a hand on her belly. "It's done its worst now. I'm mummifying. I can feel it." It was the one time she'd seemed truly terrified. He'd held her. Rose pulled back to look at him. "Would you like to?"

At first, he didn't understand. "To what?"

"A last time."

Through all of her illness, from first biopsy and bouts of treatment, the three years of remission, and the elevator plunge of the second diagnosis—those few moments had been the worst—her taking his hand, pulling it under the covers, so desperate to feel something that she pretended to want him. And he couldn't. He'd wanted to do this one thing for his wife and he couldn't. Her body wasn't her own anymore; she'd even stopped smelling like herself. Her sweat was metallic and her scalp had a petrol tinge. Her flesh had betrayed them both. They looked at each other as he eased his hand away, her eyes wide and dry, his welling and brined. That most awful moment of their marriage was also perhaps the most honest.

Soon after, she began to systematically shut herself off from one person after another. The hospice nurse said this was natural, that people begin closing out their accounts. Rose did so in ascending rank of need, starting with the grandkids, her friends, then Candy. Rose's sister Sharon, then Alpo. She'd saved Pete for last. After him, the only creature she related to was Pogo, her three-legged corgi—and she let go of Pogo only at the end when the pain meds were ramped to eleven and she'd begun the god-awful wheezing.

Alpo sometimes wonders if the disease took advantage of some fissure in Rose's nature. If he believes in anything, it might be that mind-body connection New Agers like Cathy O'Hara go on about. After all, a machine performs only as well as the operator in control of it. Not so far-fetched that shame might sicken a healthy body. If one feels they deserve it.

He'd only begun to understand Rose after she'd gone.

But he may never understand the unconditional, unquestioning way she believed in him—as if he, too were some kind of faith.

Surely Rose convinced herself there was more to him than there actually was—as if having settled on his silhouette had filled it with her own version of a husband. She assigned him mystery as if he were layered like some onion. He would insist *I'm a simple person,* and she would quote, *And I am Marie of Romania.* Was always spewing literary bits he'd have to look up.

It was Dorothy Parker.

He'd been a good-enough husband, not a great husband—never forgot to get the right gift on the right day—and was faithful as a lab (admittedly never having been tempted makes for a pretty limp feather in that cap). Could he have taken better care of his wife? No, but he might have *known* her better, peeled more layers, because in truth *she* was the onion. He could've shone more light, and not just that bedside one.

Afterward he'd hoarded her profile in the periphery like a carved cameo. In time the edges wore and dulled. These days he remembers only her features but cannot cobble them into any expression.

The plan is to do it right this time. And he'd just as soon get down to it, but checking his watch Alpo sees there's still time to waste before the ceremony. He heads behind the caretaker's shed for a leak.

Sissy isn't his first run at passion—the other is ancient history. Wanda. She'd flipped burgers at the Anchor Bar in Superior. So pretty it was easy to get past the smell of grease. She's now a circuit court judge in Milwaukee with a gray pageboy. If there is anything Facebook is good for . . . Still, Alpo cannot pass a smoking grill without his subconscious plucking the air for notes of patchouli shampoo.

Alpo shakes, and since he's wearing new wedding skivvies, gives things a bit more time to dry. Wanda had been a hippie and made love like one, with abandon. Alpo looks down and sighs, the breeze reminding him of a thing she'd done with scarves . . .

* * *

Minutes later he is huffing, zipping, exhaling the understatement, "That was tacky."

Honestly, in the cemetery where his wife is buried? Behind a shed, an hour before tripping up the aisle to his new bride. Thinking of someone else, sort of. Surely a Guinness Record for crude.

In the car he checks the rearview. Does he feel guilty? No. *Should* he? No.

Is he happy?

Damn straight he is—and lucky to have loved them all.

25

THE DAY HAS FLOWN. THE SALON HAD TAKEN FOREVER, and while her updo feels a little like a helmet, it's so pretty she can't pass a mirror without looking.

Sissy has done her toes, had a bath (which would have been longer if the hot water hadn't petered out). She's eaten a late, starchy lunch knowing she won't get through the champagne toasts without something in her. The makeup has been applied twice. Too much the first time, and the false eyelashes are ruined, but she looks like herself, finally.

And now she's zipped into the dress and faced with an hour of sitting on her hands when she can barely sit.

Poor Jeff hasn't been walked all day, only let out to the yard. She hadn't thought to take him to the dog park before getting all ready. She could kill two birds by just walking him to the church instead of driving—it's only on the other side of downtown, fifteen minutes tops, maybe twenty in the little shoes. But why not? It's gorgeous out.

She doesn't have to mince, exactly, but can't take long strides with the dress snug to her knees. They are just a block from Main Street when Jeff shapes himself into a C on the boulevard and lays a pipe of poo thick as a wrist. In front of Mr. Swanson's place to boot. Of course there's no plastic bag in the tiny purse, only her hankie and lipstick. It's all she can do to hold the purse with no strap, the bouquet, her wrap, and Jeff's leash. Looking around to see if there's something, *anything,* she spies the newspaper still in its plastic sleeve on Mr. Swanson's sidewalk.

A truck with tinted windows and Georgia plates slows and pulls over smack in front of her. Naturally someone would choose this moment to ask for directions. The window lowers and a wrinkly man points at Jeff's pile and says, "You hold on there, Miss." He has a southern accent, a gentleman's drawl.

"Ah, ok*aaay,* but . . ."

He opens the door and folds himself onto the pavement. "Don't you dare." His *dare* has two syllables. "Not in that dress, Miss." The plastic bag is already pulled from his pocket and he's bending. "Allow me." In two shakes the turd is bagged, the bag knotted, and the man is beaming her a smile.

"Well, that's very . . . *thank* you, sir."

He holds up a hand to deflect. "Aren't you a picture? I'm guessing you're off to see one lucky fella this afternoon."

"I am, actually."

He gives a stiff little bow, to which she returns a knock-kneed curtsy.

"Well, don't you keep him waiting, Miss."

The man hitches back into his truck and leans out the window. "Goodness. The ladies 'round here clean up real good, don't they?"

Sissy laughs. "We do all right."

At the statue of the French voyageur leaning on his paddle, a troop of young scouts has gathered around his huge moccasins to have their picture taken. The scout leader has set the timer on his camera, and as Sissy approaches, the little red light starts blinking. He rushes forward, urging, "C'mon guys!" But in the process of pulling them into some order, he turns his back just as the shutter clicks. "Crud. Okay, one more time." But they are distracted by Jeff.

One of the boys calls out, "Is that a wolf?"

Another asks, "What's its name?"

"He's a malamute. His name is Jeff."

"That's not a dog's name!"

"Don't tell *him* that." She taps the scout leader's arm. "I can take the picture."

"God, would you? I'm wrangling cats here. That's the button."

A boy with brown curls asks, "Are you a fairy?"

"Maybe."

"Does that dog bite?"

"No. Do you?" She sets her things on the bench to have two hands for the camera.

One says, "My mom's pretty too."

A freckled boy squints, "How old are you?"

"Smile now!" She takes several shots before handing the camera over. "That should do it."

"Hey. Get your picture took with us!"

"Please!"

The scout leader motions her to their center with a wink.

"For once I'm the tall one in the picture."

As the troop makes its way to their bus two blocks down Main, Sissy walks with them, giving each boy a turn at holding Jeff's leash. They tell her their names and she tells them hers, and upon reaching the bus they invite her on for a ride.

"That's so nice, but I have to be somewhere."

"Where are you going?"

"I am going to get married."

Halfway down the block from the bus they are still yelling. *Good luck, Sissy! 'Bye Sissy, 'Bye Jeff! Have fun getting mar-ried. First comes love, then comes marriage, then comes Sissy with a ba-by carriage!*

At the open doors of the dime store she veers in, pulling Jeff along. For a moment she stands perfectly still, blinking, not wanting to use her pretty hankie *before* the ceremony. Concentrating on the card rack and the row of stupid cartoony postcards—fish bigger than the people, mosquitos in lawn chairs—she's able to not cry, *just*. Tears, she supposes, are part of this menopause package along with the infernal toasting when you least expect it.

Simply, children hadn't been in her plan. If they had, she'd have done something about it before her eggs went stale—and now they are totally cooked, and sudden regret at not using even one sweeps hotly through her like some grass fire. She looks around before opening the ice cream case. The counter is busy with a line of tourists, no one she knows. Leaning far over as if to read the small print on the wrappers, Sissy lowers her face to meet the icy fog. The mist on her cheeks soothes, the tears that had been working their way out frost over, and her lungs fill with cool relief.

The NO PUBLIC RESTROOM sign is meant for tourists. She mops her underarms with brown paper towels and pats cold water across the back of her neck. Jeff watches it all with his head cocked. Her hair still looks very nice and the makeup is still holding; the pink is draining from her face.

Outside, she takes one step, then is jerked sideways by Jeff to miss being sideswiped by a mobility scooter. The machine screeches to a stop, then backs up. Just above the handlebars is Mrs. Mathers's pug face.

"*Jeez,* Mrs. Mathers."

She looks Sissy up and down through coke-bottle glasses, then frowns.

"Aren't you cold in that getup?"

"No," Sissy says. "And I don't think scooters are meant to lay rubber."

"In my day brides wore white. I suppose anything goes nowadays."

Sissy shrugs. "Nobody pretends to be a virgin anymore, Mrs. Mathers."

Mrs. Mathers gives her a hard glare, then laughs in spite of herself.

"You have a nice day, Mrs. Mathers."

Mrs. Mathers says, "Nice?" She lays on the throttle and is gone.

* * *

Emily is coming out of the library, wearing her best librarian smile and holding the door for a woman with a box of books. Seeing Jeff, the woman plops the box onto the bench and says, "Aren't *you* gorgeous?" To Sissy she says, "Do you mind? If I pet him?"

Before Sissy can say yes, the woman is kneeling. She doesn't just pet Jeff but takes his skull in both hands as if it's a crystal ball and looks into his eyes. "Oh you *are* beautiful. I had a beautiful boy like you. *Just* like you." The woman fuses her forehead to Jeff's and inhales hugely as if dog breath is pure oxygen.

Emily whispers to Sissy, "An *author*."

"Ah."

"Ava lost her dog recently."

"Oh? *Oh*."

Ava looks up. "Aw, your dress matches his collar? Sweet."

At the pavilion high on the hill overlooking St. Urho's, she stops. "Sit." She's speaking as much to herself as Jeff as she settles on the bench. Guests are arriving, cars are pulling into the lot. Somewhere nearby someone is smoking pot.

Alpo will already be inside—his default mode is unfashionably early. Ray and Chim are decorating his Bronco, tying a brace of cans to the trailer hitch and streamers to the antennae. She hopes the loopy stuff on the hood is Silly String and not spray cheese, which makes a holy mess. Laurie and Kitty are walking up the church steps with Louise wedged between them. Her mother looks up suddenly as if knowing Sissy is there. Sissy wriggles her fingers, but Louise is cinched at the elbows and cannot wave back.

"Hi Lou," she says, almost audibly. Turning to Jeff, she says, "Just a few more minutes. Then we're good to go."

26

GUESTS MILL ON THE STEPS AND LAWN OF ST. URHO'S. A huddle of smokers are gathered at the curb. Turning a slow circle, Pete cranes over fresh haircuts and wedding hats to catch the flash of coppery hair halfway up the hill near the pavilion. Leaning against a picnic table, Meg has edged from the fray, as usual. Always ambivalent about social gatherings, she'd explained to him once, "I look like I fit but never do, like the wrong puzzle piece."

Pete loosens his tie and heads her way.

She's looking out over the lake. The wind lazily shifts Meg's silky pants and the back of her kimono jacket is stitched with waves, giving the effect that even still she is in motion. Pete catches a whiff and hesitates. Upon sensing him, she turns and gifts him one of her rare smiles.

"Hey. I figured I'd see you."

"Hello, Meg. You smell happy. Mind if I . . . ?" He holds up the cigarette he'd bummed—not really smoking these days, but it's an excuse to approach.

"Oh, you want some of this?"

"Thanks, but just plain tobacco for me."

"Right," Meg says gravely, slipping her little pipe into a pocket. "You're a good boy now, I hear."

"That's open for debate." He nods down at the church and the crowd that represents most everyone Pete is either related to, a friend of, or acquainted with.

"Right. Would you like to sit?"

"Thanks."

She nods at his forehead and says, "You don't look as bad as I thought you would."

"Gee, thanks."

She reaches to tuck in the loose strap on his sling. "You know what I mean. I was expecting a body cast."

"Hatchet Inlet grapevine. Tell me."

She looks down at the church. "Your girls are so grown. So poised."

"That would be their mother's doing."

"Pish. The younger one?"

"Maddie."

"Right. *Maddie* told me her class saw my exhibit on a field trip to the Institute. She said no one believed that her grandfather owned one of my paintings."

"Ah." Pete bit his lip. "Sorry I didn't make it to that one."

"*Que será.*" Her shrug reminds him of that old conceit he never understood. Meg didn't seem to take much personally—slight *her*, no problem, but slight the artist at your peril. What would it be like, he wonders, to invest so much of yourself into one thing? But maybe that's the gift—or the curse—of having talent.

She says, "I heard you own the clinic now."

"More like *owe* the clinic. Bought it with loans my dad had to cosign."

"So, you're staying?"

"I am." Saying it aloud makes the decision feel final and right. "What about you? You should be living in some loft in SoHo. You could be anywhere, Meg. What's keeping you here?"

"This and that." She looks at him. "Something clicked after the accident. Something about it. And this place."

Pete nods. "That's right. You called it in, didn't you?"

"Uh-huh," Meg says. "On my way home from driving Cathy to the airport."

"Still the night driver?"

"Less so now." Meg looks to the distance. "I smelled it before

I saw it. Smoke and oil. I stopped and backed up and aimed the headlights. I knew they were dead without getting out of my car."

"How?"

"The sound—the lack of it. The van didn't even look like a van. And there were . . ."

"Were what?"

"I've never told anyone this, but there were wolves. Five wolves. They waited with me, until the sirens got close. Then they just trotted off, one by one."

"That's . . . I don't know what that is. Spooky, I guess."

"Also sort of appropriate, if that makes any sense." She looks at him. "I painted it all from memory this winter, March, when it seemed like the cold would never end."

"You painted . . . the wolves, or the wreck?"

"Both. Neither. Just the colors, mostly. Violent, shrouded. In some ways it was quite a good painting. Maybe one of my best."

"Did it help? Painting it?"

"Yeah," Meg says. "Yeah, it did."

"I'd like to see it."

"You wouldn't, actually, knowing what it is. Besides, I burnt it."

"Ah."

They look out over the lake for a while. Pete is glad to sink into the old comfortable silence—to know some things do not change. Meg's silence could be unnerving to some; Pete found it soothing. When the chime sounds from the belfry, Meg straightens and smiles. "This is lovely, yeah? Your dad and Sissy?"

"It is. It is."

"Are you the best man?"

He laughs. "I'd like to think so."

"Ha. Well, I better move if I want a decent seat."

"You go ahead. I'm gonna hang here a minute. You'll be at the reception?"

"Yeah, of course we will."

The pointed *we* would include Jon Redleaf.

The odds of Meg and Pete both winding up back in Hatchet Inlet are one thing. But resurrecting their past, maybe reviving it? As if that hope is published on his forehead for her to read, she says, "It wouldn't have worked, Pete. You know that." Her hands fall to her sides.

Pete nods. "Just out of curiosity, why, do you think?"

"Pete."

"Because you love Jon?"

"Maybe." Without missing a beat, she adds, "You know, sometimes I think I'm not quite set up for love."

"Sorry, I didn't mean to . . ."

"Maybe I'm more like Rauri. Or Vac. I don't need people very much. I wonder sometimes if I wasn't quite *finished* when my parents died." Meg meets his eye. "Hard as he tried, Vac couldn't be everything."

"True."

Before turning she captures him in one of her slow blinks sure as a shutter. *Gotcha.*

Watching her go, he lets himself drift back to their final days, when she *had* needed him, when they'd both been in ribbons. Meg, in the thick of losing Vac, had been summoned from her school in London, and Pete was realizing he'd soon lose his mother.

He would climb and descend the stairwells between ICU and Oncology, where it soon became obvious neither Vac nor his mother would recover. His mother wanted to quit treatment and live her last months at home. His father stalled, trying to peddle the idea of more chemo—almost bullying his mother into living—at least that was Pete's take on it.

During that month he and Meg were inseparable. Their need then was a thing nearly beyond them. Reunited, they grew monstrous and tender once again. Aware each passing day hastened their impending losses, they retreated, became nocturnal, gorging on each other as if storing against winter. Clinging and aching even in sleep, they woke twined like puzzle-monkeys.

For being precocious children, they'd grown into surprisingly naïve twenty-year-olds. Losing her parents, and then having Vac pulled out from under her, it made sense that Meg would go in for solid types like her staid professor, and now Jon—rather a pillar himself—a stonemason, no less.

And twenty years on, are they even the same people? Meg's bad-boy days had ended with Pete. He sees that now.

27

"IF YOU LOVE ME, YOU'LL KILL ME."

Alpo considers his tearful bride. "Honestly, Sisu?" He had not imagined this would be the first married conversation they would have, or that this would be its location. Sissy sits sideways on the toilet seat, her little suede heels braced against the stall, holding a champagne flute and a bouquet of toilet paper still rooted to the roll. Where, he wondered, had her real flowers gone?

"When I lose all *my* marbles, you will. Won't you?"

Probably left the flowers at the church before fleeing. "Sissy. No one's killing anyone."

She takes another swig. "Unbelievable."

"Well, you did want a memorable wedding."

"You think it's funny?"

"I don't."

They're in the basement of Kalevala Hall. The guests are upstairs. He eases the champagne from her hand. "I'm getting you some water." The bottle, which Sissy's drunk half of, is on the floor. As he picks it up and sets it near the sink, he scrutinizes her in the mirror. Can she know it's the nonalcoholic version? A sound escapes him.

"See? You do so!"

"Well, it is sort of funny, Sissy. Or it will be, one day. It was a nice ceremony, though."

"Right. Until it wasn't."

Is she *slurring*? "Sounds like everyone's having a good time upstairs."

Indeed, the clop of footfalls above quickens as the band does, making the wooden ceiling shake. Laughter filters down, from boom to titter, call and response. Alluring kitchen smells entice. Alpo's stomach growls.

"Where's my mother?"

"With Laurie." He has no clue. "Probably up there dancing."

He decides to test the waters. "You ready to go upstairs?"

"No." She motions for the bottle.

"Fine." He hands it over. "We don't have to."

"*You* go up?"

"And dance alone when they play our song?"

New tears threaten to erupt.

"Okay." He makes a show of locking the door. "See, just us chickens. There are plenty of other toilets in this joint."

No sooner had they been pronounced husband and wife and the recessional began playing than Sissy had rushed him down the aisle at double speed. The tears of joy had switched to vinegar by then, with more burbling when they'd had to sidestep Louise's bra in mid-aisle, landed like some gull.

Neither had actually seen Louise's dress fall from the balcony because they'd been facing the altar. Only Pastor Dan and the dozen latecomers in the last rows saw that bit of the show. They'd both heard the wrongly timed mutters along the pews. Alpo detected a stifled giggle, then saw the look on Dan's face as he rushed through the closing, his voice jumping register.

When both heard a squeal slapped short, they looked at each other and turned to see Laurie dashing to swoop up the blue dress pooled on the carpet. Above in the otherwise empty balcony, a topless Louise waved her panty hose like beige smoke.

If he hadn't had both of Sissy's wrists, she would have launched.

"Laurie has this," Alpo said, pulling her to face him. "Say you won't run, Sissy. Promise me."

She blinked.

As far as Alpo knows, only Pastor Dan had caught the full monty.

No sooner had Alpo steered Sissy into the reception line than she ducked out of it, leaving him to make excuses before ducking out himself.

He set off in the direction he'd last seen her, searched the churchyard, the little cemetery and the grounds. Finally, he'd gone next door and poked into the rooms of Kalevala Hall, basement kitchen, boiler room, and lastly this lavatory where he'd found her.

The bathroom door is gently rattled. And now someone has found them.

There's a knock followed by a loud whisper. "Granddad? Sissy?"

Alpo unbolts the door and cracks it. "Maddie."

"Is Sissy okay?"

"She's fine. Tell folks we'll be up shortly." Alpo mouths, "Louise?"

"Laurie got her dressed," Maddie whispers. "But she did drink some of the punch and gave some to Jeff." Maddie tries to peer in.

"See you upstairs." He gives his granddaughter a wink before closing the door. He turns. "Louise is fine," he lies.

"Fine?" Sissy is standing at the mirror, assessing. The tears have dried and she's taking the sort of breaths she takes before diving off the dock.

"Can we go up now?" He doesn't want to beg.

"In a few." She hands him the full champagne flute. "Since I have you, there are things we should talk about." She points to the toilet. "Have a seat."

Laurie has one eye on her mother, the other on the guy she's trying to place—lobster tan with a crew cut, wearing a Mexican wedding shirt and khakis, sandals with dress socks. (It *is* a wedding.) She tugs the mohair sleeve of the sweater she's buttoned her mother into backward. "Mom, you know who that is?"

Louise squints, then smiles. "My fuck buddy." She offers Laurie a small pile of cake on a plate.

Laurie gasps. "The cake!" Pressing her mother aside to see that it's been dug at with the punch bowl ladle. Both tiers are cratered. "Christ almighty, Mom."

"It's white!"

"Mom," Laurie groans. "The wedding cake."

Back in the church, Laurie had her back turned all of twenty, maybe thirty seconds when the gloves (and everything else) came off. She'd been digging for a tissue when she looked up to realize her mother had slipped from the pew and rushed up the balcony steps. Ignoring the mutters and stares, Laurie scooped the dress from the stairs, and in the time it took her to climb up there herself Louise had molted her entire outfit.

Since being stuffed back into her clothes, Louise had been acting subdued, almost contrite. So Laurie let her guard down once and *now* look.

"Yes." Louise smiles. "I know it's a wedding cake."

"Mom. The cake usually gets cut by the bride and groom."

"I *am* the bride."

Laurie mutters something garbled.

"What was that, dear?"

"Just repeating what you said, Mom." *Fucking wedding cake.*

Once upstairs, Alpo sets out to find Pastor Dan while Sissy goes to check the buffet and bar. Truth is, he's almost glad for the brouhaha. It's at least allowed him to avoid Pete. Just when he's thinking it, the voice comes from behind.

"Dad. There you are."

"Ah."

"Well," Pete holds out his hand. "Congrats."

Alpo looks at his son's hand, taking too long to raise his eyes.

"Dad." Pete's palm turns up before dropping to his side. "What the . . . ?"

"I'll cut to the chase. If you're drinking, I'll ask you to leave."

"Leave? Dad, what the hell?"

"Just answer. Have you been drinking? Have you had a drink?" Alpo digs in his pocket and holds up Pete's set of misplaced keys.

"No. And no. Hang on." Pete frowns at the keys. "Oh, I see . , ,"

"You went to a bar by yourself."

"I did. But I didn't drink." Pete's words are measured. "I have not had a drink."

"Don't lie to me."

Pete looks his father in the eye and says nothing, waiting.

Alpo sees it's the truth, sees Pete's eyes begin brimming.

"Christ. I'm sorry, Pete."

"Dad. I came close." He slumps.

The look, clear blue and pleading, is a look Alpo hasn't seen on his son since he was a little kid.

"I came *so* fucking close."

Alpo's jaw unclenches and he reaches for Pete, remembering just in time to be careful of his arm. Remembering.

Moments after Pete was born, before he had a name and his scalp was still streaked with birth, Alpo had been handed the infant. For having just gone through labor and delivery, Rose looked surprisingly strong, reminding him that mothers are warriors, indeed. Rose's nod implied *careful* when handing him over, saying, "Our son." Alpo's knees had gone weak with gratitude and he looked into the baby's tiny face. The blue eyes fastened on his.

And now Alpo must lean back and look up to see his son, to catch that same clear color. "I'm sorry, Pete." He enfolds his son as best he can around the sling and the girth of a grown man's chest. "I am so sorry."

* * *

Someone had found Sissy's bouquet and set it at her place at the long table. She can see Alpo talking with Pete on the far side of the room. Considering the body language, she'll stay right here, thank you. Laurie is supposed to have their mother in hand, yet their mother has the cake in hand, literally.

So much for that photo op.

Alpo did remind her she'd wanted something memorable, something different. Sissy finds the photographer and aims him. "I want shots of them. That's my sister, chewing her nails. And my mom in the backward sweater, scooping cake."

"Oh man, is that a *ladle?*"

Sissy shrugs. "It is what it is." The resignation in her own voice stills her. It *is*. What it is. And she does want pictures of this moment to look at down the road—maybe so far down the road she'll *need* photos to jog her memory, just as Louise needs now . . .

Mother with cake. May 17th.

Cathy says life isn't something that happens to you—how you choose to react to what happens is life. True. True, too, that everyone here knows the score, and Sissy needn't be embarrassed. She can let her mother's behavior ruin her wedding day, or not.

After the toasts have been toasted and pictures taken and the sappy speeches given by Joe and Erv, Cathy says some Hindu blessing and the band begins another set.

A lean little guy in his sixties with a ropey build is hanging by the bar. He wears the sort of short-sleeved shirt Ricky Ricardo might, the collar open to show a V of red skin to match his sunburnt forearms.

Pete squints, puzzling.

"Tourist?" Cathy asks. She and Veshko plop down, winded from dancing.

"Nah." Pete shrugs. "He'd be some old pal of Dad's."

* * *

Sissy has had real champagne now, a few glasses. Louise, need-ing none, climbs the stage in stocking feet and budges in next to the microphone to join in on "Let's Get It On." Guests cheer because Louise does have a voice. The Erbach Brothers are good sports and indulge her. Watching her sing, you wouldn't know she's unable to tie her own shoes or count change. In the hayfield of her memory, lyrics are one thing Louise can still reap.

A hundred years ago when Sissy wore braces she assumed all romances culminated in Princess Bride endings, and that all mothers aged gracefully into wise grannies. This is not how she pictured her wedding but if her mother belting out a slightly raun-chy Marvin Gaye tune is going to be the highpoint, so be it. As she claps and hoots, Sissy knows one thing: that nothing, but *nothing,* ever works out like you expect.

Yet everything does.

Louise sings two requests, "I Got You Babe" and "What's New, Pussycat?" Tables are pounded, hands begin to sting from clap-ping.

Alpo gives the band his signal and leads Sissy to the center of the floor as the lights dim. He's glad to see Joe has his camcorder trained on Louise when she and the Erbach Brothers sway as one to the tune of "Let's Stay Together."

After their dance, Louise performs "It's Not Unusual" as her solo encore. The tempo of the last lines slows and she winds down like a music box. Her eyes are heavy as Laurie eases the micro-phone away and leads her to the cloakroom and trundles her into her car coat. Outside she's buckled into Kitty Orjala's sedan to be chauffeured back to Senior Cedars.

Before Kitty's car has pulled away, Laurie has marched to the bar and ordered two gin and tonics. She slams one and brings the other to the table where Sissy and Alpo have collapsed among the remaining guests. Jeff is snoring under the table and Laurie kicks her shoes off to bury her toes in his fur. Anyone small, old, or demented has been taken away. Those left are a hardy few, loud, gesturing with full glasses in their hands. The buffet looks like someone's taken a rake to it. Downstairs, the teenagers have discovered the old foosball table. The annoying, nostalgic racket drifts up the stairwell until someone has the presence of mind to shut the door. The music is piped now; the Erbach Brothers are coiling cords and loading cases.

There are yawns, more guests fall away until tables are peopled by much of the same crew that get served daily in the diner. Sissy stands, holding an imaginary pad, points an imaginary pencil to Laurie's drink and asks, "Would you like pie with that?"

Laurie cracks up along with everyone else.

Seeing the little guy again, Laurie nudges Alpo. "Nobody seems to know who invited that one. Wedding crasher? Shouldn't you be defending your wife's territory?"

Hearing the word *wife,* a little hiccup of happiness escapes Sissy. She looks to the stranger, then to Joe, who only shrugs. The guy leans on an elbow at the bar as if he belongs. In the light of the revolving Schlitz globe, the man's profile is lit, then dimmed. Lit, then dimmed.

"Balls." Laurie aims a look.

Sissy says, "Don't be rude. He's *somebody's* guest." She turns and waves. "Hey, you person, come join us!"

The man begins to walk to the table, holding up his beer as if about to toast.

Which is when Alpo stands, saying, "Jesus. H. Christ."

Juri squints, then bellows, "Will you look who the fucking cat dragged in!"

"No way," Pete mutters.

Rauri is not only alive: he is shaved, shorn, groomed, hatless, and tanned, wearing smoky-lensed glasses. This isn't some poor deprived bastard who has toughed out a winter on his own. No. This hale fellow has just swaggered in from *summer.*

"Oh for God sakes," Sissy yelps. "Rauri?" She trips forward to latch her arms around Rauri's neck, repeating, "Oh my God." She plants a smack on his cheek.

Rauri it *is*.

And as Sissy has never seen him: tan as a walnut, with his thatch of hair buzzed close to reveal the shape of his skull, grinning with a mouth of polished teeth. No sooner has Sissy smothered and smooched him than she backs up a step to get a real look. That's when the gushing stops and Sissy does something so un-Sissy-like that had it not been caught on video no one would believe it.

In the span of four seconds guaranteed to go viral (caught on the still-running camcorder, as well as Janice's iPhone), the supple curve of Sissy's shoulder budges into the frame and her arm ratchets back as if pulling a crossbow. The launch of her fist is a blur, but the force behind it attests to the many hours spent making SissyBrittle; stirring vats of molten sugar to the consistency of lava, she's developed the deltoids of a bantamweight champ. Heads snap in unison like a herd as Sissy, with a decidedly unbridelike grunt, rockets her small fist to connect with Rauri's freshly kissed cheek, as if her own lipstick smear is the intended target. Rauri's beer bottle launches to shatter against the stage riser. Alpo, closest to Rauri, catches his sideways stumble.

Everyone goes still, taking a slow, collective inhale to fuel the ensuing uproar.

Laurie watches a gamut of expressions slalom across her sister's face: disbelief as Rauri staggers; horror and amazement at her own left hand before it unfurls to clap over her opened mouth; concern as she leaps to help Rauri. In the pandemonium of everyone yammering at once, Laurie and Alpo pull Rauri to his feet and guide him to the chair Sissy's just vacated.

Alpo catches Sissy's eye. In the span between two blinks, his wife wordlessly relays all Alpo will ever need of her. As joy expands within him like some sponge, instinct tells Alpo to lock down this instant in time, for he is, right now, as alive as he will ever be and this moment as good as it will ever get. He will indeed cherish and humor this woman, as promised, for however long they both might live.

Rauri's beer is mopped up, the broken shards swept. He is given another bottle. His glasses have been retrieved and dusted off and once they are back on his face he casts around suddenly as if to determine Sissy's exact location.

Sissy looks at her knuckles, curling and uncurling her fingers, shaking her head.

Rauri looks around at the room as the room looks at Sissy. "I'm fine. In case anyone is wondering." He turns to Sissy. "What the hell? I know I'm late, but that was a bit harsh."

She's trying hard not to laugh. "I know. I know. I'm sooo sorry." When she leans toward him, he leans back.

When the laughter dies down, Pete stands. "Where the fuck. Have you been?"

Rauri points to Pete's bruise and his bandage, nodding at the sling. "Where have *you* been?"

"Oh, I'll be telling you all about that, trust me."

Rauri turns a semicircle, registering the undue level of curiosity. *But anger?*

"Wait a minute." Laurie pivots. "You stood at the bar all this time and never said boo?"

"I was watching Louise sing. When I realized nobody was recognizing me, I thought I'd just be a fly on the wall for a bit."

"So, Rauri, why the disguise?" Nunce Olson taps her pen on the table as if ready to take notes.

"Disguise? I shaved."

"But where *have* you been?"

"Okay, okay. Sorry I missed the ceremony." Rauri checks his watch. "Three hours ago I was at the Cloquet Kwik Trip, getting changed."

"No no, before *that*."

Sissy hands him an ice cube wrapped in her something-borrowed handkerchief. He considers her before pressing it to the graze where she'd caught him with her wedding ring.

"It's a haul from Arizona to here. One speeding ticket in Iowa, and a piss-poor night of sleep in a motel with a dozen Harley riders. Might as well have been Sturgis. I hauled ass to get here, but had I known this would be my welcome . . ." He tests his jaw, asking Sissy, "Whatever happened to better late than never?"

Sissy only shrugs.

"So. Arizona is where you've been? All winter?" Pete asks.

"Where in Arizona?" Alpo leans.

"Sedona. Christ, what is this, the Inquisition? There's a gallery there that sells my chandeliers." He turns from Pete to Juri, then from Erv to Alpo. "I just drove eighteen hundred ninety-one miles . . . Can't a man take a vacation?"

"Vacation." Joe lets his chair crash forward. "The kitty at the diner's got you dead six ways to Sunday. There's nearly four grand in it."

"Whadya mean, *dead*?"

"Dead. *Dead.* Froze being most popular cause." Joe ticks off his fingers. "Then heart attack, drowned, head injury, propane asphyxiation, and don't forget smoke inhalation."

"People bet money on how I might've—"

"Expired. Not to forget the long shots—badger attack and spontaneous combustion."

"What?"

Laurie glares. "Yesterday everybody thought you might be in the spin cycle up at the Basin—till *that* search got called off."

"You're not saying there was a *search*?"

"Oh, lord," Sissy says. "There is, isn't there?"

"Not anymore," Janko Junior says. "I've texted Ryan over at the station."

"Rauri, why didn't you leave a note or something?"

"Why . . . would I?"

"To clue somebody in—when you knew you wouldn't be here for ice-out, knowing we'd be waiting."

"Waiting?" Rauri looks from face to face. "For *me*. Like I'm the only one that knows the date of ice-out?"

"Yes, *you*!" Sissy says. "You're usually here by now."

"I'd have been here last week but I got held up."

"Held up?"

"I've been . . . *busy*."

"Busy with what?"

"Jesus," Rauri says. "With *who,* if you must know."

Erv grunts. "You saying you nearly forfeited your islands for some piece of ass?"

"No!"

"Ah jeezus, Rauri, not a *guy*." Joe chuckles.

"Fuck off. And not forfeit, the Fed's offered a fair price."

The room goes silent; eyes not already on Rauri swivel and aim. Muttering rises and questions tumble.

"You're selling out?"

"Seriously?"

"To the Feds?"

"Selling. Not out. Besides, who are you to . . . ?" Rauri looks around. "I been out there scraping a life off those rocks for thirty-one years and change. I proved my point. I don't belong out there. Nobody should live in that Reserve 'cept what lives there now."

At that, they all look to each other, then Rauri.

This time the silence is darker, a curtain.

Sissy tries lifting it. "Who's your *who,* Rauri? What's her name? How'd you meet her?"

Rauri sighs and turns his back to the men. "Her name is Jackie. Her RV was parked next to mine. I was in site sixteen, she was in eighteen. Nice spots. We had four trees between us, good shade, brought the ambient temps down about five degrees."

"And what's Jackie like?"

"Small like you, five-two, which is good since I'm only five-four and a half." He looks wistful. "She's got curly hair—still plenty of blond in it. For someone with short legs she can get into some difficult poses." He turns. "*Yoga* poses. The park had free classes in the community room, so . . ."

"And what does she do?"

"Just retired from the library. Bought a three-acre lot in Dry

Creek Canyon. Thought we'd maybe give it a go, build something together."

"In Sedona?"

"The average January temp there is in the fifties. That's *January*. No snow. No ice." He turns back to Sissy. "She likes to hike and garden. Cooks, too. I can say I've eaten cactus now. Told her I'd be back in June to help with her building site."

When Juri stands, so does Rauri. "Really, I'm only here to get my tools, sign over my land, and collect the check."

Juri scowls.

Rauri scowls. "You wanna punch me, too? Line up. I'll tell you folks one thing, though—after driving all over this country, I can tell you there's nothing comes close to what we got in that Reserve. You want to hunt it and log it and clog it up with machines? You wanna mine the copper out of it and poison the place? If you're bent on doing that, then you're not just blind to what's coming—you can't see what's in your goddamn backyard."

Rauri looks at every face before continuing. "Thirty percent of you are morons. The other seventy percent is who I'm gonna miss." He winks at Pete and gives Jon a thumbs-up, turns to Joe, and says, "I'm gonna miss your hash, Joe. You've been like a wife to me."

That laugh, nervous as it is, settles the air some.

"I'll come back in summers, rent a houseboat, bring Jackie. He tilts his beer in the direction of the Pavolas' table, brothers and sisters and newly in-lawed Lahtis all wedged around. "You'll see me at the diner." He raises his bottle high and winks at Sissy. "Where bacon reigns."

She follows him outside.

"Don't rush off, Rauri. Please? I know that wasn't much of a welcome." She tries not to laugh.

"Getting knocked on my keister by a ninety-eight-pound bride? That's worth the story to tell Jackie. Besides, you were pretty cute throwing that punch. It's all right. I get it now."

"Raur—"

"Look at you, our same Sissy Pavola that runs her legs off at the diner, always with a smile. I remember back when you were all knees and elbows, you and your sister. Sweet and Sour."

"You're really gonna sell and go?"

He nods, a look passing over him. "You look so much like Louise did at your age."

"Yeah? Funny, actually, 'cuz there was something my mother said—"

"She told you then?"

"Told me?"

"You knew?" Rauri sighs. "I figured if you didn't know back then, Louise would eventually let that cat out of the bag, especially now that she's—*you know.*"

"Cat?"

"We did our best to keep it lowdown. Even when I'd go up to the Cedars to read to her, I would only go at odd hours and use the side door, never sign the guest book."

"Wait. You go to visit her? What do you mean?"

"Not often. When I could. Once or twice a month between thaw and freeze."

"Hang on."

"Don't be angry with your mom. She just . . . wanted privacy—a widow with teenaged girls? A town like this can be brutal."

"You were my mother's lover?"

Rauri frowns. "So you *didn't* know?"

"I do now. *Lovers?*"

"More like *friends* but with—you know—"

"—Benefits?"

"Then it got complicated, four kids clomping in and out of that house."

"Wait. Just how long . . . ?"

"Ah. Five years and two months." He shakes his head. "Poor Louise doesn't even *know* she's Poor Louise these days, does she? Hard to watch a mind like hers derail."

"Yes. It sure is."

"But by God, it was good to see her belting it out on that stage."

Not until he squeezes her fingers does she realize their hands have been twined. Sissy smiles. "Most mothers of the bride just light a candle and get weepy, right?"

"Right. How many do a striptease and sing R&B?"

They stand in a cone of streetlight on cold ground. Just as she realizes how cold, Rauri frowns. "Girl, what the hell you doing barefoot out here?"

Once he's in the car she waves, then turns to go inside. Alpo is just coming out the side door, looking very husband-like, carrying her purse and shoes and the vintage fur Laurie had given her before the ceremony—with its little gift tag, lettered *Something Old* (*Does Not Smell*). Sissy takes one step and her bare foot sinks into soft mud. She hopes it's mud.

Hiking her dress, she pulls her foot free. Almost on its own, her other foot plants itself with a *goosh*. She knows the consistency of this mud and exactly what it will feel like when she squeezes her toes—ice cream. When she closes her eyes, it does.

As if time is some zip line, Sissy is whizzed back nearly to her beginning when touch and sight made more sense than words. Squatting and tipped in the unpaved alley in midmorning sun, she'd pressed chubby fingers into the depths of a puddle. Both hands sink into red muck, cool in the already too-warm day. Laurie's hands sink deeper, next to hers. Sissy is wearing a light-yellow dress, too tight under the arms; her sister is in white, even her barrettes are white. Both wear anklets with frills and Sissy's patent leather shoes pinch.

Their mother's voice singsongs from afar. "Time for the car, girls."

Laurie's hands *schkuck* up from the mud. Sissy does not want to give up cool mud for the hot car. She makes herself heavy when Laurie reaches for her. She struggles and is lifted by her middle and is carried forward around the corner of the garage; Laurie waddles blindly and backbent underneath, muddy hands cinched around Sissy's tummy.

Their mother is clicking down the walk in her high-heeled boots, wearing the crocheted tunic Sissy likes to weave her fingers into. The car keys in their mother's hands make small music. Her other hand trails something like a little cloud. A white veil.

Laurie plops Sissy at their mother's feet like a cat presenting a mouse, and everything stops. They follow their mother's eyes and both look down to their dresses and the Dalmatian patches of mud smeared across their skirts and bodices. Laurie's arms cross—she doesn't want to go in the car either: she wants to play in the mud, as any child would.

Their mother's mouth is an empty drawer. The communion veil drifts to the grass as she finds her voice. She looks them up and down and finally says, "Jesus wept." Sissy can feel a smear of mud drying on her cheek. After a slow headshake, Louise's hands are thrown high, and she *laughs*. They are herded into the yard and peeled of their dresses. Sissy clearly recalls the feeling of the dress being pulled over her head, the sudden freedom of it, air across her bare back, the tight shoes kicked away. Louise rinses their hands with the hose; they trip out of their little frilled panties to run naked through the shallow kiddie pool and the yard. Louise chases them with the garden hose, laughing and spraying. Soon enough their mother is wet too, the crochet dress hanging around her hips. When she runs out of steam, she flops to the lawn chair while they continue to orbit her, splashing with handfuls of water from the pool. When Laurie stops long enough to arrange the veil onto their mother's too-large head, Louise laughs even louder.

And who besides children, thinks Sissy, are free to run naked through a summer morning? Who but a woman with the spirit of a child would peel her clothes off in a too-warm church?

This is what Sissy's been searching for—the essence of her mother. It doesn't matter if it happened exactly as remembered.

When it comes to love, facts and order are meaningless. The Louise laughing and helpless on her lawn chair was, and is, Sissy's true mother.

Alpo stops short. Sissy has bunched her dress into silken handfuls at her hips and is planted in the mud, pedaling down one foot then the other as if pressing grapes—rocking, smiling, her eyes closed.

He carefully lays her things on the sidewalk and unlaces his shoes.

And why not?

It's a start.

ACKNOWLEDGMENTS

Thanks to the wonderful team at the University of Minnesota Press: Erik Anderson, Louisa Castner, Emily Hamilton, Heather Skinner, Matt Smiley, Laura Westlund, Daniel Ochsner, and the rest of the gang.

Funding and time to write this novel came from many sources, including the Minnesota State Arts Board and the Oberholtzer Foundation (hooray, Beth Waterhouse!). Sheila Smith and Perry McGowan donated time at their beautiful Dragonfly House. Sisters with cabins gave many days of peace in which to write near the water—thank you, Val and Tom, Julie and Jerry.

The St. Croix Watershed Research Station and the Science Museum of Minnesota granted me a month-long residency, and during the final stretch of completing this book Write On, Door County kindly hosted me.

As always, I'm indebted to those readers who urge me to keep the stories coming. Thank you for supporting my work, writing reviews, and inviting me to your book clubs: you remind me why I do this. Thanks to Pamela Klinger-Horn, fairy godmother to writers, for tirelessly championing the books and careers of authors.

To Minnesotans who voted for the Legacy Act of 2008, thanks for assuring Minnesota's two most vibrant resources continue to sparkle—clean water and the arts.

Thanks, Monkey! And last but never least, love and gratitude to the handsomest man alive, Jon.

SARAH STONICH is a northern Minnesota native. Her novels include *The Ice Chorus* and *These Granite Islands* (Minnesota, 2013). *Vacationland* (Minnesota, 2013) is the first book in her borderlands trilogy, followed by *Laurentian Divide*. She is the author of a memoir, *Shelter: Off the Grid in the Mostly Magnetic North* (Minnesota, 2017). She also writes under the pen name Ava Finch; *Fishing with RayAnne* and *Reeling* are the first novels in her fem-lit trilogy. Both Sarah and Ava live in a repurposed flour mill on the Mississippi River in Minneapolis.